THE BOOKISH LIFE OF NINA HILL

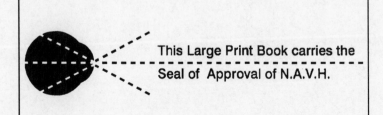

This Large Print Book carries the
Seal of Approval of N.A.V.H.

THE BOOKISH LIFE OF NINA HILL

ABBI WAXMAN

THORNDIKE PRESS
A part of Gale, a Cengage Company

GALE
A Cengage Company

Farmington Hills, Mich • San Francisco • New York • Waterville, Maine
Meriden, Conn • Mason, Ohio • Chicago

Copyright © 2019 by Dorset Square, LLC.
Thorndike Press, a part of Gale, a Cengage Company.

Thorndike Press® Large Print Women's Fiction.
The text of this Large Print edition is unabridged.
Other aspects of the book may vary from the original edition.
Set in 16 pt. Plantin.

LIBRARY OF CONGRESS CIP DATA ON FILE.
CATALOGUING IN PUBLICATION FOR THIS BOOK
IS AVAILABLE FROM THE LIBRARY OF CONGRESS

ISBN-13: 978-1-4328-6348-7 (hardcover alk. paper)

Published in 2019 by arrangement with Berkley, an imprint of Penguin Publishing Group, a division of Penguin Random House, LLC

Printed in Mexico
1 2 3 4 5 6 7 23 22 21 20 19

For my stepfather, John, who came late to the party, but stayed to clean up. I love and respect you with all my heart.

And for all the booksellers and librarians, who care about writers and readers in equal measure, and put them together every day. The world would be so much lonelier without you.

Solitude is independence.
— HERMANN HESSE

Independence is happiness.
— SUSAN B. ANTHONY

Happiness is having
your own library card.
— SALLY BROWN, PEANUTS

today is the day

DATE Tuesday, April 30th   M T W Th F S Su

⬡ ⬡ ⬡ ⬡ ⬡ ⬡ ⬡ ⬡

SCHEDULE

7 > 8
8 > 9
9 > 10   Work
10 > 11
11 > 12
12 > 13
13 > 14
14 > 15
15 > 16
16 > 17
17 > 18
18 > 19   Spin
19 > 20
20 > 21   TRIVIA

▷▷ ▷ ▶ ▷▷ ▷ ▶ ▷▷ ▷ ▶

TO DO LIST

- ☐ Buy water bottle
- ☐ Get paperclips
- ☐ Stapler
- ☐ Cat food
- ☐
- ☐
- ☐
- ☐

GOALS

DRINK MORE WATER !!!

NOTES

Finish Oliphant

➡➡ ➡➡ ➡➡ ➡

✚ BREAKFAST Smoothy 😇

✚ LUNCH Subway ?

✚ DINNER

✚ WORKOUT Spin before Trivia ?

ONE

In which we meet our heroine and
witness a crime of thoughtlessness.

Imagine you're a bird. You can be any kind
of bird, but those of you who've chosen
ostrich or chicken are going to struggle to
keep up. Now, imagine you're coasting
through the skies above Los Angeles, cough-
ing occasionally in the smog. Shiny ribbons
of traffic spangle below you, and in the
distance you see an impossibly verdant
patch, like a green darn in a gray sock. As
you get closer, the patch resolves into a
cross-hatching of old houses and streets,
and you have reached Larchmont. Congratulations, you've discovered a secret not even
all Angelenos know. It's a neighborhood like
any other, but it boasts a forest of trees,
planted generously along semi-winding
streets that look like they were lifted whole-
sale from a Capra movie, and were actually

11

all planted at once in the 1920s.

The houses are big but not showy, set back with front gardens that make the streets seem even wider than they are. Even today, most of the houses look the way they always have, thanks to historical preservation and a general consensus that the whole thing is hella cute. The trees have grown into truly beautiful examples of their kind; magnolias drift the streets with perfume, cedars strew them with russet needle carpets, and oaks make street cleaning and alternate side parking a necessity.

Larchmont Boulevard is the linear heart of Larchmont Village, populated by cafés, restaurants, boutiques, artisanal stores of many kinds, and one of the few remaining independent bookstores in Los Angeles. That's where Nina Lee Hill works; spinster of this parish and heroine of both her own life and the book you're holding in your lovely hand.

Knight's has been in business since 1940, and though its fortunes have risen and fallen over time, a genuine love of books and a thorough knowledge of its customers have kept it in business. It is like all good independent bookstores should be, owned and staffed by people who love books, read them, think about them, and sell them to other people who feel the same way. There is reading hour for little kids. There are visiting authors. There are free bookmarks. It's really a paradise on earth, if paradise for you smells of paper and paste. It does for Nina, but as our story opens, she would happily go back to the part where we were all being birds and poop on the head of the woman in front of her.

The woman was staring at Nina in what can only be described as a truculent fashion, jangling her extensive, culturally appropriative turquoise jewelry.

"I want my money back. It's a very boring book; all they do is sit around and talk." She took a breath and delivered the coup de grâce. "I don't know why the manager told me it was a classic."

Nina looked around for Liz Quinn, the guilty party. She could hear the distant rustling of washable silk as Liz went to ground in the young adult section. Snipe. Nina breathed in hate and breathed out love. She smiled at the customer. "Did you read it all the way through?"

The woman didn't smile back. "Of course." Not a quitter, just a whiner.

"Well, then we can't refund your money." Nina curled her toes inside their fluffy socks. The customer couldn't see that, of course, and Nina sincerely hoped she looked calm and resolute.

"Why not?" The customer was short, but she managed to draw herself up a couple of inches. All that Pilates finally paying off.

Nina was firm. "Because we sold you a book and you read it. That's pretty much the whole life cycle of bookstores right there. If you didn't enjoy it, I'm very sorry, but we can't do anything about it." She looked down at the book on the counter. "You really didn't like it? It's generally considered one of the greatest novels of all time." Nina resisted the impulse to pull out her imaginary blaster and blow the woman's head off, and got a microflash of the bit in *Terminator 2* where his silvery head splits in the middle and waves about. Liz was always telling her to be warmer toward the customers, and to remember they could go online and buy any book on the planet faster than Knight's could order it. Nina needed to make it a friendly and personal experience, so they liked her enough to give the store a) more money and b) more time than they had to give That Other Place. Independent booksellers called it the River, so as to avoid saying it out loud. But as Nina often thought, denial ain't just a river in South America.

The woman made a face. "I don't know why; the heroine sits around and gazes out of the window. If I spent all my time sitting on my butt pondering life, I assure you I wouldn't be as successful as I am." She shook back her long blond hair, with its carefully casual beachy waves, and had another thought. "If I don't like the food at a restaurant I can send it back and get a refund."

"Not if you've eaten it." Nina was confident on this one.

"Can I get a store credit at least?"

Nina shook her head. "No, but may I suggest a library card? At a library you can borrow the book, read it, and give it back totally free of charge." She forced a smile. "There are actually two within walking distance of here." She was sure Liz would be happy to lose this customer. Pretty sure.

"Walking?"

Nina sighed. "There's parking at both." She slid the book back across the counter. "This is still yours. Maybe you could try it again sometime. I've read it about twenty times, actually." (This was a gross understatement, but Nina didn't want to blow what was left of the customer's mind.)

The woman frowned at her. "Why?" She looked Nina up and down, not unkindly,

15

just trying to work out why someone would do something so strange. Nina was wearing a pale green vintage cardigan over a blue dress, with a cardigan clip across the collar. Apparently, this clarified things for the customer, because the woman's expression softened to sympathy. "I guess if you've got a boring life, other people's boring lives are reassuring."

Nina stepped on her own foot and seethed as the woman dropped *Pride and Prejudice* carelessly into her fancy handbag, bending the cover and dinging the pages.

Two minutes later, Liz appeared over the top of the graphic novels shelf. "Is she gone?"

Nina nodded, viciously tidying a pile of bookmarks and trying to forget the callous book treatment she had just witnessed. "You're a craven coward and wouldn't even emerge to defend your second favorite nineteenth-century writer. For shame."

Liz shrugged. "Ms. Austen needs no defense. You did fine, and besides, I've never forgotten a long conversation I had with that particular customer about LSD and the boundaries of consciousness." She straightened some copies of *Roller Girl*. "I thought I was asking about her vacation, but it turned out she'd stayed home and gone further than she ever thought possible." She tipped her head down to peer at Nina over her glasses, her short, dark hair barely touched with gray, despite the several careers she'd had, and the many cities and lives she'd been part of. "There was a long portion about the deep inner beauty of yogurt when viewed through the lens of hallucinogens that put me off Yoplait for life."

Nina regarded her carefully. "I find that story almost impossible to believe."

Liz turned and walked toward nonfiction. "I should hope so, seeing as I completely made it up."

Nina looked down and smiled. She'd never felt more at home than she did at Knight's, with the plentiful sarcasm and soothing rows of book spines. It was heaven on earth. Now, if they could only get rid of the customers and lock the front doors, they'd really be onto something.

As the only child of a single mother, Nina's natural state was solitude. Growing up, she saw other people with fathers and brothers and sisters, and it looked like fun, but generally she thought she was better off without a crowd. That might be overstating it; sometimes she'd ached for them, especially in middle school. There were lots of kids who had older brothers or sisters in the high school, and those kids had a protective glow around them she envied. Older siblings would wave at recess, or even stop by to chat and confer greatness. Then, in high school, Nina would listen to the kids with younger siblings complain about them but wave, or go over and chat. She saw the relationship, the shared address, and wondered about it.

Nina's mother, Candice, had had her after a very brief liaison with some guy she met in those strange times before Google (1988 BG?), where all you had to go on was what someone told you in person. Nina often shook her head over the crazy risks those Gen X-ers took. No online database of criminal records, no checking social media for wives and children, no reading back through months of feeds looking for clues. They would have to physically talk to a stranger without knowing any backstory. They could pretend to be a whole new person for everyone they met, without the effort of creating a matching online profile; the potential for dishonesty and deceit was shocking. Anyway, Nina's mom wasn't even sure of the guy's name and wasn't worried about it. She was a news photographer; she traveled the world and took lovers whenever they presented themselves, without guilt or complications. *I knew I wanted you,* she would say to Nina. *God only knows if I would have wanted him.*

At first, Candice had taken Nina everywhere with her, carrying her under one arm and putting her to bed in hotel room drawers. After a year or two, however, Nina got inconveniently big and wriggly, so Candice found a nice apartment in LA, and an even nicer nanny, and left Nina to get on with the business of growing up. She'd show up three or four times a year, bringing gifts and strange candy and smelling of airports. Nina had never really gotten to know her, though Candice had loomed large in the child's imagination. When Nina first read *Ballet Shoes,* as a child, she'd realized her mother was Great-Uncle Matthew.

Her nanny, Louise, had been a wonderful parent; funny and interested and bookish, loving and gentle. She'd created a peaceful life for Nina, and when she'd come to Nina's college graduation, she'd hugged her, cried a little, then moved back South to help her own, older daughters raise their children. Nina had been far more devastated by Louise's departure than she'd ever been waving good-bye to her own mother. Candice had started the race, but Louise had carried Nina over the finish line.

Nina hadn't missed her mother as much as she'd missed having a father. She wasn't entirely sure what fathers actually did, day to day, but she'd seen them standing on the sidelines at peewee soccer, or showing up at the end of the school day with their hands in their pockets. In middle school, they'd become totally invisible, but then in high school they'd reappeared, driving the car for late-night pickups and avoiding everyone's eye when a crowd of teenage girls piled in, smelling of drugstore body sprays and showing liberal amounts of nascent cleavage. Nina found them mysterious. Visiting other people's houses, she would see their moms — often, in fact, become friendly with their moms — but she left high school without ever truly getting the point of dads. They were a nice bonus, like a pool, or a cute dog, or a natural predisposition to clear skin.

"So, what's tonight?" asked Liz. "Delicate Ladies Book Club? Transgender Support Bridge Night? Decoupage Devils?"

"You think you're very funny," replied Nina, "but truthfully, you're just jealous I have a wide variety of activities to keep my mind alive."

"My mind needs no encouragement," said Liz. "In fact, I'm taking up hard drugs in the hope of killing off some brain cells and leveling the brain/body playing field."

This was actually true for Nina, too. Not the hard drugs, but the part about her mind needing no encouragement. As a child she'd been told she had ADD, or ADHD, or some other acronym, but her school librarian had simply clicked her tongue and told her she was imaginative and creative and couldn't be expected to wait for everyone else to catch up. She'd started giving Nina extra books to read and encyclopedias to gnaw on. This approach, Nina now realized, was in no way medically recommended, and didn't do anything at all for her math skills, but it did mean she arrived in high school having read more than anyone else, including the teachers. It also meant she thought of books as medication and sanctuary and the source of all good things. Nothing yet had proven her wrong.

Nina eyed her boss. "Tonight is Trivia Night." She knew Liz wanted to join her trivia team but couldn't work up the energy for the required late nights and weekly study sessions.

"They didn't ban you yet? I thought they

were going to ban you for winning all the time."

"They did ban us from one place, but there are plenty of bars where they've never heard of us."

Liz raised her eyebrows. "You're a trivia hustler?"

Nina shrugged. "Living the gangster dream."

Liz looked at her. "Go on. Do it."

Nina shook her head.

"Please."

Nina sighed. "You have to give me a category."

"Marine life."

"Too easy. A hundred-pound octopus can squeeze through a hole the size of a cherry tomato."

"Kurt Vonnegut."

"He opened one of the first Saab dealerships in America."

"Jupiter."

"Has the shortest day of all the planets. Can I stop now?"

"Does it hurt your head? Do you see auras around things?"

"No, but your expectant expression is low key stressing me out."

Liz cackled and walked away. "You have no idea how amusing that party trick is," she added over her shoulder. "Don't forget to dress nice tomorrow. Mephistopheles is coming in."

"OK." Nina frowned after her, then tried to remember how long Jupiter's day actually was. She couldn't help it; it was . . . 9 hours and 55 minutes. Thank God for that. Not being able to remember something was, for Nina, torture. It was like an itch on the roof of your mouth, or when you get a bug bite between your toes. You have to go after it, even though it's almost too much sensation to deal with. Liz thought all the clubs and activities Nina did were a way to be social, but she was totally wrong. Left undistracted, her brain tended to fly off the rails and drive her insane with endless meandering rivers of thought, or constant badgering questions she needed to look up answers to. The trivia, the reading, the book club . . . they were simply weapons of self-defense.

Two

In which we learn a few things
that irritate Nina.

Nina walked home in the golden light of her evening neighborhood, the magical hour beloved of lighting directors and single people dreaming their plans for the night. Around her, people walked their dogs after work, talking on their phones, oblivious to the slanting sun glinting on windows and door knockers, the colors of the pastel sky as gauzy as any red-carpet lineup. Nina often reflected that LA was not a pretty city, architecturally speaking, but the sky made it beautiful several times a day. As with all things Hollywood, the lighting guy is God.

For example, at this time of day the sun made a great deal of her dark red hair. Had Nina known how pretty it looked, she would have taken a photo of herself, but sadly, she was thinking about pickles — sliced, whole, or relish, discuss — and missed the opportunity. In general, she wasn't the kind of woman who turned casual heads; her looks were an acquired taste, and her resting expression suggested you weren't going to be given much chance to acquire it. She was small and slender and gave the overall impression of a baby deer, until she spoke and you realized you'd been looking at a fox all along. As her good friend Leah once said, she wasn't mean; she was painfully accurate.

Nina rented the guesthouse of one of the larger houses on Windsor Boulevard. It was a charming little place, completely separate from the main house, with its own entrance. Absolutely perfect for Nina. The owners were friends of Nina's mother, and when Nina finished college had miraculously just finished renovating their guesthouse. They generously offered to rent it to Nina, who couldn't have been happier to accept.

Her cat, Phil, was sitting on the gate waiting for her. Phil was a tabby of the brown and cream variety, with a black tip to his tail and white feet. He jumped down as the gate opened and preceded her up the stairs, the tip of his tail forming a jaunty accent like the marker flag on a toddler's bicycle. Nina noticed he'd left a large but very dead worm on the doormat. He stood next to it casually, like, oh yeah, I'd almost forgotten, I brought you a worm. Nothing special, just a deadly worm I captured with my own paws and brought back for you. Thought you might fancy a little smackerel of something after work, you know. (He was apparently channeling Pooh Bear.)

Nina bent down and stroked his head. "Thanks, Phil. This is an incredible worm." Phil rubbed against her legs, totally stoked with himself. Other cats might stay in all day, lounging around and licking their butts, but he was out and about Getting the Job Done. "I'm going to save it for later, though, if that's all right with you." Phil shrugged.

Nina opened the door and walked in, kicking off her shoes and surreptitiously placing the worm on the kitchen counter to be thrown away when the cat wasn't looking. She looked up at the giant clock on the wall; still an hour before the trivia thing started. She turned on the kettle; time to chill and tidy. She loved her apartment, even if calling it an apartment was a bit of a stretch. It was basically one big room, with a tiny kitchenette and bathroom, but what it had in abundance was light and bookshelves, and really, what else does anyone need? Big double windows on the south and west walls filled the place with sun and color, and the shelves went from floor to ceiling. There was an oversize armchair near the window, where Nina could — and did — sit for hours and read her butt off. The Persian rug was all reds and oranges and tigers and birds, a souvenir of some trip of her mom's, and had shown up a week or two after Nina had moved in her stuff (a bed, a chair, six boxes of books, a kitten, a coffee maker, and a large bulletin board). The note attached had read, *Hey, had this in storage for years, thought you might like it. Let me know if you want the rest of the stuff.*

Rest of the stuff? Nina had called her mom immediately. "Hey, Mom. Where are you?" This was her standard greeting.

"I'm in London right now, darling. Where are you?" Her mom was Australian, but her accent had softened over the years to the occasional hint. She said *sockAH* instead of soccer, or lollies instead of candy, but it wasn't like she walked around in a hat with corks dangling from it.

Nina had smiled to hear her mother's voice, the part of her she was most familiar with. "I'm in Dubai, Mom, at the top of the Burj Khalifa."

"Really?" Her mom sounded excited. "How's the view?"

27

Nina had sighed. "No, I'm in Los Angeles, right where you left me."

"Oh." Her mom was clearly disappointed Nina hadn't inherited her wanderlust. She didn't say it in so many words, but she didn't have to.

"What's with this carpet?" Nina had asked, poking the rolled-up rug with her foot.

Nina could hear her mom sipping tea. She had probably been doing three or four things at the same time as taking Nina's call. One thing at a time? Where's the fun in that? "Well, I lived in LA when I was pregnant with you, remember?"

"Of course." Nina knew her own origin story by heart, as everybody does. Her mother hadn't been a slut, exactly, but she hadn't been interested in romantic relationships. Nina had asked her many years earlier why she'd chosen not to have an abortion, and Candice had laughed in her usual way.

"Because I thought it would be an adventure, and it was." *AdvenchAH.*

"The rug is gorgeous. What's the rest of the stuff like?"

"Well, I think there's all kinds of things. Go look if you want." She'd told her where the storage unit was, and now, as Nina looked around her happy little place, she

28

was looking at furniture she might have peed on as a baby. A small kilim sofa, an ottoman from Rajasthan, which Phil thought was his, and as much of her mom's art collection as she could drag out of storage. The one wall that wasn't covered with books was covered with photographs; images by Ruth Orkin, Henri Cartier-Bresson, Inge Morath and a few snapshots Nina liked that she'd taken herself; posters and magazine covers featuring the TV shows and celebrities of her childhood; her "visualization corner," with its bulletin board and calendar (don't mock; you only wish you were as organized as Nina); photos of Nina's mom and Phil as a kitten. A single Malm bed from IKEA — with the optional storage drawers, please note — was tucked against a wall. By the way, the plural of Malm is just "Malm," like deer; "Malms" sounds wrong, although it also sounds like a delicious marshmallow candy — ooh, are those chocolate malms?

Stooping to pick up the mail, Nina fed Phil and poured herself a glass of wine. Then she wandered over to her visualization corner and stood there, frowning at her bulletin board, with its inspirational images, quotes, and life hacks she never actually put into practice. She enjoyed being organized but always felt there was so much room for more. She loved having color-coordinated folders and lists and spent half an hour each morning reviewing her planner, setting her goals and intentions for the day, and generally pondering. This was time she had, of course, set aside for that purpose in her planner. She only wished there was more to actually, you know, *plan*. She sometimes made lists of things she'd already done solely so she could cross them off, which she couldn't help feeling was pretty pathetic but strangely satisfying.

She'd graduated from UCLA with a useless but interesting degree (Art History, thanks for asking) and took the job at Knight's while she worked out what she wanted to do now that she was grown up. She spent the next few years actually growing up; having short-lived love affairs and one slightly longer love affair and then some more short ones, and Getting in Shape and Being Vegan and Paleo and then Giving Up And Eating Everything Again. She took up yoga, then Spinning, then a combination yoga and Spin class she inwardly referred to as Spoga, then decoupage and knitting and a series of those evenings where you drink wine and paint, but she had a niggling suspicion she was underperforming in some way. Surely her purpose in life wasn't simply to read as many books as possible?

Many of her friends were in long-term romantic relationships, but Nina was single. She liked sex; she enjoyed people with different points of view; she dated. But dating in LA was an Internet-enabled contact sport, and after a dozen evenings that established new lows for interpersonal behavior, she'd decided to Take a Break from Dating. It had been a lot easier than the time she'd tried to give up caffeine.

Nina worried she liked being alone too much; it was the only time she ever fully relaxed. People were . . . exhausting. They made her anxious. Leaving her apartment every morning was the turning over of a giant hourglass, the mental energy she'd stored up overnight eroding grain by grain. She refueled during the day by grabbing moments of solitude and sometimes felt her life was a long-distance swim between islands of silence. She enjoyed people — she really did — she just needed to take them in homeopathic doses; a little of the poison was the cure.

In solitude she set goals and made them, challenged herself and accepted the challenge, took up hobbies and dropped them, and if she periodically cleaned off her bulletin board and stuck up new goals and plans and dates and budgets and bought a new planner in the middle of the year and started over, so what? Nina leaned forward and crossed off that day's date on the calendar, even though it wasn't fully done yet.

See? One hundred percent ahead of the game.

Nina's trivia team consisted of her and her three closest friends and was called Book 'Em, Danno, because why not? They were unassailable on books (Nina), history and geography (her friend Leah), contemporary popular culture (Carter, an ex-boyfriend of Leah's who'd been too smart and funny to completely let go of), and current events and politics (her other friend, Lauren). All of them were equally good, in true millennial fashion, at classic popular culture (1950–1995, Lucy Ricardo to Chandler Bing) and identifying international snacks. Despite the fact that Nina was a football fan, their Achilles' heel was still sports. In an effort to broaden her athletic knowledge, Nina had started reading *Sports Illustrated,* but so far all it had done was give her dirty dreams about a Norwegian snowboarder whose name she couldn't even pronounce.

Having been thrown out of their last

regular bar for never letting anyone else win, Book 'Em, Danno was now cautiously testing a new venue. Sugarlips was in Silver Lake, had been open two months, and served a vast selection of sodas (international and domestic) alongside the traditional panoply of craft beers. It was also making a name for itself by serving bowls of dry breakfast cereal as bar snacks, which presumably explained the name.

"How is it?" Lauren was watching Carter try a prickly pear soda. Lauren had dark hair, dark eyes, and a dark soul that delighted in humor other people might consider sardonic. She reminded Nina of a really good loaf of sourdough bread — crusty on the outside, with a soft and rewarding interior.

Carter shrugged. "You know, I've never had anything else prickly pear flavored, so I realized halfway through I didn't have a frame of reference. But it tastes like . . . watermelon bubble gum?" He took another sip. "It's kind of awesome, but I should probably be stoned to truly enjoy it." He didn't look like the kind of guy that got stoned; he looked like the kind of guy who helped old ladies across the street and regularly took Communion, but, as we all know, appearances are very deceptive. He had the symbol of the Rebel Alliance tattooed on his arm, and the Force was strong in his family.

"No." Nina shook her head. "Keep your head in the game. You know the rules."

"It might make me quicker."

Lauren snorted into her beer. "Yeah, because that's something people say all the time: We need to move with maximum speed and efficiency; break out the pot."

The trivia contest began, and Book 'Em kicked butt for an hour or so. Then a late entry arrived to harsh their mellow.

"Oh crap," muttered Carter. "Look who it isn't."

Nina craned around. "Who isn't it?"

"Dammit," said Leah. "It's You're a Quizzard, Harry."

Nina kept a straight face, but inwardly she was vexed. Quizzard was really the only challenge they had in the East Los Angeles bar trivia world, which, admittedly, is an extremely small world, but Nina was competitive.

They watched as Quizzard, which was three guys and a girl, like the bizarro-world version of them, sat down at a table across from them. The team leader was clearly the tall guy who narrowed his eyes at Nina, and then raised his hand in mock salute.

Nina held his gaze for a second, then yawned hugely.

"Nice," said Lauren. "Subtle."

"He annoys me."

"Is it his cuteness or the fact that he knows so much more about sports than you?"

"He's not cute. And he knows more about sports because he's a dumb jock. Have you noticed he never answers a question about anything other than sports?"

"That's not true; he answered a question about supermodels a few weeks ago."

"Pah, swimsuit issue," said Nina.

Lauren and Leah looked at each other over her head. "I think it's the cuteness, personally," said Leah. "I think you two are destined to fall in love and run off together on a trivia honeymoon."

"Which would take place where?"

"The Culver City studio where *Jeopardy!* is filmed?"

"Washington DC, so you can geek out at the Library of Congress?"

"Hawaii?"

They all looked at Carter. "What has Hawaii got to do with trivia?" asked Lauren.

Carter shrugged. "I don't know. I was focusing on the honeymoon part."

Nina sighed. "He's objectively attractive but subjectively repulsive, on account of his overwhelming self-confidence."

Carter nodded. "That's right, because women hate a confident man. That's why Luke is so much more attractive than Han."

Nina said, "Sarcasm gives you wrinkles." She looked at the Quizzard team leader, surreptitiously. He had dark hair that seemed uncombed, which was good, and a bony, lean face that only just missed being traditionally handsome because he'd clearly broken his nose at some point. "Besides, he looks like he fights, and I'm a pacifist." Neither of these things was strictly true, and Carter rolled his eyes.

The quizmaster tapped on his microphone. "OK, we have a new team joining the fray, You're a Quizzard, Harry. The current leader, Book 'Em, Danno, is ahead by ten points, but we've still got three rounds to play, and, per the rules, late teams don't get any extra credit, so, good luck, everyone."

Nina checked that everyone had their pencils handy, and spare paper for notes. No one else needed paper and pencil, of course — she was the one who filled in the answers — but she liked everyone to be prepared. What if she suddenly had a seizure and broke her pencil? Her brain smash-cut to a slo-mo of her falling to the ground, the pencil snapping under her, pieces of wood and graphite flicking across the floor. She really needed to get laid; this kind of daydreaming couldn't possibly be a good sign. She looked over at the Quizzard guy who, she had to admit, was totally sexy and probably as dumb as a stump. No, brain, no, she told herself, to which her brain responded that she was not in any way responsible for the issue at hand, and suggested Nina address her complaints to a lower authority.

"Are you paying attention, Nina?" barked Leah. "They're handing out the quiz sheets."

"Yes, yes."

She took the sheet from the quizmaster, who leaned over and said, "Ten dollars Quizzard beats the crap out of you."

Nina frowned at him. "Howard, get a grip. We're already one round ahead. It'll be hard for them to catch up."

Leah leaned over and poked the guy in the chest. "Hey, just because I wouldn't go out with you, there is no need to drag trivia into it. This is an honorable sport, played by honorable people."

"In honorable bars," chimed in Carter.

"At honorable times," concluded Lauren.

They all knew Howard because he traveled from bar to bar, running quiz nights. He called himself the King of Questions but was referred to by everyone else as QuizDick. He loved to wield his power, which was solely based on his having all the answers, and the team suspected he was responsible for getting them banned from the last place. "You guys are drunk. They're going to wipe the floor with you."

"I am not drunk," said Nina. "I am stone cold sober, and I am going to take your bet and then I am going to take your money."

Howard sneered, which was even less attractive than you might think, and sauntered away.

Over at the Quizzard table, the girl member of the team, Lisa, was making fun of Tom, the tall guy who Nina thought was dumb as a stump.

"You like that girl, don't you?" She inclined her head half an inch in Nina's direction.

Tom shook his head. "Not at all. She's full of herself. And she's really short." He could have gone on to say she had skin like a peach and hair the color of an Irish setter and a mouth that was higher at one corner than the other and ankles that tapered just so . . . but he thought it might undermine his position.

Jack, another Quizzard, made a face. "You're jealous because she knows more than you do."

"She doesn't."

"Yes, she does. She seems to know everything."

"No one knows everything."

"I heard she works at a bookstore," said Paul, the final member of the Quizzard team.

"Isn't that cheating?" said Jack.

Tom looked at him. "I don't think having a job is cheating, Jack. Lots of people have jobs."

"Not me," said Jack proudly. There was a pause while he considered whether or not that was something to boast about, but ultimately decided he was cool with it. "I'm an artist."

"You're a vandal," said Lisa. "You write your name on the sides of buildings."

"I'm exercising my right to political protest," said Jack.

"You'll be exercising your right to do community service," replied Paul. He was a lawyer; he couldn't help it.

Lisa, who had known Tom since high school, watched his face. He definitely liked that girl, the Book 'Em team leader. She looked over at the girl, who really was pretty in an unusual and interesting way, and wondered if they knew anyone in common. It was time Tom started dating again; enough time had passed since the last . . . disaster. She made a note to ask Jack which bookstore it was.

Howard tapped the microphone again. "Teams, let the battle commence. Pencils at the ready; the time starts . . . now."

today is the day

DATE Wednesday May 1st   M T W Th F S Su

⬦ ⬦ ⬦ ⬦ ⬦ ⬦ ⬦ ⬦

SCHEDULE

7>8	
8>9	
9>10	Dress nice!!
10>11	
11>12	
12>13	
13>14	Work
14>15	
15>16	
16>17	
17>18	
18>19	
19>20	Book Club
20>21	

TO DO LIST

- ☐ Sports illustrated sub.
- ☐ cereal
- ☐ popcorn
- ☐ Marshmallows
- ☐ cocoa
- ☐ milk
- ☐
- ☐
- ☐

GOALS

Improve Sports knowledge

NOTES

Horse racing wiki

＋ BREAKFAST

＋ LUNCH

＋ DINNER

＋ WORKOUT

THREE

In which Nina is surprised, not
necessarily in a good way.

Mornings were a bit of a challenge at Nina's
house.

In Nina's imaginary life, which was the
one she wished she were leading, rather
than the one she'd been handed at birth,
she would get up, wash her face with a variety of responsibly sourced products, shower
in one of those showers with multiple heads
(though she often wondered what happened
when you bent down for the shampoo —
Did you get a blast of water full in the face?
That seemed rude), and then dress herself
in comfortable but stylish clothes made of
natural fibers picked by well-paid workers.
Are you following all this? Then she would
breakfast on fresh fruit and whole grains
and yogurt made from milk freely donated
by goats who had more than they needed

for themselves. She would be grateful and mindful and not in any way blemished.

It was actually more like this: Nina would get up and her head would hurt because she drank wine that was at least 30 percent sulfites or whatever it is that causes headaches. Her mouth would feel like the inside of one of those single socks you see on the street sometimes, and her hair would be depressed. She would stand slightly crouched by the coffee maker and shiver until the coffee was done. Sometimes her glassy eyes would rest on her visualization corner and she would resent the steady way the planet whirled around the sun without consulting her at all. Day after day, night after night, rinse and repeat. Basically, until the first slug of caffeine hit her system, she was essentially in suspended animation, and she'd been known to drool.

Once she was caffeinated and showered, she was a whole new person. That person would take a second cup of coffee to the big armchair and pull out her planner and pencil box. She would decide what to eat and how she was going to exercise. She would make a shopping list. She would feel like her life was controlled and organized and heading in the right direction. It was the most satisfying part of her day.

Today she had a book club meeting, after which her plan was to come home and read until bedtime. She laid out some extra-fluffy pajama pants and socks in preparation. She made a note to get popcorn. She made a note to get mini marshmallows to go in her cocoa. And then she made a note to get cocoa. And milk. And then she looked on eBay for an interesting vintage cocoa mug, but then she noticed the time and closed everything and rushed off to work.

On the way to work, Nina felt pretty chirpy, and put in her earbuds and pretended she was in a movie, smiling at all the people who passed her and saying hello to the dogs. She had this fantasy a lot, that her life was like *The Truman Show*, that audiences all over the world were enjoying her playlist and hairstyle as much as she was. She would angle her face to the sun to help the lighting guy, or look over her shoulder to give the camera back there something to do. In public Nina was a quiet, reserved person; in private she was an all-singing, all-dancing cavalcade of light and motion. Unless she was a quivering ball of anxiety, because that was also a frequently selected option. She was very good at hiding it, but anxiety was like her anti-superpower, the one that came out unbidden in a crisis. The

Hulk gets angry; Nina got anxious. Nina had a lot of sympathy for Bruce Banner, particularly the version played by Mark Ruffalo, and at least she had Xanax. He only had Thor.

Nina reached Larchmont Boulevard, with its artisanal hat and cheese shops (two different shops; that would be a weird combination, especially in warm weather), and turned into her favorite café to grab a gluten-free low-fat bran muffin. Just kidding, it was a chocolate croissant.

"Hi, Nina," said Vanessa, a friend of hers who worked there. "What's new?"

"Surprisingly little," Nina said. "I'll have a chocolate croissant."

"The breakfast of champions."

"French champions."

"Champignons?"

Nina said, "I think that means mushrooms." She sounded more confident than she was.

Vanessa shrugged. "Look, I've only had two cups of coffee. I'm barely alive."

Nina took her croissant without a bag and ate it as she crossed the street. Multitasking and eco-sensitive all at once. Not even 9 A.M. and already ahead for the day.

Liz looked up as she walked in. "Ooh, did you get one of those for me?"

Nina turned and went back across the street.

A minute later she had returned. "Yes, I did, funnily enough."

"That's so nice of you. How was the trivia thing?"

"We lost."

Liz stared at her. "What? You never lose."

Nina kicked a bookcase. "Well, we did last night. It came down to a tiebreaker and the topic was horse racing and we lost. Did you know all racehorses have their birthday on January first? No? Neither did I."

Liz frowned at her. "Don't kick the bookcase. I'm sorry your fund of general knowledge stops short of the sport of kings, but damage the fittings and it's coming out of your wages." She turned to walk away, clicking her tongue, but then suddenly turned back. "And don't forget to make a pile of books in case of Mephistopheles." She walked on, then stopped again. "Oh, and I forgot in the shock of your losing, you missed a call."

Nina swept the buttery crumbs from her sweater, glad none of them had lingered long enough to leave a stain (which always made her think of The Simpsons: "Remember . . . if the paper turns clear, it's your window to weight gain"), and frowned at

46

her. "A call? A customer?"

Liz shrugged and bit into her croissant, adding crumbs to her own shirt. "I don't know. A man. He asked for Nina Hill, which is you, and when I asked if he wanted to leave a message, he said he would call back." The phone rang. "Maybe that's him."

But it wasn't; it was someone else entirely, and Nina had already forgotten about the call when the man who'd placed it walked into the bookstore a couple of hours later.

He stood out immediately, because he was wearing a suit of a cut and kind not often seen on Larchmont Boulevard. A serious suit. A white shirt with starch. A pocket square. Most of the people in Larchmont worked in one creative field or another, and tended to wear hooded sweatshirts and high-tops. The more successful they were, the shabbier they looked. This guy looked like an alien. "Nina Hill?"

Liz pointed at her, although Nina had already looked up when she'd heard her name, like a cat hearing a distant can opener. She'd been happily shelving new nonfiction, and at that very moment was holding a book about earthworms and thinking fondly of Phil and his generous nature. She looked over at the guy and decided he was probably bad news.

He approached her, gliding as if he were on casters, and said, "Miss Hill? Nina Lee Hill?" It was too late to run for it, and as far as she knew, there were no outstanding warrants for her arrest, so she nodded.

He smiled. "Is there somewhere we might speak privately?"

Definitely bad news.

The office at Knight's was very small and mostly filled with cartons of books, oversize poster board advertisements for books, and piles of books that threatened to tip and spill at any moment. There was one chair, which was supposed to be adjustable but wasn't, and the man gestured in a "go ahead" kind of way, so Nina sat. That turned out to be super weird, because her face was basically on the same level as his crotch — see: broken chair — so she stood back up. He didn't sit down, either, as there really wasn't room to get past her, and so they stood there, about four inches too close to each other to be comfortable. Nina wanted to take a big step back, and possibly assume a defensive stance, but the moment had passed, and if she did it now it would seem rude. Oh my God, she thought, it's hard to be human sometimes, with the pressure to be civilized lying only very thinly over the brain of a nervous little mammal.

Maybe other people's layer of civilization was thicker than hers; hers was like a peel-off face mask after it had been peeled. Through the edge of the door she could see Liz hovering, in case she needed help. Feeling better, she decided to take the plunge and smile.

"How can I help you, Mr. . . . ?"

"Sarkassian. I'm a lawyer for the estate of William Reynolds."

"OK." Nina waited. She'd never heard of the guy. Was she supposed to know the name?

"I'm afraid I have some bad news." The lawyer paused.

Nina kept waiting. If it were really bad news, the police would have shown up, right?

"I'm sorry to tell you that your father has died."

After a brief pause during which Nina checked for double meanings or maybe a language difficulty, she shook her head. "I'm sorry, there must be a mistake. I don't have a father." That sounded wrong. "I mean, of course I have a father, but I've never known him. We're not connected in any way, I mean. I don't know who he is."

"He is, or rather was, William Reynolds."

"I don't think so."

49

The lawyer nodded. "He was. The estate has a letter from your mother, Candice Hill, confirming his paternity and absolving him of all parental liability and responsibility under the proviso he never attempt to contact you."

Nina sat down on the chair after all. "I don't . . ."

Mr. Sarkassian was balding on top but with hair around the sides and back, like someone wearing a brown woolly hat with everything but the brim removed. He spoke quickly and firmly, and Nina wondered if he'd been practicing on the way over. He couldn't possibly have to break this kind of news all the time, surely? "Mr. Reynolds clearly abided by your mother's wishes during his lifetime, but you were nonetheless included in his list of beneficiaries."

He paused, but Nina looked at him without replying, largely because she had absolutely no response to that.

"I'm here to invite you to attend the reading of the will, which is actually in a few weeks." He looked apologetic. "It's taken me rather longer than I hoped to find you, as you could have been anywhere." He shot back a French cuff and looked at his watch. "Imagine my surprise when you turned out to be half a mile away in Los Angeles."

"Why?"

He smiled, relieved to finally have some good news to share. "Because this is where the rest of your family lives, of course."

Nina shook her head like Phil did when she put drops in his ears. "My family?"

The lawyer patted her on the arm, and she was too weirded out to even bridle. "I'm sorry, I had no idea your paternity would be news to you." A momentary expression of judgment crossed his face, and Nina spoke.

"My mother clearly didn't think Mr. Reynolds would have been a good father."

Another expression crossed Sarkassian's face, though this one was harder to read.

"Well, she may have been right. It was a long time ago. Here's my card — my office address is on it — and we'll be in touch with details of the will reading." He paused. "In the meantime, I'm afraid you may be hearing from your brother and sisters. I had to let them know about you, because they wanted to know why the will reading had to wait."

Nina stared at him. "My what now?"

"Your brother and sisters."

"I have a brother and sisters?"

He coughed. "I'm afraid your father was married three times."

"Just not to my mother."

"Right." He nodded. "But to other women. You actually have three sisters and a brother, two nephews and two nieces, and two great-nieces and a great-nephew. Plus two stepmothers still living, though you don't need those, I imagine." He looked at his watch. "I've asked one of your nephews, Peter Reynolds, to get in touch and explain the whole family to you, because it's complicated and he's the only one everyone is always talking to."

Nina stared at him. "I'm sorry, but can I pretend you never told me? I don't really want any more people in my life. I've done fine without them for nearly thirty years." She felt her breathing start to get shallow and willed herself to slow it down so she wouldn't hyperventilate and topple to the ground.

The lawyer had clearly not considered this option and looked puzzled. "Mr. Reynolds was an extremely wealthy man, and the fact that you're a beneficiary means he presumably left you something of value."

Nina tried to focus. "Well, not to look a gift horse in the mouth, but unless it's a butt load of money, I really don't care. I'm not sure I care even if it is a butt load of money."

"Of course you do," said the lawyer. "Everyone cares about money." Again with the watch. "I have to go. Peter will contact you shortly. None of them were very thrilled to hear about you, I'm afraid. Except Peter."

"He's supportive of illegitimate children?"

Sarkassian turned to leave. "He's an anthropologist."

Four

In which Nina observes other people and talks to her mother.

Well, obviously after that kind of news, Nina walked out of the store and wandered the streets sightless with shock, rending the air with lamentation. Actually, she went back to work, because they had Preschooler Reading Hour that afternoon and she was nominally in charge. Life will throw you major curveballs, but it's rare you can do much more than duck.

Liz was not a lover of children, describing them as sticky little book-chuckers, so the store's schedule of kid activities was Nina's to run. She took it seriously, and had developed quite a program:

Baby and Parent Reading Time: In this activity, which happened three mornings a week, newborns and lap babies lay like

54

slugs while the parents listened to an impoverished young actor read to them. To be fair, most of these parents were basically asleep with their eyes open, and the babies often rolled off their laps onto the *Reading Is Cool* rug. The actor was usually hoping at least one of the parents was an agent or something, and ever since one reader had been plucked from obscurity to star in a pilot that actually went somewhere, there had been a waiting list to read. Nina did her best to keep things fair, but she had been known to succumb to bribery (See's Candies were her weakness, in case you're wondering).

Preschooler Reading Hour: Three-to-five-year-olds and nannies, throwing books around (the kids, not the nannies), with the nannies doing the reading, and extremely popular. Firstly because the nannies could relax and chat a bit, and secondly because parents could say, oh, the nanny takes Aubergine and Salamander to reading hour every day, and feel better about preferring to be at work with people who knew how to use a fork. Daily, at three thirty.

Elementary Book Club: This was Nina's

pet project. Larchmont was a neighborhood filled with kids, and the girls in particular were very Big on Books. The boys were, too; they just preferred not to talk about them, whereas the girls were all about the chatter. These little girls were strong and confident, mostly, because of when and where they were growing up, and because puberty hadn't smacked them across the head yet. They unapologetically and voraciously read books about fairies and witches and female heroines who didn't need rescuing, and would open a book to check it out and then still be standing there reading an hour later when their parents reappeared. It was wonderful to watch a kid get tugged ineluctably into a different world.

Nina had developed a special fondness for these kids, because she knew the world would soon begin telling them other things were more important than the contents of their heads. So she started the elementary book club, and once a month after the store had closed at seven, she would sit there with a group of eight-to-twelve-year-old girls and talk about books for an hour. It was the club she wished she'd had when she was their age, and if she occasionally sat there making friendship bracelets and talking about *A Mango-Shaped Space* with even more enthusiasm than the ten-year-olds, what's your point?

Young Adult Book Club: This one was all Liz. She loved a darkling teen.

There had been some discussion of starting a regular, adult book club, but Nina didn't have time, because she already belonged to a weekly adult book club — of which more later — and that commitment, along with the elementary book club, her exercise regime (if you can call sporadic exercise classes and fervent promises to do better a regime), and of course the trivia team, meant she had no free time. Liz refused to do it, and the part-time girl who worked there, Polly, hated reading. Why does she work in a bookstore, you ask? It's a long story.

Anyway.

Despite not having a child herself, Nina enjoyed watching other people handle the unsuspected responsibilities of parenthood. The baby wasn't the biggest problem at all, it turned out; it was the other parents. There was a definite learning curve over the first few years, and Nina had a ringside seat, because so many of Larchmont's parents were parishioners at the Church of the Dust-Jacketed Hardback and brought their kids in all the time. She'd watched dozens of little kids graduate from *Goodnight Moon* to *Bedtime for Frances* to *Junie B. Jones* to whatever YA series was trending, and with them went their parents, learning to navigate the intricate social networks of neighborhood and school.

Take when two moms met in the store at reading time. Standard school-mom rules of engagement applied: If your children were friends and you met while both of you were standing, you hugged, of course. If one of you was sitting on the floor already and your kids were *good* friends, with an actual, out-of-school playdate under their tiny rainbow belts, then the one sitting would start to stand but the other would wave her back down and bend from the waist to half hug. If your kids were *really* good friends, with multiple playdates and maybe a sleepover in their shared past, then the one sitting would scooch over to make room for the other, and they would hug once both were down. Nina studied these things, because they didn't come naturally to her. And working in a store where people tended to aimlessly wander around looking at books gave her ample opportunity for observation.

Nina's special favorite was watching people handle introductions. It played out like this: A woman would be browsing in the store, trying to decide whether she had the balls to get something vaguely pornographic or if she'd have to stick with something worthy (note: this is where that online bookseller really triumphs, undercover purchasing), and notices someone she knows has come in. In a split second she has to decide whether or not to acknowledge their existence, the decision depending on how well she knows them, how well they know her, and whether or not she can get away with ignoring them (i.e., they definitely haven't seen her yet, or she's disguised as a pirate).

Their eyes meet, and now she has to decide whether to say hi and keep browsing, or actually approach and greet. She decides she can't get away without actually greeting, but then realizes the other woman has someone else with her, someone who looks vaguely familiar, but she can't remember why. Nina had seen this scenario so often she'd gotten used to the flicker of panic in a woman's eyes as she walked forward while desperately wishing she weren't. It was hilarious, but only when it wasn't you. Anyway, now the friend is committed, too, whether she likes it or not, so she says hey, the original woman says hey, hug regulations apply as previously described. Then the friend says, so, whatever your name is, this is Bindy Macaroon, I think you two might already know each other. (Moms of a certain age know dozens and dozens of people through various channels, so they have to perform this human equivalent of canine butt sniffing all the goddamned time.)

ORIGINAL WOMAN: Oh, hi, Bindy. *Do* we know each other? (Here there would be a lot of head movement and facial expressions that alternated between friendly openness and self-abasement, playing it safe until the connection is clarified. If it turns out they know each other because one of them slept with the other one's boyfriend in college, then, you know, awkward.)

BINDY: I think we do! You look so familiar! (Similar head bobbing and approach/withdraw body language.) Do you have a kid in Miss Rectangle's class?

ORIGINAL: No . . . My daughter, Elephantine (pronounced the French way, of course), is in Mr. Elevator's class. Does your child do swimming at the YMCA with Professor Bubbles?

BINDY: No . . . Art class on Saturdays at Brushlicious?

ORIGINAL: No . . . Preschool? We were at Harmony House of Love and Kindness, were you?

BINDY: No, Urethra went to Mandarin Immersion Buddhist Chakra Preschool. In the Valley.

And with that they would give up and shrug and would never, ever realize they knew each other because one time they bumped cars in traffic and stood on the street for ten minutes exchanging insurance information.

If you had walked into the bookstore after lunch that day, you would have seen Nina making a pile of books on the counter that might have struck you as dangerously unbalanced, and shortly before two in the afternoon she suddenly knocked it to the floor. It made an incredible noise.

The man who'd just walked through the door paused and narrowed his eyes at her.

"Is Liz here?"

Mr. Meffo was their landlord. Larchmont Boulevard was broadly owned by three or four people. A large family had owned properties in one section of the boulevard since the '60s, and they were generally mellow and much loved. Another landlord was an investment bank that kept out of it, for the most part. And the third was Mr. Meffo. He was a popular villain on the boulevard, but of course he was just a regular businessman trying to make a profit, which would be the actual point of business. If he'd been a sheep farmer, he would have been carrying a lamb around and wearing a bonnet, but as he was a landlord, he was carrying an iPad and a cell phone.

Unfortunately, the rent had gone up precipitously, and business hadn't followed suit, so Liz had taken to hiding whenever he came around. She paid the rent, more or less; she just took generous advantage of space and time. She also called the poor man Mephistopheles, which wasn't nice.

"Sorry, Mr. Meffo, she just left." Nina hoped the book fall had been sufficient warning. Once Liz had been trapped with a customer when Mephistopheles walked in and had had to pay the rent on time.

Mr. Meffo sighed. He wasn't a bad man; he was simply a good businessman. "Can you tell her to call me, please? The rent is overdue."

Nina nodded and smiled, glad she'd worn a nice, professional outfit. Liz had told her they needed to look successful, so it wouldn't cross Meffo's mind to cancel their lease. "I'm sure she knows, Mr. Meffo. We've been very busy with lots of customers lately."

He looked around at the empty store. "Really?"

"Oh yes, you just missed a rush."

"Did I?" He looked at Nina, doubtfully. "Well, tell Liz I've had several inquiries about the store, and one or two buyers interested, which is appealing." He sighed. "Being a landlord isn't as much fun as you'd think."

Nina said nothing, having never thought being a landlord would be fun.

He left, and Nina waited ten or twenty minutes until Liz peered around the office door.

"Is he gone?"

Nina nodded. "You must pay the rent," she said.

"I can't pay the rent," replied Liz.

63

"You MUST pay the rent," Nina insisted.

"I can't pay the rent," said Liz, again.

Nina assumed a Dudley Do-Right voice. "I'LL pay the rent!" and Liz sighed, "My hero!" and then they went about their day.

Later that day, Nina finally reached her mom. She had to get the timing right in order to catch her mother when she wasn't ignoring her phone, which was most of the time. Candice Hill had grown up in the darkest Australian wilds of the 1980s, where, reportedly, the women glowed and the men plundered, but no one had a cell phone. These days, she was remarkably cavalier about turning hers on. "I don't want to make myself too easy to find, darling," she would say, as if being thousands of miles away wasn't enough.

Nina had decided 7 A.M. in China was a reasonably good bet, so she stepped into the bookstore office a little before four in the afternoon, before the high school kids came in to moon around the graphic novels and peep at one another over the shelves. The phone rang and rang, and Nina was getting ready to leave a sarcastic voice mail when her mother picked up.

Of course, modern telecommunications made it sound like she was across the street.

"Good morning, lovely!" Candice yelled, as she often did. "Everything OK?"

"Well, mostly," replied Nina.

"What can I do you for, my love? I have to be at work in an hour. Spit it out." She issued an order in Mandarin, multitasking as usual.

"William Reynolds is dead."

There was a pause, then the sound of her mother exhaling. She gave it a shot, though. "Sorry, who's that then?"

"My father, William Reynolds."

Candice could tell Nina was mad, but she was still blasé, because she'd been born that way. "Oh, *that* William Reynolds. Yeah . . . I was hoping you'd never find out about him."

This was one of the things Nina actually loved about her mother. She would lie or make up crap and then, if you caught her at it, simply admit defeat and move on. She didn't seem to experience shame or regret in any form.

However lovable her mother was, though, Nina was being firm with her. "Well, I did, so how about you fill me in? Why on earth didn't you tell me I had a father? You knew I wondered. Why did you think it was a good idea to keep us apart? I have a brother and sisters!"

"You do? That's nice."

Nina's voice went up an octave. "Mom, I have more than half a dozen relatives living in the same city as I am! Just think of all the playdates and birthday parties I missed out on."

Her mother laughed. "You didn't need anyone to play with; you were fine. Other people are overrated."

"I generally agree, Mom, but I would have liked the option." Nina noticed her other hand was clenched tightly, and reached for a pencil. She twirled it back and forth through her fingers, a nervous habit she'd refined into a party trick. Assuming she was at the kind of party where pencil twiddling would be impressive.

Her mother paused, then said defensively, "He wouldn't have been a good dad, Nina. He was a player, he was full of himself, he had a wife."

"A wife is not a character trait, Mom. And what about you, sleeping with a married man? What the hell? What about hos before bros, dude?"

"I beg your pardon? Nina Lee Hill, did you just call me a ho?"

Nina laughed, suddenly, and tossed her pencil away. Her mother always made things seem lighter. It was partly her Australian accent and general "let's get on with it and

66

stop making a fuss" approach to everything, and partly her personality. Candice Hill had no patience for drama, or overblown feelings, really, of any kind. Which made her superficial and frustrating if, like Nina, you wanted to have a conversation about emotional topics like discovering your entire life had been a lie, but which also made things clunk back into perspective.

"No, Mom, I didn't call you a ho, but please could you take a second to think about how this might feel to me?"

Candice clicked her tongue. "Nina, this all happened nearly thirty years ago. Your father was very handsome; we met on a photo shoot of some kind, I don't even remember; we stayed in my apartment for a long weekend; and then I found out he had a wife, who was actually pregnant at the time if I remember rightly; so I cut him off and moved on. Two months later, I found out I was pregnant and decided to keep you. He wasn't really part of any of it except for a sweaty forty-eight hours at the start."

Nina badly wanted to cover her ears and say la la la, but she was holding the phone.

Candice continued, "I had enough money and time to take care of you, and I didn't want him involved, because I didn't know him at all and he'd already exhibited bad judgment by cheating on his wife, so I made him sign something promising to leave you alone and that was that. I never saw him again. I'm amazed he even remembered my name."

"Well, to be fair, Mom, your name might have been slightly less memorable than the fact he had an actual child. That one's a little harder to forget." *Not everyone finds it as easy as you did.*

"What a pain in the ass. I knew he was bad news."

"It would have been better if he hadn't been news at all. I hate surprises; you know that."

"Yeah, I know, which is something you must have inherited from him, because I love surprises."

Nina rolled her eyes. "We were talking about me."

"I have to go. Are we done here?"

"Yeah. Any chance you're going to say, 'Sorry, Nina, you're right, I should have prepared you for this sudden shock'?"

Her mother made a huffy noise. "None. I didn't expect him to break his word after three decades. If anyone owes you an apology, it's him."

"Well, he's dead."

"Serves him right." Candice sighed. "I'm

sorry he was a loser, Nina. But you're a big girl now; you can handle this." And with that she hung up.

Nina sighed and wondered if she would ever be a mom herself and, if she were, would she be any better at it than her own mother was. As a child, Nina had been sad her mother wasn't there, because everyone else seemed to think it was sad. Then, as a teenager, she'd been angry with her absent mother and blamed her for her own anxiety and shyness. Now, as an adult, she'd come to the conclusion that her mother being away all the time had probably been a blessing. Her nanny, Louise, had been a wonderful mother, and her mother had been a wonderful photographer. Biology is not destiny, and love is not proportionate to shared DNA. Of course, she reflected, as she put down the phone and returned to the store, she could be totally wrong about this. She was wrong about so many things.

FIVE

In which Nina attends a book club
meeting and gets an e-mail.

Nina went home after work and Googled
the crap out of William Reynolds. It was a
common name, but she decided he couldn't
have been a professional tennis player from
the early twentieth century, or an English
lord of the seventeenth century, and was
more likely to have been this lawyer guy
who lived in Los Angeles until he died a
week or two earlier. She guessed she'd
missed the funeral. Seeing as she'd missed
everything else, this wasn't a stinger. All the
obit said was he'd been seventy-eight and
was survived by a widow and young daughter. She knew the last part wasn't accurate,
although she'd already forgotten how many
children there actually were. She found a
few pictures of him online, usually attending a charity function of some kind, always

in a tux. He didn't remind her of herself, but, to be fair, she was a slender twenty-nine-year-old woman with dark red hair and freckles, and he had been a rounded old man with white hair and wrinkles, so it wasn't exactly apples to apples. More like grapes to raisins.

Nina wondered if she and her siblings would like each other, and if they'd have things in common, like a fondness for *The Simpsons* and sandwiches. Maybe they'd become good friends, or maybe they'd start a family feud like a TV reality show. She drifted off for a moment creating title sequences for *Reynolds vs. Hill: Sibling Wars,* which for some reason had mid-'80s synthesizer theme music and the kind of credits that whoosh in from the side. Would she appear as herself, or would she be played by someone more telegenic? She didn't photograph well, which was a bigger problem for her generation than it had been for any generation prior. Her friend Leah, who was all about Building a Personal Brand, had told her to keep still more often.

"Your face is too mobile," she'd explained.

"I'm talking and laughing and being an Active Listener," Nina had replied.

"Well, quit it, because you look like you've been poked with a pin in every picture."

She'd pulled some faces to illustrate her point.

"I do not look like that," protested Nina.

"You do. I have photographic evidence. You might only look like that for a few seconds at a time, but that's when the shutter clicked, so to speak, so that's what you look like online."

"Well, great, I can use it as a first line of defense. If a guy doesn't look beyond my pained expression to see the real, pain-free me, then he's not good enough to date me."

Leah had shrugged. "Or you'll filter out the regular guys and be left with those that like seeing women in pain, and then who's going to be sorry?"

Remembering this conversation now, Nina decided William Reynolds must have had similar advice, because if he'd ever smiled or laughed or actively listened in his life, the photographer never caught it.

It had taken Nina quite some time to investigate the state of Los Angeles book clubs, and after months of study, she'd decided to form one club that discussed a different genre each week, rather than four different clubs that each met once a month.

First Wednesday of each month was Book Bitches (contemporary fiction).

Second Wednesday was Sneaky Spinsters (Golden Age mysteries).

Third Wednesday was District Zero (young adult fiction).

Fourth Wednesday was the Electric Sheep Grazing Club (science fiction).

If there was a fifth Wednesday in the month, she would wing it, because she liked to live dangerously. Book nerds are daredevils, as you know.

Nina would have liked a classic literature club and a romance club as well, but God saw fit to deliver a limited number of hours in the day, and days in the week, and she needed to balance her books, so to speak, with other activities.

Because she advertised her book club widely, membership varied, but it was basically a reliable core team of women who lived for books and were eclectically nerdy enough to want to discuss a different genre every week. She'd met her trivia teammates Leah and Lauren through her book club, and Vanessa, her friend from the café on Larchmont, had joined. The other reliable team member, Daisy, worked at a big chain bookstore, and often brought leftovers from their in-house café, which was a plus. The five of them were completely committed and came every week, taking turns to host and trying to set new standards for snacks. Occasionally, a new member or visitor would show up, and then they would actually have to talk about the book and be completely focused.

That evening's club was Book Bitches, which was contemporary fiction, and the gang was discussing a worthy tome shortlisted for the Man Booker Prize. The ladies had, however, wandered from the topic.

"Really? An actual photo shoot?" Nina was skeptical.

"Yeah, really." Vanessa was flipping through her phone. "Not just one, but five. From several different angles, different lighting, moody black and white, sun flare filter, the whole nine yards."

"Yards? I hope you mean inches, because a nine-yard penis would be . . ." Lauren trailed off, and frowned. "How many inches in a yard, again?"

Everyone looked at Nina. They were familiar with her memory.

"Thirty-six. A yard is three feet." She paused. She wanted to stop, but she couldn't. "It's an imperial unit of measure based originally on a physical metal bar in England, which itself was based on the size of a quarter of a cow's hide." She took a breath, but Lauren — who could see when

74

a rabbit hole was about to be explored — held up her hand.

"That's enough. If you keep going, we'll forget the mental image of a twenty-seven-foot penis, which would indeed be worth looking at."

Leah snorted. "Although presumably harder to fit all in one frame."

Nina giggled and sipped her wine, trying to forget the rest of the facts she knew about units of measurement (did you know a "moment" is actually a medieval term for a minute and a half, for example?). She loved being at book club, because although they did talk about books and stories and writers and readers, they also chatted about other interesting things. Dick pics, for example, or the dating life of single women in Los Angeles (the two are sadly related).

"Here's the thing," said Daisy, who had brought two dozen cake pops and may have been high as a kite on sugar. "Someone needs to take men aside and whisper in their ear, 'Dudes, your penis is not the most photogenic thing about you.' Let's be honest: The out-of-context penis is not an attractive item. It's a naked mole rat wearing a beanie."

"Yeah. If I walked into my kitchen at night and flicked on the light and saw a penis lying on the ground, I would definitely scream and hit it with a broom. At the very least, I would climb on a chair until it rolled away." Vanessa had clearly given this topic some thought.

Nina objected. "But isn't that true of any body part? If you flicked on the light and a leg was lying there, you'd also be alarmed."

"Yes," agreed Vanessa, "but at least you'd recognize it as a leg. If there was a disembodied penis, you wouldn't necessarily place it at once." Vanessa turned up her hands in exasperation. *"I'm not sure what it is, but its single eye is staring at me, and it's too big to squash with a rolled up newspaper . . . Oh, wait, hang on, it's starting to look familiar . . ."*

Nina was still not buying it. "Wouldn't you be more concerned there was someone walking around missing a penis?"

"Nope," replied Vanessa. "I don't think I'd get that far. I think I'd get stuck on the penis, if you'll excuse the phrase."

Leah was more practical. "Why don't men ever send me a picture of them holding a puppy? I'd be so much more interested in that. Or even their smile, or their forearms, or a witty text that doesn't ask me if I'm wet."

"Which isn't a good question to ask, either." Nina had tackled this one a few times. "Because it offers up too many opportunities for sarcasm: 'Am I wet? Because you sent me a badly composed picture of your mediocre man meat? No, I'm not wet. I'm not even mildly moist around the edges. I'm a veritable Sahara of repulsion.' " She turned to Daisy. "Do lesbians do this?"

"Send dick pics?" Daisy raised her eyebrows. Daisy's whole aesthetic was fifties' retro pinup, and her eyebrows were perfect for raising. "Only if we're breaking up with someone and want to make sure they block our number forever."

"So, anyway, what did you say to the photo shoot dick guy?" Nina turned to Vanessa, who shrugged.

"I had already said yes to a date, so I felt bad canceling after he'd shown me the goods." She grimaced. " 'I know I said yes to a movie, but now that I know you have that monstrosity nestling in your pants, I'm no longer interested.' Too hurtful."

"Why were you being considerate of his feelings when he had just visually insulted you?"

"Because I'm not a horrible human being." Vanessa was occasionally too nice, although she was working on it. "But I do wonder if penises look completely different from the male point of view. Is there, like, an aura or something around it, or a tiny halo? Do they think, 'Wow, that's a handsome penis; simply the sight of it makes me horny. Let me send a photo of it to this girl and it will make her horny, too'?"

The women collectively sighed. "They're simple creatures, men," said Lauren. "If they like something, they think everyone else will, too."

"So you're going out with him?" Nina was sticking to the original topic.

Vanessa nodded. "Yeah, we're going to the *Aliens* screening at the ArcLight in a couple of weeks. I left plenty of time in the hopes he meets someone else in the interim."

"I'll be at that screening!" said Nina. "Shall I come over and tell him I've heard his penis looks really good in black and white?"

"Please don't." Vanessa paused. "Although if he takes it out during the film, I promise to text you for help."

Leah snorted. "That is absolutely the last movie you want to take your dick out in. Too much similarity to those things that burst out of people's stomachs. Take your dick out at the wrong moment and you could cause a stampede for the doors."

"Oh my God, that would be a great Halloween costume; you could dress as John

Hurt from the first movie and have your own dick sticking out of a bloody hole in your T-shirt. Totally convincing." Nina reconsidered. "Mind you, you'd have to keep it hard and menacing looking the whole time, which might be difficult in late October."

"Can we get back to the book?" Daisy asked, giggling but trying to hold it together. "We're nearly out of time."

"Who are you going to *Aliens* with?" Vanessa asked.

Nina. Nina nodded at Leah and Lauren. "These two losers, plus Carter."

"Are you seeing someone right now?"

Nina shook her head.

Lauren coughed. "She likes a guy at trivia, but she's too chicken to talk to him."

Nina frowned and shook her head. "He's cute, but he may not be worth talking to. He knows too much about sports. He probably doesn't even read."

Lauren added, "And that's apparently her deal breaker."

Nina looked around. "Isn't it everyone's?"

Lauren shook her head. "Not mine. Mind you, I'm not a bookstore employee, so it's not like nonreaders threaten my livelihood."

"It's not mine, either, and I do work at a bookstore," said Daisy, tucking her blond curls behind her ear. "I draw the line at non–animal lovers. Or girls who ostentatiously use hand sanitizer after going to a public bathroom. Soap and water should be enough. What are they going to do after sex, a full body scrub and chemical peel?"

"I won't date someone who talks about politics within the first two hours of our meeting," said Leah. "It used to be a good filter, but now everyone talks about politics, so maybe it's too fine a mesh. I might need to lower my window of exclusion."

"Rudeness to waiters, total veto," contributed Vanessa.

"Backward hats, or, actually, any hats. I hate hats." Leah looked firm.

"Men who call me by my last name. Unless they're my high school gym coach, it's not cute."

"People who blow their straw wrappers off in public."

"People who say, 'Can I come with?' as if it's a complete sentence."

"Calling soda 'sody pop.' "

"Asking for water with no ice in a restaurant."

"Pussy Whisperers."

There was silence. "I'm sorry?" asked Lauren.

Vanessa blushed. "You know, when a man

gets down there, so to speak, and then says stuff like, 'Hello there, gorgeous' or 'You like that, don't you, baby?' except they're talking to, you know, *her* and not you." Pause. "It's like when you think a guy is interested but it turns out he's only trying to get to your hotter friend."

"You're jealous of your own snatch?"

Vanessa was now bright red. "No, but if you give me your thoughts on my vagina, I'll make sure they get passed along, OK? We're the same person."

All the women gazed at her for a moment, then Nina said, "You know what I hate? Men who assume women are scared of spiders. And mice. And snakes."

"Men who like *Star Trek* but not *Star Wars,* or the other way around. As if they're so incredibly different. Or who only like the original *Star Trek.*"

"Or who use the word 'canon' without irony when talking about comic books."

"Hey, can we get back to Nina's love life, and then the book we're supposed to be discussing?" Daisy really did like to stay on schedule.

"There's nothing to discuss about my love life. I can't see myself dating someone who doesn't read books. What would we talk about?" Nina was also ready to get back to the book.

"I think it's good to date people who spend time in the real world." Everyone turned to look at Vanessa, who was still blushing a bit from the pussy-whispering part. "Look, last year I dated a guy who could actually hang a picture."

"Really?" Lauren was surprised.

"Yeah. He changed his own oil."

"Olive or automobile?"

"Car oil. He cooked. He had a dog he'd trained to do stuff. Impressive stuff, like jump off the guy's back and catch a Frisbee."

"Huh." Nina was interested. "But he didn't read?"

Vanessa shook her head. "No. He was too outdoorsy. He didn't like to sit still for very long, you know?"

"And that worked?"

Vanessa nodded, suddenly looking a little sad. "Yeah, it really did. He didn't care I was less outdoorsy. He went off and did his thing and I went and read books and it was fine."

There was a pause, and then Leah asked the obvious question. "So, what happened?"

Vanessa shrugged. "He broke up with me and started dating a personal trainer who competed in that competition where they do the crazy obstacle courses."

Silence.

"She could scale a rope wall in eight seconds."

Silence.

"I bet she had no imagination," Nina said, comfortingly.

"Yeah," Vanessa replied. "Shall we get back to the book?"

So they did. Because, as Neil Gaiman once memorably said, "Books were safer than other people, anyway."

When Nina got home from book club, she had an e-mail from Peter Reynolds.

"Hey there," it began. "This is a weird thing to say, but I am your nephew and until recently neither of us knew the other existed. Sorry about that. Sarkassian thought I might be able to help you understand the family you inherited, and I'd certainly be happy to try. Would you like to have coffee or something? Let me know. Your little nephew Peter, ha ha."

Nina looked at it for a long time. She could always ignore it. She really had things pretty much together right now; she didn't need any new complications. Then again, what if there was a very sporty member of her new family who could help her edge out

Quizzard? And why was that guy getting under her skin so much, the big, good-looking dumbass? She decided her friends at book club were right: She was being a little Lizzy Bennet about him. I care not one fig, she told herself firmly. I am not in any way intrigued. And besides, I have plenty of other things to think about.

"Dear Peter," she wrote. "I must admit this whole thing has been a bit of a shock, and I have no real comprehension of what just happened. It would probably be helpful to get my head around it with someone who understands it all. Here's my number. Why don't you text me if Friday lunchtime works for you. Love, Aunty Nina, which is hilarious even to write." Then she put a smiley face so he'd know she was joking, and hit send.

See? Not distracted by the guy in any way. Totally focusing on more important things. One hundred percent not thinking about him. Or his hands. Not at all.

today is the day

DATE Friday May 3rd

M T W Th F S Su
△ △ △ △ △ △ △

SCHEDULE

7 > 8	
8 > 9	
9 > 10	Work
10 > 11	
11 > 12	
12 > 13	LACMA lunch
13 > 14	
14 > 15	
15 > 16	work
16 > 17	
17 > 18	
18 > 19	
19 > 20	
20 > 21	

GOALS

No!
More!
surprises!!

NOTES

Research William
Reynolds

TO DO LIST

- Order birth certificate
- hummus
- carrots
- chocolate
- bread
- ~~fruity pebbles~~ BRAN BUDS!

+ BREAKFAST
smoothy

+ LUNCH
lacma

+ DINNER
Chipotle?

+ WORKOUT
spin class?

SIX

In which Nina feels less alone, but not
necessarily in a good way.

Peter Reynolds and Nina had agreed to
meet for lunch at the Los Angeles County
Museum of Art, the modern art museum in
mid-Wilshire. It was right next to the Tar
Pits, with their disturbing, life-sized models
of mammoths stuck in the tar-filled pond.
Nina remembered standing by the fence
around the pond as a child, agonizing over
the baby mammoth. He (or she; it was hard
to gender-identify a mammoth at fifty feet,
probably even for other mammoths) was
standing at the side of the pond panicking
because his parents were having a problem
he couldn't understand. Nina had been a
child with a rich imagination and way too
much empathy, so after a few tearful visits,
her nanny, Louise, had stopped bringing
her.

"It's only a model, baby," she had explained. "It's not real."

"I know," wailed eight-year-old Nina. "But it could be real, right? Mammoths did get stuck in the tar. That's why all their bones are here, right?"

Louise had nodded.

"Well then," cried Nina. "This is a model, but it's Real Life, too, and a real baby mammoth might have watched his parents get stuck and starve because they couldn't get out and days and days would go by, and they'd keep telling him to go find food, or somewhere safe, and he would say, 'No, Mommy, come out of the tar,' and then she would say, 'I can't, baby,' and she would have cried and he would have cried or maybe some nasty dinosaur would've come and eaten him and his mommy wouldn't have been able to help and it would have been awful . . ." And then Louise, who didn't think it was the right time to point out dinosaurs and mammoths hadn't lived at the same time, realized it really would have been awful, and then the Tar Pits were ruined for her, too.

It was the same way with everything Nina experienced; fictional characters were as real to her as the people she met and touched every day. Eventually, she developed a tougher skin and a more critical appreciation of literature, but she still cried at endings, happy or sad. Certain books had left an indelible impression, and Liz never let her forget the occasion she'd been explaining the plot of *Flowers for Algernon* and had started crying in the middle of the store. Not that Nina needed reminding.

She'd arrived a little early for her appointment with Peter Reynolds and had taken a table where she could watch the door. Sipping her coffee, she examined the people coming in. Every arrival was scrutinized carefully for familiar mannerisms, walks were studied, and of course she missed her actual nephew completely. A man approached her table, a broad grin on his face.

"Oh my God, you must be Nina. We totally have the same hair." He sounded as giddy as a kid opening a packet of Pokémon cards and finding their favorite.

Nina goggled at him. He was very tall and handsome, and debonair would be the only word to describe the tweed jacket and black turtleneck he was wearing. It was true, though: His hair was the same color as hers, though his was definitely more stylishly cut.

She nodded and started to stand up. He waved his hands at her.

"Don't get up. I walked from La Brea, and

if I don't sit down I'm going to fall down. I really need to get in shape." He smiled and sat, reaching across the table to shake her hand. "Peter Reynolds, your fabulous gay nephew, and how bizarre is that?"

Nina shook his hand, grinning back. She'd always enjoyed the company of gay men, and finding out she was related to one was honestly a bit of a bonus. "I'm Nina, your single heterosexual aunt, which doesn't seem possible."

"The single part, or the heterosexual part?"

"The aunt part."

He turned up his palms. "But that's the only part that's easy to explain. Heterosexuality you can't do anything about, of course, and the single part is presumably by choice, because you're very pretty, although maybe you have a terrible personality . . . Do you?"

"Awful," said Nina.

"OK, well, you'll have to work on that if we're going to be friends, because I have a very low tolerance for irritating people."

"Me too."

He seemed delighted. "Ah! Another similarity. I love it. Genetics are so fascinating."

Nina reached for her coffee. "Wait, do you want something to eat? We are in a café, after all."

"Of course," he exclaimed. "I was so excited I forgot. I'll be right back." He got up and went to fetch food. Nina watched him charm the checkout girl, the older tourist couple he was next to in line, and the possibly also gay guy waiting for someone. There was something about Peter that was just . . . open, in a way she wasn't. She found herself smiling at him as he came back.

"Aren't you so excited?" He hugged himself. "I am beyond thrilled. When Sarky called, I thought it was Christmas. You're totally going in my syllabus."

"Sarky? Sarkassian the lawyer?"

"Yeah, we call him that."

"Do you see a lot of him?"

"More than you would think. I'm afraid you've inherited one of the more bizarre family setups. Did you eat? You're going to need all your mental faculties."

"Oh," said Nina, faintly. She reached for her coffee. "I wasn't hungry."

"Here, have half my panini. No one needs a whole panini." He looked around the room and spotted the guy who had smiled at him earlier. "I think that guy is checking you out."

"No," said Nina, "he's checking you out." She picked up half of his sandwich and bit into it. Pesto ran down her chin and Peter handed her a napkin.

"He's not, but it doesn't matter. I'm spoken for."

Nina giggled. "You are?"

Peter nodded. "I'm betrothed."

"How old fashioned of you."

"Here's the thing," said her nephew. "I am an old man in a young and, let's face it, gorgeous man's body. I was born fifty-six. It was very hard for me to be young. I hated it. It's only very recently I feel like I'm becoming who I was supposed to be, which is a middle-aged professor of Anthropology with elbow patches."

Nina looked at his jacket and raised her eyebrows.

He made a face at her. "OK, so this jacket doesn't have them, but I will find one that does, or find patches I can add, or something. That's not really the point; I'm wearing patches on my elbows all the time, even when I'm naked, metaphorically speaking." He shrugged. "The professor part is fine — I'm on the faculty at UCLA; and the age part is fine — I'm thirty-three. Not yet in my prime, but getting there." He suddenly looked concerned. "Do you understand what I mean, or do I sound completely nuts?"

Nina shook her head at him. "No, I totally get it. I think I was supposed to be born in the nineteenth century, or maybe Edwardian England. I should be wearing empire-waisted tea dresses and sitting in a window seat watching for carriages."

"How old are you?"

"Twenty-nine. I'm your aunt, but younger than you; how is that possible?"

Peter stared at her, then frowned. "When's your birthday?"

"June 30."

He let out a low whistle. "Oh crap. That's not going to make things any easier." He leaned down and started rooting around in his briefcase, a large brown leather messenger bag that looked like it had seen some heavy use. He finally found what he was looking for and unrolled it onto the table: a long, laminated piece of paper covered in some kind of diagram. It was highly complicated.

"You laminated it?" asked Nina. Not that she didn't love a laminator — she really did; she could frequently be found randomly laminating pretty pieces of fabric or paper to use as bookmarks. "Your margins are really even."

"Thanks," he said. "No one's ever noticed my margins before."

"You have beautiful margins." Nina smiled. "But I'm still not sure why it's laminated." She paused. "I'm not completely certain what it is."

Peter looked surprised. "It's us. I mean it's our family. It's laminated because I use it in class to explain how to construct a kinship diagram."

"A kinship diagram?"

"A family tree is what we call it in the West, but in many cultures, degrees of kinship extend way beyond immediate or even secondary family."

"Ah," said Nina, having no response to that.

"However," said Peter, pointing to parts of the chart, "our chart is actually relatively shallow but very wide, which makes it interesting." He noted her bemused expression. "Perhaps only to me. Our family is extremely matrimonially extended, so it's a good demonstration of how interpersonal relationships are affected by changes in legal status." He shrugged. "Or not, as the case may be."

He was clearly serious about this, but then he looked at her and grinned. "And now I get to redo the whole thing and add you, and as you are illegitimate — no offense — it's even better. I get to use dotted lines!"

"No offense taken. Can you give me a broad overview? I still don't understand the whole family bit." Nina was starting to wish she'd brought notepaper. "I'm having a hard time believing it."

Peter nodded, finished his coffee, and said, "I can imagine it's a bit of a shock." Then he pulled a dry-erase marker from his bag.

"I have that brand," said Nina. "I find they streak so much less."

"They really do, and I can't believe we're discussing it. Just think, we would be friends even if we weren't related, drawn together by our love of quality office supplies."

He leaned forward and poked his pen at the top of the chart. "OK, so here's William at the top, and here, ranged from left to right, are his three wives. The main reason the family is so wide is that he married for the first time at twenty and the last time at sixty. He had kids each time, and those big gaps of time allow for three generations to be born, obviously."

Nina had no idea what he was talking about, but nodded. "Obviously."

Peter looked at her keenly, clearly used to students pretending to understand him. He sighed and reached into his bag again. "Here, let's try this instead. It sometimes helps."

94

He slid a piece of paper across to her and handed her a pen. It was a FriXion, she was pleased to see, and then she was mildly embarrassed that she even noticed.

"Put William at the top, and then draw a horizontal line all the way across."

She did so.

"Now, from left to right, leaving space, write Alice, then Rosie, then your mom's name — what is it, by the way?"

"Candice."

"OK." He made a note on his laminated chart, the tip of his tongue poking out happily, like a little kid. "And then finally Eliza. Done that?" He looked over and nodded. "OK, now draw another horizontal line under their names, and put a big ONE on the far left."

Nina did so, feeling on familiar ground now that she was dealing with paper.

"I like your lettering," said Peter. "Now, under Alice write Becky and Katherine. Under Rosie write Archie. Under Candice write Nina, and under Eliza write Millie. Then put another horizontal line."

He sat back and puffed out his breath. "That is your generation. Those are your siblings, and they range from the oldest, my mother, Becky, who is fifty-nine, to the youngest, Millie, who is ten."

Nina gazed at him. "No way."

"Way."

"But . . . how is that possible?"

He shrugged philosophically. "It's possible because men can father children until they're really old, and for some reason — and this is less easy to explain — your father was so charming he persuaded three women to marry him and at least one other that we know of to sleep with him. Mind you," he added judiciously, "I only knew him as an old man; he was pretty handsome in his youth."

Nina said dryly, "I imagine my mother wasn't the only one."

Peter shook his head. "I imagine you're right, but so far you're the only child out of wedlock we know about." He looked serious for a moment. "But here's the problem: Archie is thirty, and his birthday is in January."

Nina looked at him, confused. "So?"

"So you were born while his dad was still married to his mom. In fact, based on your birthday, William slept with your mom while his wife, Rosie, was pregnant with Archie."

"Oh." Her mother had been right. So much for not remembering all that much about it.

Peter nodded. " 'Oh' is right. And Rosie,

96

sadly, is dead. Of cancer. A decade ago. And William and she seemed very happy together, and that's been the story all along, that Rosie was the love of his life, that they would have stayed married and had more kids and it was all a big tragedy. And now it turns out he cheated on her and we have living physical proof. Which is you."

"Awesome."

"Yeah," said Peter. "Not entirely sure how Archie's going to feel about it, but there's not much we can do to change it."

Nina was silent.

"Shall we carry on?" asked Peter. "There are two more generations to go."

She nodded. "Let me get more coffee and maybe a bun of some kind."

"Excellent idea. Grab me something fattening while you're up there, will you?"

Nina went and stood at the counter. She was feeling something new, something she was finding it hard to quantify. She turned and looked at Peter, who was texting on his phone and smiling at something. She liked him so much already, not in an 'I wonder if we'll be friends' kind of way, but in a . . . she wasn't sure what it was. She got two more lattes and two chocolate éclairs.

"Ooh, good choice. I can see genetics are still working in our favor. There is nothing

— nothing — that isn't improved by laying a thick piece of chocolate frosting on top of it."

Nina nodded and realized what it was. They were related. She'd never experienced a relative before, apart from her mom, and Candice had never really warmed to the role. Presumably, if she and Peter had hated each other on sight it would have sucked, but she knew already that they were going to be connected forever. There was no confusion, no potential attraction, no time limit. It was a relationship she could understand and rely on. She felt . . . relaxed. Which of course made her feel slightly worried. It shouldn't be as easy as this to like someone, right?

"Shall we continue?" She drew a third horizontal line, some way below all the names, and put a big two on the side.

"What an excellent student you are," Peter said, around a mouthful of éclair. "OK, so Becky had Jennifer and then me, Peter." He waved at himself, even though they were two feet apart. "Katherine had Lydia, which is somewhat amazing, because my aunt Katherine is a piece of work. She may have eaten her husband; he disappeared completely. According to my mother, one day he was there and the next day he was gone, leaving all his worldly possessions and his car keys behind."

"That's weird."

"Yeah." He paused. "He took the dog, though."

Nina nodded. "Not a total loss then."

Peter continued, "My grandmother, Alice, is a nightmare. She looks like Miss Havisham, you know, from Dickens, but talks like something out of a Coppola movie. My mom is great, proving genetics aren't everything, but Aunt Katherine continues to be a strangely dressed homicidal maniac."

"Wow, don't hold back. Say what you really think."

"You'll see. My sister Jennifer is awesome — you'll love her — but my cousin Lydia is a fiend in human form, despite being a genius. Or maybe because she's a genius. She's not as bad as her mom, but let's call her challenging. OK, let's get on with the chart. We have years for backstory." He licked the last of the chocolate off his fingers. "But remember, don't go near my grandmother without a shiny shield to look into. One direct glance and it's masonry all the way."

"Damn."

"True story. Anyway, let's press on. Draw another line and put a three."

Nina did so.

Peter turned his head to see her piece of paper. "You could totally take my class. OK, we're nearly done. Now you've reached my group; me, my sister, and Archie's little boy, Henry, who is two. No one else has any kids, so that's it for nieces and nephews."

"Great." Nina pushed the piece of paper away, but Peter pushed it back.

"Oh no, you're not done. You need another horizontal line. I don't have kids, but my older sister Jennifer has three, Little Alice, JoJo, and Louie. They're nearly teenagers, and they are — drumroll, please — your great-nieces and great-nephew."

Nina looked at him. "Wait, I'm someone's Great-Aunt Nina?"

Peter laughed. "Yes. You are their Great-Aunt Nina. Which would be amusing to them if they didn't already have a Great-Uncle Archie, and a Great-Aunt Millie, who's younger than they are." He pointed his finger at her. "And THAT is unusual, even to me." Then he pushed his cup and plate away and started to roll up the chart. "I'm exhausted. Shall we go to the gift store? I hear they have paper clips shaped like rabbits and those old-fashioned pencils with all the colors inside one on top of the other."

So that's what they did.

William

	Alice	Rosie	Candice	Eliza
1	Becky Katherine	Archie	Nina	Millie
2	Jennifer Peter Lydia	Henry		
3	Little Alice JoJo Louie			Peter's chair

After the shopping was over, Nina and Peter exchanged hugs, and Nina headed home. She felt anxious about a potentially angry brother she hadn't even met yet and worried that, through no fault of her own, she had ruined someone else's life. It was a whole new level of awkward, and she was someone who was pretty familiar with awkward. It had taken her previous record — the time she'd attended a Bar Mitzvah by accident when she'd walked into the wrong synagogue (Beth EL is not the same as Beth AM, in case you were wondering) looking for a friend's wedding — and

101

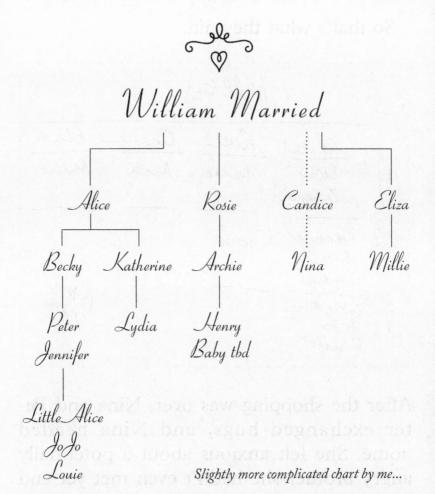

William Married

Alice	Rosie	Candice	Eliza
Becky Katherine	Archie	Nina	Millie
Peter Lydia	Henry		
Jennifer	Baby tbd		
Little Alice			
JoJo			
Louie			

Slightly more complicated chart by me...

smashed it completely. She felt discombobulated, to use a word Liz liked, as if millions of voices had suddenly cried out in — no, wait, that's *Star Wars*. She felt like she'd had a heart transplant. The original organ that usually felt stable in her chest, beating its way along and only occasionally skipping a beat (hello, Michael Fassbender), had been replaced by something that didn't feel as though it had been installed correctly.

Nina told Phil the cat all about it, and he was horrified. "Your dad isn't Richard Chamberlain from *The Thorn Birds*?"

She stroked his head and shook her own.

"Or Magnum, P.I.?"

Nina looked over at her wall. Phil wasn't really saying any of this, of course, because he's a cat and cats don't talk, but his voice in her head was listing her dream dads. She had head shots of all of them on her wall; a tribute both to their stellar work on television, and to the hopeful and imaginative little girl she'd once been. The two he'd mentioned were there, but also Commander Riker, whose real name she could never — no, wait, Jonathan Frakes; Bruce Willis (*Moonlighting,* not *Die Hard*); Alan Alda in *M.A.S.H.;* and her personal favorite, Mark Harmon from *St. Elsewhere,* though his character ended up dying of AIDS, which was a bit of a blow at the time. For her, not him.

Throughout Nina's childhood, TV had been her second best friend, after books, and she had watched what her nanny Louise had watched, which meant mostly '70s and '80s shows, not counting *Star Trek: TNG* because Louise was a die-hard Trekkie. She even liked *Deep Space Nine.*

When Nina had been around ten, she'd gotten it into her little head that maybe one of these characters was her dad, and it became a game, sort of. She liked calling it a game, anyway, because if she actually thought about how much effort went into researching whether or not the potential dads in question were in Los Angeles when she was conceived, that would seem weird. Once she'd clarified that they were, she would cut out their picture and stick it in a box she had for the purpose. The Dad Box had become a bit of A Thing for a while, because Nina had been an anxious kid, and had frequently needed to sit on the floor and dream about possibilities outside of her daily experience.

Not that her daily experience was dreadful; it wasn't like she was ice fishing in the Bering Strait, or using her tiny child fingers to pick solder out of abandoned electrical products, but sometimes walking down the halls of elementary school had been terrifying. She had panicked a lot, and could still remember the time Louise called her mom and talked to her in a quiet voice about it. Then she'd hung up, turned to Nina, and said, your mom says breathe in a paper bag and tough it out. Then Louise had sat and rocked Nina on her lap, and she'd cried —

little Nina, not Louise — and a few days later Louise had gone out and bought a laminating machine and laminated the dads. Nina would take one to school with her every day, rotating through the roster so none of them would get upset, but anyway, that's not the point. The point is none of these witty, urbane, caring men were her dad. Her dad was just some guy who sounded like a total phallus.

Phil pointed out that the sins of the fathers are not the sins of the child, and Nina replied that the apple doesn't fall far from the tree, then they both fell asleep on the sofa. It had been a difficult day.

today is the day

DATE Saturday May 4th   M T W Th F S Su
⬡ ⬡ ⬡ ⬡ ⬡ ⬡ ⬡

SCHEDULE

7 > 8	
8 > 9	
9 > 10	
10 > 11	work
11 > 12	
12 > 13	
13 > 14	
14 > 15	
15 > 16	
16 > 17	
17 > 18	
18 > 19	work on mood
19 > 20	board
20 > 21	

GOALS

Make new goals :)

NOTES

wiki hereditary conditions :(

TO DO LIST

- [ ] order book on genetics
- [ ]
- [ ] ICE CREAM
- [ ] red vines
- [ ] tampons
- [ ] advil
- [ ] socks
- [ ] bacon
- [ ]
- [ ]
- [ ]

＋ BREAKFAST bacon

＋ LUNCH pizza

＋ DINNER ICE CREAM

＋ WORKOUT no.

SEVEN

In which Nina meets a brother.

As was often the case, Liz got hung up on the details.

"You're the love child that's going to derail the whole plot of their lives?"

Nina nodded. "I'm afraid so. I didn't do it on purpose."

"Of course not, but how often does one get a chance to be Jon Snow?"

"Does that mean I know nothing?"

"I think that was always the case; your illegitimacy has no bearing." She smiled. "But maybe you'll inherit a million bucks and we'll be able to pay off Mephistopheles." She pointed her finger at Nina. "You could be like Little Lord Fauntleroy. Characters in books are always inheriting a fortune."

"It doesn't usually end well. Think of Charlie Kane in *Citizen Kane*. Or Isabel

Archer in *The Portrait of a Lady.*"

Liz shrugged. "You're forgetting the greatest family of inheritors ever, the Beverly Hillbillies. Elly May Clampett's life was filled with joy. Joy and plenty of gingham." She looked Nina up and down. "You could totally pull it off."

Nina asked, "Do we actually owe Mr. Meffo a million bucks?" She hoped not; she loved her job at the store. Loved everything about the store, in fact.

Liz shook her head. "No, it just feels like it."

It was still pretty early. The store was open, but the only customer they had was a guy who lived nearby and had some kind of developmental disability. His name was Jim, and he had the sweetest smile and often hung out in the natural history section for hours looking at pictures of animals. Everyone knew him on the boulevard, and watched out for him and said hi, and as far as Nina knew, he thought he was a prince occasionally visiting his fiefdom to check on the peasants.

The door to the store opened and Polly came in. Liz turned and frowned at her.

"Good afternoon, Polly."

Polly grinned. "Liz, it's nine thirty. There's no one in the store except you two and Jim, and Jim's here often enough that if there had been a rush — which there never, ever is — he could have filled in for me."

Liz clicked her tongue but let Polly come over and hug her extravagantly, then went away hiding a smile. Polly was the other spinster of this parish who worked at Knight's, although spinster wasn't as accurate a description of her as it was of Nina. Polly was an actress. She worked at Knight's as a way to actually support her passion for movies, both being in them and watching them.

Polly had come to LA when she was nineteen, a beautiful and hopeful girl with lots of charisma and even more talent, and then spent ten years *nearly* making it. If she'd never gotten anywhere she might have given up and been content to have given it a shot. However, in common with thousands of others, Polly would occasionally get a part in a commercial, or a pilot. She was always auditioning and getting called back, and would be frequently "on avail" (meaning that she was short-listed for something and had to keep her schedule free for a day or so while they made a final choice between two or three girls). It's this occasional hit of success that makes for a real addict. The breakthrough was always imminent; there was always something about to happen. In the dim interstices between flashes of hope you make your life.

Polly had been working at Knight's for a little over a year, and she and Nina had become friends, despite the fact that Polly never read books and only knew about plots from movies. For example, in the *Harry Potter* series, she had no idea Peeves the poltergeist even existed, or that Ludo Bagman wasn't a luggage outlet, because those characters were totally cut out of the films. Being a lover of drama, Polly was deeply amused by Nina's sudden family situation.

"Oh my God, you should write a screenplay!" She laughed out loud. "Not that anyone would share screen time with so many other people. You'd have to pare down the cast."

"The whole point is the numerousness of them," Nina said, dryly. "Numerosity?"

"There are a lot of them." Polly nodded.

"Yes, there are. I've only met one of them, although he was pretty awesome." She told Polly about Peter.

"Lucky," Polly said. "I had to borrow a gay relative from our neighbors." Her eyes misted over. "He took me shopping for prom." Another thought came to her. "Are any of these new family members handsome single men?"

"I have no idea. I'll have to ask Peter and consult my chart."

"There's a chart?"

Nina nodded. "It's laminated."

"Well, did you Google your dad at least?" She didn't wait for an answer, but pulled out her phone and got to work. Nina was used to her and kept on unpacking book deliveries that had arrived that morning. There was no point telling Polly she'd already looked online, and besides, Polly was a whiz at searching.

Her patience was rewarded. "Wow," said Polly with the air of that guy in the movie who is finally going to tie all the pieces of the plot together and whose refusal to do so up till then has led to either comical misapprehensions or mortal peril. "William Reynolds, your dad, was a very social butterfly."

Nina nodded. "Thus the three wives."

"Plus possibly innumerable girlfriends?"

Nina turned up her hands, both of them holding books. "Unproven, but suspected."

"With evidence."

"Sitting on the floor in front of you."

Polly turned her phone to face Nina. "Here's the most recent wife, by the way. The actual widow." She digressed. "If you're not married to someone and they die, are

112

you an ex-widow?"

"I don't think so," said Nina, looking at the image on Polly's phone. "What's her name? I can't read it from here. I knew I should have memorized that chart."

"It's Eliza," said Polly. She read, "William and Eliza Reynolds attend the blah blah blah." Eliza was beautiful, and not as young and bimbo-ish as Nina had imagined. Why had she imagined a bimbo? she chided herself. Honestly, had feminism taught her nothing? Why shouldn't a younger woman fall in love with an older man? Despite his enormous wealth and success?

"I don't know why you're not more curious about your dad," Polly said. "This is precisely why the Internet was invented."

"To research fathers?"

"Yes."

Nina sighed. "I did look him up; there wasn't all that much there. He was a serial cheater and abandoner of children. What more do I need to know?"

Polly shrugged. "Maybe he was really good at skiing and you've never even tried it and you could have had an entire Olympic career because you're naturally disposed to be good at it." Polly was charming, but not super grounded in reality. "Or," she said, warming to her theme, "what if he had some inheritable condition?"

"I did think about that, but male-pattern baldness isn't something I'm concerned about."

"What about hemophilia?"

"Well, firstly, hemophilia is carried by women and only dangerous to men, so I would be fine . . ."

"Think of your children!"

". . . and you'd think anything important would have cropped up by now."

"And there's where you'd be wrong. I think you should talk to all of them carefully and see what kind of hand you've been dealt."

"I think you're nuts."

Polly shrugged. "That might be true, but it doesn't mean I'm wrong."

Polly apparently had more pull with Fate than either of them realized, because that afternoon she and Nina looked up to see an incredibly handsome man walk through the door and approach them both with a great deal of purpose.

They all looked at one another, and then the man said, to Nina, "You must be Nina Hill."

Polly audibly hissed, but Nina wasn't going to let her down. Chicks before dicks.

114

"Yes, I am, and this is Polly Culligan."

He looked at her and, to be fair, did pause for a half second, but then he came back to Nina.

"I'm your brother. Archie Reynolds. Our father slept with your mother when my mother was pregnant with me."

It's possible that someone somewhere has written cogent advice about how to respond to a statement like that, but if they have Nina had never read it. So she stuck out her hand and said, "Pleased to meet you." Then she said, "Your mastery of pronouns is impressive," and regretted it. Struggling to recover, she added, "I'm sorry about the infidelity thing, but you know, I wasn't there at the time."

He nodded. "I understand that. You presumably arrived a few days or so later."

"Are you an obstetrician?" asked Polly, curiously.

"I'm sorry?" said Archie.

"Well," Polly shrugged, "we seem to be talking about the pacing of conception, and I thought maybe you had some expertise or something, because you know, we just met and usually men like to take girls out to dinner before they talk about making babies."

There was a pause. Nina hadn't been able to stop herself from imagining a *School-*

house Rock!–style sperm and egg animation, so she didn't have anything to say, but her brother laughed and had the courtesy to blush. His hair was very dark red like Nina's, and, like her, he blushed well.

"You're right, I'm being incredibly rude." He looked around, as if suddenly realizing he was in a public place, but fortunately for him the store was empty. "I only just found out where you worked and . . ." He trailed off. "I'm sorry, I shouldn't have marched in like that."

Nina shrugged. "I would probably have done the same."

"But you didn't," he said. "Are you able to come and have a cup of coffee or something?"

Liz had Apparated, as she frequently did. Honestly, she could be McGonagall's sister. "Go ahead, Nina," she said. "We'll struggle along without you. It will be hard, but we will try."

Nina made a face at her and reached under the counter for her phone/wallet combo thingy.

Archie and Nina went across the street to the Belgian place, and Vanessa grinned at Nina when she handed them menus.

Nina burst her bubble. "Vanessa, this is

my half brother, Archie."

Her dark eyes took him in, and after a second she nodded. "I didn't know you had family in town."

"That makes three of us," he said, before Nina had a chance to. She narrowed her eyes; a brother who stole her lines was something she hadn't considered. They both ordered, also the same thing, then sat there and looked at each other with open curiosity.

"You look like me," Nina said, after a minute. "A guy version, obviously."

"Thanks for clarifying," he said dryly, "and, actually, you look like me. I'm a few months older, remember?" He pulled out his phone and flicked to the gallery. "And to be truthful, we both look like our dad." He handed her the phone. Their father, apparently, standing with his arm around the shoulder of a younger Archie, smiling for the camera in a pro forma way: point, smile, click, move away, drop the smile, get on with whatever important thing you had to do. You know the smile. William Reynolds had been handsome; his hair was thick and the same color as hers and Archie's, but his eyes were difficult to read. Maybe they'd been easier in person, but Nina was never going to find out.

She said, "I don't recognize him at all. I never saw a picture, never heard his name, never even knew my father was American." Their food arrived. "The whole thing is blowing my tiny little mind." She shook out her napkin, her mouth watering at the smell of her *croque madame.* Grilled cheese in any form was her spirit animal.

Archie pronged a lettuce leaf and chewed it thoughtfully. "Yeah, me too. Can I ask you about your mom?"

Nina nodded, also chewing. She watched her new brother, noticing additional similarities between them: the cheekbones, the eyelashes. How strange, to have a brother all of a sudden. She remembered a friend of hers who had an older brother in high school and how awesome that had been for her and all her friends. A steady supply of boys one or two years older, paraded through the house for their inspection. Damn, that would have been nice to have; maybe it wouldn't have taken her so long to lose her virginity.

Archie sipped his water. "What's she like, your mom?" He paused. "The home-wrecker."

Nina frowned at him. "That's not fair; she didn't wreck your home at all. In fact, she had nothing more to do with your dad once

118

she found out he was married."

"True. I withdraw the home-wrecker comment. But what is she like?"

Nina thought about it. "She's cool. She's a well-known photographer; you can look her up online. Candice Hill. That's how I usually find out where she is and what she's up to. She's Australian and travels all over the place, which is why I never knew where my dad came from. She never, ever mentioned him, except to say she wasn't sure who he was. Apparently, it was more preferable for me to think she was promiscuous than it would have been for me to know my father, which is a weird choice.

"I didn't see much of her when I was a kid, and see even less of her now. She loved me, I guess, but she was busy." Nina took a bite of her *croque madame* and shamelessly talked while chewing. "She carried me around everywhere when I was the size of a loaf of bread, but once I needed regular meals and got too big to sleep in a hotel drawer, she found an apartment here and hired Louise."

"Louise?"

"The greatest nanny in the world. Her own kids were at college, and her husband irritated her, so she moved into our apartment to take care of me. Once I went to college, she moved to Georgia, to be closer to her grandchildren. She's my family, my regular cast member. My mom is more like a guest star."

"And now our father is like a character the other ones talk about."

"Right, but one that never shows up. He's Godot. Or Guffman."

"Charlie in *Charlie's Angels*."

"Norm's wife in *Cheers*."

Archie smiled. "Well, he was around all the time when I was little. He worked a lot, but when he was there, he was really there. He had that way of making you feel you were the only person in the world. As long as you were right in front of him."

"He was a lawyer, right?" Nina had seen that online but wasn't sure she was remembering correctly.

"Yeah, entertainment lawyer. He and ten thousand other guys in this town. He inherited money from his parents, then made lots more, threw parties, went to parties, drank a lot, glammed around, the usual thing. He was larger than life and really smart. I loved him. When my mom died, he was devastated." He frowned. "But now all I can think of is how he had you the whole time and never paid any attention to you at all."

"I think that was my mom's doing, not

his." Nina paused. "Do you think your mom knew about me? Do you think he told anyone?"

"Well, he told Sarkassian, because he put you in the will. He must have thought about you. He was pretty buttoned up; it's highly unlikely you slipped his mind."

Nina waved at Vanessa and ordered an iced coffee. Archie did, too. "Are you ordering the same thing as me on purpose?"

He shook his head. "No, I guess we like the same things. We're like one of those twin studies, where they look at twins who were raised apart and yet turn out to have both married a woman named Darla."

"Not the same woman, hopefully."

"No, that would really be too coincidental. Were you a happy kid? Did you have a good childhood?"

Nina shrugged. "More or less. I was shy. I'm still shy. I wasn't good at making friends. I got anxious a lot. Honestly, it would have been nice to have sisters and brothers and cousins and stuff back then. Now I'm not really sure what to do with you, although it feels nice to have a family for the first time." She looked at him thoughtfully. "But maybe it's too late for me to really be part of yours."

He shrugged. "If you got married you'd

join one."

"True." Nina thought about that. "I could always pretend I married into you, so to speak."

"We could throw a wedding." He laughed. "One thing that can be said for our family is that we love a wedding, or a birthday, or really any excuse for a party. We're a sociable lot, mostly."

Nina fake shuddered. Or at least, she faked a fake shudder, because inwardly she was actually shuddering. "I am not a party person. I'm an introvert."

"Don't worry," Archie responded. "You can always say no."

Nina went back to his question about her childhood. "You know, as a kid I felt alone a lot, but I also really liked being alone so, you know, it was fine. I spent a lot of time reading and lying on the living room rug watching TV. What about you?" The iced coffee arrived, and they toasted each other instinctively.

Archie took a sip and sighed. "It was happy at first. I remember hanging out with my mom a lot, and kids from the neighborhood, but then my mom got sick and it got sad. I was still pretty young, but old enough to feel bad I couldn't do more to help. I got good at making tea. I got good at giving foot rubs." He looked at the table. "I think I did more physical caring for another person during that period than I've ever done since, although I love my wife and son very much." He met her eyes again. "Not sure what that says about me."

They paused to consider this, then Nina plowed on. "And what about Eliza, your stepmother and now the widow?"

Archie shrugged. "We only really got together — all of us — at the holidays, usually at our dad's instigation, so I don't know if we'll even do that anymore. I don't know her very well; they live on the other side of town."

"Santa Monica?"

"Worse: Malibu."

"Might as well be Mars." They both nodded. Los Angeles is a big city, as everyone knows, but there is an even bigger divide between the West side and the East side. To get from east to west you have to cross under the 405 freeway. There's a stretch of Olympic Boulevard where you can see the 405 just ahead, a parking lot in bridge form, where it can take you over an hour to go one or two blocks because a portion of the traffic is going up the ramp to get on the freeway and blocking the way for everyone else. People have gone insane on that stretch.

Whenever Nina was stuck there, which was rarely, because she would rather have filled her ears with flaming dog turds than go to the West side, she thought of that Andrew Wyeth painting *Christina's World,* where the young woman is lying on the hillside, dragging herself up toward a barn in the distance. That same sense of desperation and struggle and reluctant acceptance permeates the very air in that part of town. It is purgatory. Or limbo. Sartre said hell was other people, but that was only because the 405 hadn't been built yet.

"How long were they married?" Nina realized she'd probably have to meet this woman; she might as well know more about her.

"Oh, a long time. Since 2000, maybe? Millie is ten, and she was born quite a few years after the wedding." He shrugged. "Sorry, I'm not so good at dates."

"Millie is our half sister?"

He laughed. "You get used to it. We end up just using everyone's name and not worrying exactly how they're related unless someone asks."

"Do people ask?"

"Sometimes. People will say, is this your

son, or is this your father, and you have to say, no, the little one is my brother and the older one is my nephew. Most people ignore it, but some people think about it for a minute and either demand a full explanation, which is a pain, or realize for themselves it means your father never stayed married for very long, and it gets awkward."

Nina looked at him. "Like now, you mean?" It actually didn't feel awkward; it was as it had been with Peter. A weird feeling of knowing someone already; a total absence of the usual pressure she would feel with an attractive man; a kind of comfort.

Archie's expression grew cooler. "Yeah. That was dad's dark side, unfortunately. He was funny and handsome and charming, but he was also a narcissistic loser. He married and left three wives and didn't seem to lose a night's sleep over any of it."

"He didn't leave your mom. And he didn't leave Eliza."

"But he cheated on my mom, and who knows about Eliza. The fact that you exist means there might be more of us out there." Archie shrugged. "He always seemed so loving, but it was like he was two people: the one who was there in front of you, and the one he turned into the minute he left the room."

"The one in front of you loved you, at least."

"Yeah, but the other guy always won in the end."

He reached up his hand and called for the check.

Back in her apartment that night, Nina sat in front of her bulletin board and stared at it. She looked up other people's visualization and organization practices on Pinterest and realized hers was woefully in need of updating. At the very least, she was now a different social being, someone with a family. Someone who might need to write down more birthdays, for example. Or have more invitations to decline.

Concerned, she started looking at bullet journaling instead, to see if maybe that would work better for her new, wider circle. Honestly, you couldn't turn your back on the Internet for a minute. There were, like, fourteen thousand pins about bullet journaling, which was a way of laying out a daily planner to be more . . . something. Prettier? More efficient? Nina leaned back against the wall and started daydreaming. How did this whole thing come about? Who was Bullet Journalist Zero? Who was struggling to capture and condense everything about their life using traditional journaling methods (which are what . . . lists? calendars?) and thought, hey, wait, let's do it This Way Instead and spawned a worldwide phenomenon?

Nina imagined a young woman, let's call her Brooke, the kind of Basic Girl that Nina both despised and envied, a woman who understood contouring and highlighting, and followed people on Instagram who cared passionately about tiny niche verticals such as, for example, contouring and highlighting, and who had a boyfriend with a YouTube channel about his crazy life with his three husky puppies and his hot, contoured, organized girlfriend. Imaginary Brooke considered herself a Boss, but at the same time enjoyed the girlie things of life, the cushions, the candles, the body glitter, and the trending Starbucks drink.

Having created the concept of bullet journaling, Brooke would then spend months perfecting her art, learning awesome new calligraphy styles, taking fantastic photos and posting them, and watching the rest of the Internet take her idea and run with it. Finally, she would start a company selling blank notebooks, Japanese pens, tiny stickers, and templates so her followers could bullet journal in their own, unique way within a Brooke-approved design frame-work. BrookeCo would spawn a whole life-style channel on some upstart streaming network, and Brooke would retire at forty, having married and divorced Husky Guy (who, it turned out, only really liked young dogs), and live a life filled with Meaning, Joy, and Meaningfully Joyful Accessories. Nina hated her.

Having invented and disposed of Brooke, Nina decided to love the one she was with, and stick with a regular bulletin board. She sat there a second, considering her goals.

OK, brain, keep it simple. She wanted to drink less wine and more water. Nina wrote that down, then refilled her wineglass. Baby steps.

She wanted to exercise more. This is easy, she thought; it turns out I have lots of goals. She looked up Couch to 5K plans and printed one out, pinning it to her board. She considered buying new running shoes. Then she found an article that said walking was as good as running and felt good about saving $100 by not buying running shoes.

She wanted to eat more vegetables, so she printed out a picture of broccoli and stuck that up. Why was broccoli the poster child for all vegetables? It must have a good agent or something, because she saw it everywhere. Big giant heads. Little bouncy florets. Kale had given it a run for its money for the last couple of years, but broccoli stayed focused and maintained its brand. Good for it. Nina put a prettier push pin on the picture of broccoli and felt supportive.

She wanted to date the guy from Quizzard.

She drank her wine and considered that. She hadn't realized it was a goal, per se, until that moment, which proved that mood boards were good for something, haters be damned. Then she searched for "good first date restaurants on the East side of Los Angeles" and printed that out. Then she threw it away and printed out a picture of a baby penguin. Then she added a picture of a baby Russian dwarf hamster sitting in someone's hand, because it made her go "squee." Then she spent a full, fat twenty minutes looking at photos of small mammals and baby animals in general, then drifted into videos of soldiers returning from war to their dogs, which made her cry. Then she realized she was vampiring other people's feelings, and that made her feel bad about herself, and suddenly the whole mood board made her cry and so she went to bed.

Why did she want to go out with that guy,

anyway, when she could barely make it through an evening alone? A boyfriend was the last thing she needed. Therapy was what she needed. Therapy and maybe a Boston terrier. Or a French bulldog. One of those ugly yet adorable dogs.

Tomorrow would be better. At the very least, tomorrow would be different.

today is the day

DATE _Saturday May 11th_   M T W Th F S Su
⬭ ⬭ ⬭ ⬭ ⬭ ⬭ ⬭

SCHEDULE

7 > 8	
8 > 9	
9 > 10	
10 > 11	work
11 > 12	
12 > 13	
13 > 14	
14 > 15	
15 > 16	
16 > 17	
17 > 18	
18 > 19	autha's night
19 > 20	
20 > 21	movie

▷▷ ▷ ▶ ▷▷ ▷ ▶ ▷▷ ▷ ▶

TO DO LIST

- ☐ Broccoli
- ☐ Fruit
- ☐ Kale
- ☐ nuts
- ☐
- ☐
- ☐
- ☐
- ☐
- ☐
- ☐
- ☐

GOALS

VEGGIES 🌱

NOTES

Don't forget tickets!

✚ **BREAKFAST**
Smoothie

✚ **LUNCH**
Unclear

✚ **DINNER**
Even less clear

✚ **WORKOUT**
does a movie count?

EIGHT

In which Nina views other people's inner animals, then goes on safari.

The next week passed uneventfully, which is not to understate the high level of energy that normally prevails on Larchmont Boulevard. A third juice bar opened. The hat store had a sale on berets. Rite Aid changed their seasonal display to bunnies and chickies. It wasn't exactly a never-ending cavalcade of light and motion, but it was change.

However, the high spot was definitely the Author's Evening at Knight's, on Saturday night. Author's Evenings meant setting out a load of chairs, which meant moving bookcases and putting out plastic cups of warm white wine or plates of crackers and sweaty cheese, then standing there ready to sell multiple copies of the author's books so he or she could sign them. It wasn't hard, and sometimes the authors were fun, but occasionally Nina wasn't in the mood, and this was one of those evenings.

It didn't help that the staff weren't supposed to drink the wine, but that night Nina was so cranky Liz actually urged her to break her own rule. "You're being a pill, Nina," she said. "Have a drink and chill out. This book is fun, the author is hopefully fun, and you're not a child soldier in Rwanda, so get a grip."

Liz was right, of course. She had a variety of these comparisons: Aside from the child soldier, Nina had also not been a twelfth-century Catholic martyr, a tribute from a forgettable district in *The Hunger Games,* Scout's Halloween ham costume, and the first one voted off the island. You had to stay on your toes with Liz; she could throw any number of references at you, and you had to be ready for them.

Nina tried to pull herself together. She'd been irritable all week. Either her period was coming or she had a brain tumor, and at that moment the tumor felt more appealing, which probably meant it was her period. "OK, you're right. What's the book again?"

Liz sighed at her. "*Unleash Your Inner Animal* by Theodore Edwards."

"Teddy Edwards? His inner animal is presumably a stuffed bear?"

Liz looked at her employee and narrowed her eyes. "One drink, Nina."

Theodore Edwards turned out to be the least cuddly-looking Teddy that Nina had ever seen: tall and angular, with a tiny goatee and an actual pair of pince-nez on a long handle. Wait, that might make them lorgnettes — hold on, yes, lorgnettes are the ones with handles. Anyway, he had a pair of those, plus the aforementioned tiny beard, and the overall effect was one of a highly affected praying mantis who was going to peer at you closely before biting your head off and dabbing his chin with a handkerchief. You might not have felt this way about him, but Nina had a rich imagination to compensate for her lack of spending money.

As the crowd started to filter in, Nina noticed that they were mostly older women, and by older she meant fifties and up. She was as biased as the next person, unconsciously or not, and made the assumption that this was going to be a quiet evening. She looked around for Liz, saw her engrossed talking to a customer, and slipped a second cup of wine. Shuddering, because it really was piss poor and warm to boot, Nina dropped the cup in the trash and kept herself busy walking around with the rest of the tray. Everyone helped themselves, and the atmosphere warmed up. People seemed to know one another. There was a lot of hugging and eye widening.

Liz checked her watch, then stepped up to the front of the room, where Theodore Edwards was already perched on a stool, cleaning his antennae. Not really, just joking. His antennae were already clean. Nina found herself wanting to giggle and realized she should have stuck with one glass of wine.

Liz said, "It's my pleasure to present Theodore Edwards, whose book *Unleash Your Inner Animal* hit the *New York Times* bestseller list this week." Everyone applauded, and Nina took a closer look at the book. It seemed to be a nonfiction, self-help kind of thing. She put it down and paid attention, like she was supposed to.

Theodore cleared his throat. His voice was surprisingly deep and attractive, and made him seem less like a praying mantis and more like a bear or something, dressed as a praying mantis.

"Welcome, fellow animals," he said. "What a pleasure to see so many of you here, ready to look inward and encourage your secret animal to come out and be free."

Nina wondered idly if she should have put out a litter tray.

Teddy amped up his delivery. "Civilization has crushed so many of us and driven us away from our place in the natural world. It's hard to even remember we are mammals, just part of life's great chain of being, fearful of predators, hungry for our prey, lusting for our fellows."

Nina looked at Liz. Her eyebrows had contracted slightly, and Nina saw her flip over her copy of the book to read the description, as she herself had. Theodore continued.

"As I had hoped, people are embracing both the book and their inner beasts, and around the country, chapters of humanimals, as I call them, have sprung up to reacquaint themselves with their wilder side."

Oh God. Nina had a bad feeling about this.

"So, let's take a moment to greet each other properly, shall we?" And with that, but without any further warning, he tipped back his head and roared like a lion. Liz and Nina froze, their jaws dropping open as the entire room erupted into growls, bellows, and, impressively, convincing whale song.

Nina looked frantically at Liz, who had backed up against the nearest bookcase. She caught Nina's eye and mouthed, *Save me,* but there wasn't anything the younger woman could do.

Theodore stopped roaring and raised his hand to his ear, encouraging his readers (willing acolytes in the Temple of Crazy) to bellow louder. They complied. Nina covered her ears and started giggling uncontrollably. People were stopping in the street; a crowd was forming outside the door. It was a pity she hadn't set out more chairs.

And then, "Humanimals! Let's prance!" Theodore leaped from his stool and started prowling about, and with a resounding crash of wooden folding chairs, his audience followed suit.

It was pretty much downhill from there.

After the animals had left, the chairs had been folded and returned to the back room, and Liz had taken four Tylenol, Nina was allowed to leave.

"It's Saturday night," Liz said to Nina. "You should run along before I have a coronary and you have to waste the entire night in the emergency room."

"Do you think you actually might?" Nina paused. Liz wasn't old, but it had been a somewhat challenging Author's Evening.

"I doubt it. Run along, little doggie." She waved her hands. "I see someone trampled cheese into the carpet in the young adult section, and it's going to be relaxing digging it out with my fingernails. Off you go." Nina made a break for it.

Saturday nights Nina had a ritual: She went home, fed Phil, had a shower, got dressed, and headed out into the night to sink her teeth into the neck of any virgins she could find. Clearly, this isn't true: There are no virgins out on Saturday night in LA. No, Nina would grab her camera and go out to take pictures.

One of Nina's few early memories of her mother was when Candice had taught her to recognize a moment worth photographing. They'd sat together in a crowded spot, and Candice had pointed out the images that appeared every so often in the patterns of people around them. It was a pleasant memory, and although Candice tended to take photos of war zones, starving children, or miners covered in toxic chemicals, Nina preferred to take photos of her hometown. Los Angeles was famous for its intoxicating mix of riots and red carpets, but the city she saw was very different.

Bear in mind, Los Angeles is an unnatural oasis. It was built in and on the desert floor of a long mountain valley, which slopes gently east to west into the Pacific Ocean.

Native American tribes settled the valley over seven thousand years ago and lived in relative peace until the Spanish showed up and ruined it all. Eventually, the movie industry arrived, driven there by Thomas "Grabby" Edison, who held a monopoly on all things movie related on the East Coast, and wasn't averse to breaking a few legs to maintain it. The movie business really caught on. Those people who move like jerky ants in old footage built studios and houses and bigger houses and then swimming pools, and before you knew it . . . the Kardashians.

This is a blatant simplification and compression of over a century of development, but the point is that people basically arrived and laid a carpet of tarmac and trash over the top of a beautiful but somewhat surprised natural world. Too polite to point it out, nature simply continued to go about her business and ignored us the way we largely ignore her. But she's still working, like the experienced old performer she is.

Hike up into Griffith Park in spring, for example, and you'll suddenly find yourself alone apart from four squillion birds, winding down from their day and chattering over a postprandial brandy or whatever it is birds wind down with. A buttercup filled with dew? A half acorn filled with honey? It's more likely they're sipping rainwater from the crumpled edge of a Coors Light can, but whatever it is, it's rocking their world, because they are singing their feathery little butts off. Sometimes, if she were sitting very still, Nina would see a raccoon, or a coyote, or a jackrabbit, all trying not to be seen and freezing when they noticed her, then dissolving away like Homer Simpson sliding back into the hedge.

As the light dwindled, palm trees and distant buildings would become black silhouettes against an impossibly rosy backdrop. Sunsets are beautiful in California, the cornflower blue of the sky diluting as the light fades into a teenage girl's pastel palette of nail colors. The whole world is familiar with Big Bold Daytime LA, the blinding sun, the girls in shorts and roller skates, the traffic. They know Nighttime Glamorous LA, too, the paparazzi with their shouts and flashes, the starlets with their cleavage and heels. But only Angelenos get to see LA as she's waking up and going to bed, and like many beautiful women, she looks best with her makeup off.

That evening, Nina could see the jacarandas were having their usual giddy effect: Every May, jacaranda trees burst into flower in an improbably riotous display of color. Ranging from deep purple to the palest violet, they bloom together on some pre-arranged schedule, so one night Angelenos go to bed in Kansas and wake up in Oz. They're all over the city, hundreds of them, but until they bloom, they're totally unre-markable. Like dozens of transformation scenes in movies from *My Fair Lady* to *Mean Girls,* jacarandas are the previously plain girl who suddenly gets a makeover and emerges triumphant to turn everyone's head. They don't last long, but while they're there, people smile more. They flirt more. They feel spring in their step and summer in their underpants.

Nina hid behind her camera and watched people crowd together, or sail alone down the street, looking at one another from the corners of their eyes, noticing and seeing and ignoring like any herd congregating around a water hole. She never felt more contented than she did when she was seeing and taking pictures and being invisible. She thought maybe owls felt the same way, but she couldn't turn her head 270 degrees, which was a total bummer.

Anyway, once the light had gone, she would take this happy feeling of peace and purpose with her to the movie theater, where she would sprinkle herself with heavily buttered popcorn and then spend the whole movie picking it out of her teeth.

The ArcLight was a Hollywood institution, a movie theater with great seats and amazing sound, plus the usual healthy range of unhealthy movie snacks. Nina loved going to the movies alone, even though Saturday night was always crowded.

It turned out it wasn't Polly who had the pull with Fate, it was Nina, because the first person she saw as she walked into the movie theater lobby was the guy from You're a Quizzard, Harry.

No, she said to herself. Ignore him. But then he looked up and saw her and smiled. Unbeknownst to her, he'd seen her, thought she was someone he knew, smiled, then realized she *was* someone he knew, she was that quiz girl who knew everything and not actually a friend of his, but by then it was too late because she was smiling back at him. Uncertainly, but definitely smiling.

Crap, thought Tom. She's really so pretty.

Crap, thought Nina. He's gorgeous.

Crap, thought Lisa, the girl from Quizzard, who had walked into the lobby to meet Tom to see a film and immediately saw Tom and Nina smiling at each other in a strained fashion across a twenty-foot distance. Go!

142

she thought to herself, or rather to Tom, go talk to her. But he wasn't moving, and the girl wasn't moving, and so Lisa decided she needed to take matters into her own hands.

"Hey, Tom!" she called out, raising her hand.

Oh thank God, thought Tom, though he was also a little annoyed with himself. Why couldn't he have gone and said hi, made a new friend? What was this, kindergarten?

Ah, thought Nina, he IS dating that girl from his team (which we all know is suicide for team cohesion) and that's that. Not that there was any *that* there in the first place, of course . . . And then she realized the girl from Quizzard was walking toward her with a big, broad smile on her face. Behind her, Tom was wobbling in his trajectory, thrown by Lisa's sudden darting movement. His sneakers squeaked on the polished concrete floor.

"Hey there, I know you, don't I?"

Nina was a full adult, capable and competent in many ways, but this simple greeting made her blush and get flustered. "Uh . . . well . . ."

"From trivia league, right?" said Lisa, holding out her hand. "I'm Lisa. Our team beat your team last week."

Nina nodded, shaking her hand. "Yes, I

remember. I'm Nina." She paused. "January the first."

"I'm sorry?" Lisa shot a quick glance over her shoulder to make sure Tom was coming over. He wasn't. She micro-frowned at him, and he started to move.

"Racehorses. January the first. That's how you won."

"With racehorses?"

"Yes. You won with a question about racehorses." Nina was starting to feel a little desperate for this conversation to be over. The good-looking guy was approaching; it was too late.

"That's right," said Lisa, smiling at Nina as if the two of them had known each other forEVS. Then Tom joined them and Lisa revealed herself as the manipulative mastermind she truly was. "Oh, hey, Tom, this is Nina. Do you remember her from Quiz League?"

"Of course." Tom had had an additional fifteen seconds to compose himself, and felt utterly capable of exchanging pleasantries and walking away. "I'm Tom. Nice to meet you properly, if you know what I mean."

Nina shook his hand, feeling her systems coming back online. "The feeling is mutual." *(No, Nina! What the hell was that? Why do these stupid phrases come out of your mouth? What's next, gum would be perfection?)*

"So, here's the weirdest thing," said Lisa. "I can't see the film after all, so here, have my ticket and you guys can go together." She pushed her ticket into Nina's hand and started to back away.

"No," Tom yelped. *(Great, Tom, attractive noise. Let's hope she's got a secret fetish for yodeling.)* "Why? You texted me like ten minutes ago saying you were looking forward to it."

"I have a sudden headache," said Lisa.

"I have Advil in my bag," said Nina, also in a somewhat higher voice than normal.

"I can't take ibuprofen. Sorry, upsets my tummy." Lisa looked apologetic, but she was still unmistakably backing away.

"I also have Tylenol," said Nina, starting to rummage.

"Can't take acetaminophen, either. Deathly allergic."

"Allergic to Tylenol?" asked Tom, trying to remember if she'd mentioned this in the nearly twenty years they'd been friends.

"Yes, terribly. I'll drop dead on the spot." Lisa shrugged, which Nina thought made for a pretty casual reference to sudden death.

"Maybe you need caffeine?" suggested

145

Tom. "Or something to eat?"

"Or you can get a rain check?" suggested Nina, looking now to Tom for support. They didn't want to see a film together, did they?

Lisa looked at the clock above the movie board. "Too late! Movie starts in three minutes. Run along."

"I don't think that's how rain checks . . ."

"Gotta go," said Lisa, clutching her head. "Starting to lose consciousness. Got to get to a darkened room and an ice bag ASAP. See you guys." And then she turned and essentially ran away. Not literally running, obviously, because that would have been bizarre, but definitely speed walking.

Tom and Nina stared after her. Then Nina looked down at the ticket in her hand. *Space Spiders on Mars?* She raised her eyebrows and looked up to see Tom watching her.

"Not a sci-fi action movie fan?" he said, with a note in his voice that suggested he wasn't surprised. He looked up at the board. "I bet you were going to see *Miss Eglantine Expects,* weren't you? One of those movies where the corsets are tighter than the fight choreography."

Nina frowned. He was right, but she wasn't going to admit it. "No, actually, I'm here for *Bloody Deadly Blood Death III: The Blood Rises.*"

146

"Really?" He had started the word sounding surprised, but by the end of it he was sarcastic.

"Yes." She gazed up at him, Popsicle cool, though she suddenly wished she hadn't gone in this direction and had simply offered to buy the popcorn. He was really attractive, and now he thought she was . . . She didn't know what he thought. His expression was unreadable, not that she was all that good at reading people, anyway. She started to feel the familiar signs of imminent panic. Tingling hands. Mild nausea.

Tom was thinking he didn't believe Nina about *Blood Death III,* but it was clear she didn't want to watch a film with him. He wanted to stop bickering with her but wasn't sure how. He opened his mouth to suggest something, and then she suddenly thrust the ticket back at him and turned and walked out.

He watched her go, realizing for the first time that he really was attracted to her and that she apparently hated him so much she was willing to break all social conventions and walk away without a word.

As she walked toward Vine Street, Nina realized she had done exactly what Lisa had done, and giggled a little, somewhat hysterically. She was starting to calm down, but her palms were still tingly. Her anxiety had gotten better in the last several years, once she'd started to use a planner and keep a schedule and basically try to control every aspect of her life, but it was always curled up at the base of her spine like a sleeping cat. Any step off the normal path, any deviation from standard, and it started lashing its tail.

Suddenly, she wanted to cry. She'd been doing so well, but clearly she wasn't one of those people who could be spontaneous, and that was going to have to be OK. She didn't want complexity in her life, and with work and the new weird family thing, she definitely didn't have space for a boyfriend.

Time to go back into hiding.

today is the day

DATE **Monday May 13th**

M T W Th F S Su
△ △ △ △ △ △ △

SCHEDULE

7 > 8	
8 > 9	
9 > 10	
10 > 11	Work
11 > 12	
12 > 13	
13 > 14	
14 > 15	
15 > 16	
16 > 17	
17 > 18	
18 > 19	Elementary book
19 > 20	club
20 > 21	

TO DO LIST

- [ ] get snacks
- [ ] ice cream
- [ ] pick next book
- [ ]
- [ ]
- [ ]
- [ ]
- [ ]
- [ ]
- [ ]

GOALS

Stay Calm
♡

NOTES

Herbs for anxiety?
Get a 2nd cat?

✚ **BREAKFAST**
Smoothy

✚ **LUNCH**
Sandwich

✚ **DINNER**
goldfish?

✚ **WORKOUT**

NINE

In which Nina gets schooled by
well-meaning but ill-informed children.

"You did what?"

"I just turned and walked away."

Polly stared at her. "But, wait, I thought
you liked this guy. Or rather, I thought he
was cute and, therefore, you might like him
once you got to know him. There was the
possibility of liking."

Nina nodded. It was the following Monday, there were no customers in the store
yet, and Polly had shown up on time for
once.

Polly continued, "And yet, when you had
a chance to talk to him, you walked away."

"Right."

Polly narrowed her eyes. "So I'm struggling with this. Talk me through it."

Nina sighed. "I went to the movies, alone.
I saw him there. Weird circumstances involv-

ing a girl on his trivia team meant suddenly the two of us had tickets to the same movie, then I freaked out and walked away."

"Without a word?"

"Silently, yes."

"No pathetic excuse, even? No 'I have a headache'?"

Nina shrugged. "The other girl beat me to that one, and I was freaking out, remember?"

Polly shook her head. "It's amazing to me you ever get laid at all."

"It's amazing to me, too."

"When was the last time?"

"We're not talking about this."

"We are. I can hear us."

"No." Nina walked away toward the stock area to grab some books that needed shelving, or something. Anything.

"Well," said Polly's voice from behind her, "if it's any consolation, you have a great walking away view. Walking away makes your butt look awesome."

"Good to know," called Nina. "I'll make sure I always keep attractive men behind me." She paused. "You know what I mean."

"Sadly," said Polly, "I do."

At the end of the day, Nina started to set out the beanbags for the elementary book club. She'd been feeling irritable and sad all day, but she knew the generous application of little girls would distract her perfectly.

"All right, young one," said Liz, pulling on her battered Dodgers baseball hat. "It's an important game, and I am so out of here I am basically a dot on the horizon."

Nina frowned at her. "You're still very much in front of me."

Liz replied, "And yet my heart is already in the stadium, a hot dog in its hands, ketchup on its chin."

"Does a heart have a chin?"

"Some have several. I, however, am slender and lissome, so mine only has the one." And with this utter ridiculousness over, Liz touched the brim of her cap and left the store. Nina stared after her for a moment and shook her head. Honestly, that woman was a lunatic.

"Do you need any help?" Nina looked up to see Annabel, one of her book club ladies, as she called them. Annabel was ten, a serious child, with deeply held beliefs and unwavering suspicions.

"Sure," said Nina. "Can you grab the extra beanbags from the office?"

Nina had started out using regular chairs, but everyone had been silent and reserved. Beanbags worked much better. Annabel knew where they were kept; this was the first book club she'd joined, but she was one of those kids who was geared toward mastery. She wanted to know how you did it, then she wanted to do it herself.

Logan came in. Logan was also ten, though she went to a different school than Annabel. They looked at each other and Logan smiled first. Annabel smiled back and said hi. Logan followed her back into the office, and they both came back with the final pair of beanbags, not saying anything. Nina was often surprised by how tentative and shy ten-year-olds were. She had been like that herself, but all the other girls had looked so much more confident than she'd felt. They would greet one another enthusiastically, play together at recess, argue passionately, and hug. She had always marveled at them and wondered if maybe her mom had been supposed to apply for some kind of training for her, something she'd forgotten to do because she was so busy. Other people's moms had clearly equipped them better. Then she would feel guilty for feeling that way and retreat further into her books and TV shows and solitude.

The door flew open and Nora and Una came in, full of chatter and giggles. They were the same age and had known each other since preschool. Just behind them were Asha and Ruby-Fern, another pair of friends. They were all dressed in regulation girl-power ensembles, with fully empowered whimsical touches: rainbows, fake fur, glitter, unicorns, pictures of Ruth Bader Ginsburg or Amelia Earhart, enamel pins of donuts or sloths or foxes. Check, check, check. This age was the last hurrah of individualism; already they dressed like one another, but usually because they saw something and loved it. Icons or fabrics blew like a breeze through every classroom in the land, and parents, happy to get a request they could fulfill with a simple trip to Target, went out and bought every *Girls Rule the World* T-shirt they could.

Nina wondered how much good it would do once hormones rolled up and kicked the doors down; her own observation of middle school girls was that they dressed alike in order not to be separated from the pack and eviscerated online, which was an entirely different motivation than "OMG, that sloth is so cuuuuuute!" She looked at her watch; it was time to start. She locked the front door — nothing was more distracting to book club than customers wandering about — and went to the office to get the Goldfish crackers and bottled water that constitute the mortar of childhood.

"Who wants to start?" she asked when she returned and sat down on her own beanbag. The book that month was *The Mysterious Benedict Society,* one of her favorites. Seeing as she got to pick the books they read, this was hardly surprising.

Nora stuck up her hand. Nora was a highly creative little girl, who never hesitated to share her thoughts. As they were usually sharp and insightful, nobody minded, and in this group the kids had clearly decided she was the leader.

"I loved this book, but it made me really frustrated. Why is it always kids who have to solve stuff?"

"Please clarify," requested Nina.

Nora tipped her head to one side. "Well, in real life kids don't get to do anything much on their own, right?" She looked around at her peers, all of whom nodded. "Parents drive you places; there are teachers and babysitters and whatever. But in books, little kids are always doing things. In this one, they take weird tests and join a secret society and save the world."

"They don't have parents," said Logan. "Not proper ones. None of the kids in books do." She counted on her fingers. "They're usually dead, or evil, or distracted and busy."

"Junie B. Jones has parents. Ramona Quimby has parents," Nina said.

"Yes," replied Logan, "but those kids do regular stuff. I'm talking about when the kids do awesome stuff. Stuff that nine- or ten-year-old kids never really get to do.

"Like fly on a bat and fight rats like Queen Luxa in the *Gregor* books."

"Or travel through space like Meg in *A Wrinkle in Time.*" Annabel clearly agreed with Logan on this one.

"Let's try and stick to this book." Nina sometimes let them ramble on about all the books they loved, because she enjoyed that conversation as much as they did, but she was trying to be more grown up about it.

"Sticky has parents, though." Asha waved her copy of the book. "Right?"

Logan nodded. "He does, but he thinks they don't want him anymore."

"Which is worse than not having any," said Annabel.

"Definitely," said Ruby-Fern.

"And Kate has a dad, but she doesn't know it."

"What about Miss Perumal?" asked Nina. "Isn't she like a mother to Reynie?"

There was a sudden knocking on the store's front door, which scared the applesauce out of all of them. One of the girls

156

actually squeaked.

From where they were on the floor, they couldn't see the door, but Nina stood and saw a man standing outside. The early-evening sun was behind him, so she couldn't get a good look at his face, but she started over to let him know the store was closed. The parents wouldn't be here to pick up the kids for nearly another hour, but maybe it was one of them.

It wasn't. It was Tom. From Quizzard. That Tom.

What. The. Actual. Heck?

"Is that a friend of yours?" asked Ruby-Fern, from a foot or two behind her. Nina turned and discovered the whole book group had followed her to the door, drawn helplessly by their adaptive need to stick their beaks into anything new.

"Not really," replied Nina. She reached the door and smile-frowned at Tom, wondering why he was there.

Tom, who was wondering exactly the same thing, waited until the door was open and then held up the movie ticket. "This is yours. I was in the area, so I thought I'd bring it back."

"Uh," said Nina, "we're closed." *Yes, Nina, let's open a conversation with a non sequitur. Stylish.*

Asha said, "Are you Nina's boyfriend?" She was a tall, clear-eyed child who stuck to the point.

Tom, who was a little confused by the six girls who were now all staring avidly at him, shook his head.

"Are you a boy who is also a friend?" Ruby-Fern wasn't going to let him slip by on a technicality.

"Uh . . ." said Tom.

"Maybe he wants to be her boyfriend," suggested Logan. "And Nina doesn't want him to be?"

"Or maybe she wants him to be, but hasn't told him yet." All the little heads swiveled to look up at Nina, who was approximately the color of a strawberry.

"Ladies," she said in her firmest voice, "please return to the book club area and wait quietly. I won't be a minute."

"No, it's OK," said Nora. "We're fine here."

Nina looked at them with her best laser beam eyes, and they all backed away.

Tom was starting to lose focus. "Anyway . . . I thought you might want to go see another movie sometime." He held out the ticket, and Nina took it, trying to decide if he had asked her to "go see another movie sometime *with me*" or had simply been

158

making an observation: "I saw you at the movie theater, *alone,* so here's a ticket you can use in the future, *on your own.*"

"Thanks. But this is really your friend's ticket. She bought it."

He shook his head. "No, she gave it to you, so I turned it in for a rain check." He smiled suddenly, and Nina felt her hands start to prickle with a combination of anxiety and attraction. He appealed to her so much. He was very tall and strong, all bones and mass; he made her feel like she wouldn't be up to the task of even holding his hand, let alone anything else. And why was she thinking of anything else?

He spoke again, slightly more hesitantly. "You left somewhat abruptly."

She blushed. "Yeah, sorry about that. I, uh . . . had to leave."

"Somewhat abruptly?"

"Yeah." There was no way she was going to explain any further; it was bad enough already. "Anyway . . . thanks." She smiled back at him and went to close the door. "I have to get back to my book club." *Before I start hyperventilating and have to breathe into a bag.*

"Oh, they're not all your children?" He tried a smile. He could smell her shampoo, honey and lemons. He was having trouble

159

with this simple social transaction; her shiny hair, her tiny hands and feet, her very small-ness made him feel clumsy and awkward, like he should be carrying a bale of hay with a straw between his teeth and saying things like "Shucks, ma'am, I have to move the she-cow back to pasture." She was smiling at him. *Keep your head in the game, Tom.*

"I'd have to work pretty hard to have six kids the same age." Her eyes were hazel, he saw; a warm brown with a darker ring around her iris. Distracting.

He said, "Modern science?" *Really, Tom, you're talking about fertility treatment? What's next, asking her what brand of tampon she prefers?*

"Well, sure." They stood there smiling at each other, both frantically trying to think of something to say that wouldn't make them look as stupid and confused as they felt.

"See?" said Asha, from behind the book-case. "They're definitely flirting. My older sister looks like that when she's texting sometimes." She sounded gleeful. "Usually just before my mom takes her phone away."

Tom and Nina looked over; six little heads were peeping over the bookcase, like a row of ripening avocados on a windowsill. They ducked down again, and giggling was heard.

She looked back at Tom and shrugged. "Sorry, they can't help it. I have to go."

He nodded. "Yes, well, anyway . . ."

She said, "Yeah . . ."

He said, "See you at trivia?"

She said, "Sure."

He said, "Bye then."

She said, "Bye, thanks for the ticket."

He said, "It was yours. I was returning it."

She said, "I know, but still."

He said, "Got it. Bye."

She said, "Bye."

He said, "See you."

She said, "Yeah."

She closed the door and turned to face the kids. They had popped back up and were looking at her over the top of the bookcase again. Nora was the first to comment.

"Sister," she said, "you need to work on your banter."

When Annabel's mother, Lili, came to pick her up, she seemed stressed. Nina had always liked this mom; attractive without working at it, casually dressed, funny and mellow. But this evening she was rushing. Her hair was escaping from her bun in a way that had moved from messy to imminently undone. Nina itched to tuck it all in but managed to keep her hands to herself. Not everyone enjoys symmetry and control like you do, she reminded herself.

"Bel, come on, baby, we've got to hustle." Lili was hunting in her giant handbag for something.

"Why?" asked Annabel. She wasn't giving her mother attitude; she was just wondering.

"Because I need to get home and finish those forty individualized packets of seeds to use as place markers at Tanty's wedding." Lili finally pulled out her car keys and looked at her watch. "And I literally need your help and you have to go to bed like an hour ago, which means I have to use child labor while also breaking child labor regulations about sufficient sleep."

Annabel frowned at her. "There are no child labor regulations about sleep in California."

"Oh, I'm sure there are," chimed in Nina, who was picking up the beanbags. "You can't work at all until you're fourteen."

"But what about the sleep part?"

Nina looked at Lili over Annabel's head. "I think those regulations vary from state to state."

Annabel turned from Nina to her mom and narrowed her eyes. "What exactly does helping involve?"

"Coloring in, tying ribbons, stickering, checking things off a list . . ."

"Ooh, that sounds awesome," said Nina, unable to help herself. Seriously, Lili had just rattled off four of her favorite activities.

Annabel grinned. "Well then, there you go. Nina can help you and California won't get mad."

Lili appeared embarrassed. "Bel, I'm sure Nina has plenty to do this evening."

"Actually, no," said Nina. "You live in the neighborhood, right? I don't mind helping. I love all that crafty and organizey stuff."

"You do?" Lili looked almost comically grateful. "It's not my game at all. Well, the crafty part is OK, but I keep freaking out that I'll forget someone or something and it's really important."

Nina laughed. "Well, let me put away the rest of the stuff and close up the store, and I'll meet you out front in ten minutes?"

"You're a goddess in human form," said Lili.

"She's not very good at flirting, though," said Annabel, firmly. She looked at Nina. "My mom has a boyfriend. Maybe she can help you."

Lili looked at her daughter in mild horror. "We're going to get ice cream. We'll see you

163

in a little bit."

As they walked out of the store, Nina watched them pause after a few steps and tried not to lip-read Lili telling her daughter not to comment on people's personal lives. Good luck with that, she thought.

TEN

In which Nina is helpful.

Lili lived fairly close to Larchmont, but nonetheless they drove, because it was Los Angeles. Besides, Lili had groceries, art supplies, and a giant bag of dog food to carry inside, so it was just as well Nina was there.

"Oh, you have a dog!" said Nina, thrilled. She would love to have a dog, even though Phil the cat might not approve. She couldn't stop herself from squatting down to greet Lili's clearly ancient Labrador.

"That's Frank," said Lili. "He's a shameless food whore; yours for a single kibble."

Frank gazed into Nina's eyes, trying to convince her to run away with him to a butcher's shop. She smiled at him and rubbed his ears until he made grumbly noises at her.

"Coffee?" asked Lili, putting away the groceries. Annabel had disappeared, presumably into her room. Another little girl appeared, younger than Annabel.

"No, thanks," replied Nina. "It's too late for me."

"Too late for you because you're dying or too late for you for some other reason?" asked the little girl, interestedly.

"This is Clare," said her mother. "Try and ignore her."

"Yes," said Clare, smiling at Nina like an angel, "you can try."

"I meant it was too late for caffeine; it will keep me awake."

"Really? My mom drinks it all the time. But she's much older than you, so maybe she's more tired. People's bodies wear out, you know." She reminded Nina of Ramona Quimby, with her shiny little bob and big brown eyes. Not to mention her apparent lack of filter.

Lili sighed. "I think they're doing a biology project on decomposition or something; she's all about death right now."

"Did you know," said Clare, ignoring her mother, "that you have tiny insects living on your eyelashes, right now, eating your eyelash juice?"

Nina raised her eyebrows. This kid had picked the wrong target. "Yes," she said, "and not only on your eyelashes; the adult

166

face has a thousand or so mites living on it at any one time. Did you also know," she asked Clare, "that the entire world is covered in a microscopic layer of poop?"

"Yes," said Clare, "and did you know that tapeworms can grow eighty feet long?"

"Yes, and did you know people produce a liter of snot every day?"

"On a regular day!" said Clare, with relish. "And did you know the shiny coating on jelly beans is made from insect poop?" She paused. "Or it used to be. I don't know if it still is."

Nina nodded, but Lili was done with this conversation. "That's enough," she said. "Honestly, you're revolting, Clare."

"I'm not," said Clare. "I'm learning." She went closer to Nina. "Who are you?"

"I'm Nina. I work at the bookstore where your sister does her book club."

Clare considered this. "Do you have a book club for littler kids?"

"How old are you?"

"Six."

"No, not yet. When you're older you can join one."

Clare narrowed her eyes at Nina, as her older sister had done. "If we can read, we should be able to come."

"You might be bored."

Clare shrugged. "I'm willing to take that risk," she said.

Lili had finished putting away the groceries. "Time to get crafty," she said, and led the way to the living room. Clare trailed after them.

Lili spoke over her shoulder. "I have an office in the garage, but I've been doing this stuff in here so I can watch TV at the same time. Is that OK?"

Nina nodded and Lili pulled out a basket containing a load of seed packets, each of which was different. They were all painted with flowers, and names had been worked into leaves and petals, vines and twigs. They were gorgeous.

"Where did you get these? They're great." Nina turned them over in her hands.

Lili smiled. "I made them. I'm an illustrator. These guests are confirmed, so now I need to thread this piece of ribbon *here*" — she demonstrated — "and then add an extra sealing sticker on the back flap *here* so the packets don't burst open. The seeds are really, really small."

"Like poppy seeds?"

"Exactly like. They're California poppies."

"Cute."

"Inexpensive." Lili grinned. "But also cute."

"Can I help, too?" asked Clare.

"You're supposed to be getting ready for bed."

"This looks more fun."

Lili considered her younger daughter for a moment, then smiled. "Sure, you can do the stickers."

They sat in a circle and started working.

Nina asked, "So, who's getting married?"

"My aunty," answered Clare, while her mother's mouth was still opening. "She's marrying a man she met in the street."

Nina looked at Lili, who was shaking her head. "My sister Rachel met her fiancé at the Grove, but for some reason Clare enjoys embroidering the truth."

"Maybe you're a writer," Nina said to the little girl. "They make up stuff for a living."

"Really? And it's not lying?"

Nina shook her head. "No, it's called fiction."

"Huh." Clare looked thoughtful. "Anyway, she's marrying Richard, who's very nice and tall."

"Do you mean nicely tall, like, he's nice and tall, meaning really tall, or nice and also tall?"

Clare looked at her and frowned.

"Never mind," said Nina.

"He's very tall," Clare said slowly, "and

169

he's also nice. And he has a dog, too, and he makes my aunty laugh all the time, almost as much as my mom does."

Nina glanced at Lili, who was working on a blank seed packet with some watercolor pens. "You and your sister are close?"

"Super close." Lili was focused on her work, but continued. "She's my best friend, which is why I don't want to mess up her wedding by forgetting anyone. And she keeps randomly inviting more people."

"Well, that definitely makes it harder."

Lili sighed and waved the packet to dry it. "She's very friendly. She'd be happy if total strangers came, honestly; she isn't paying that much attention. I think if it had been up to her she would have eloped. She had a big wedding the first time she got married." She turned her head and pretended to spit on the ground, which made Nina jump. "Sorry, family tradition; her first husband was a loser. Anyway, she had the big wedding, and the marriage was a disaster, every day of the five weeks it lasted. So she's superstitious about it. She left it up to me."

"Did you have a fancy wedding?"

There was a tiny pause, then Lili nodded. "Pretty fancy."

"My dad is dead," piped up Clare.

"Oh," said Nina. "I'm sorry, I didn't know."

"No problem," said the child. "I don't think it matters anymore."

"It's always going to matter, honey, but it's been a long time." Lili didn't look up from her painting, but Nina could hear wistfulness in her voice.

"Sam in my class has no dad, either." Clare was clearly pursuing this topic.

Lili raised her eyebrows at her daughter. "Sam has two moms."

"Bethany has no dad."

"She does; her parents aren't together anymore, but she still has a dad. Totally different. Divorce is not the same as someone dying, honey."

"Why not? They're still gone." Nina realized Clare must have been very young when her dad died and didn't have memories of him. She hoped Lili wasn't finding this difficult to talk about. She busied herself with her ribbons.

"Not really. Even if they aren't very nice, they're still around. Once someone has died, that's it. All gone."

There was a pause while Clare considered this. Then, "Mom has a new boyfriend now, anyway. Edward. He's even taller than Richard, and even nicer. He brought me a tiny house for the garden. Do you want to see?"

"When we're done, sure." Nina grinned at Clare. "You seem very interested in how tall people are." Nina was happy to change the subject.

Clare looked at her in surprise. "Of course. I'm forty-three inches tall."

Then she suddenly got up and walked out of the room. "I'm going to go and write a book now," she said. "Bye, Nina. See you at the wedding."

With a thump, Frank the dog jumped off the sofa where he had been sleeping and lazily followed Clare. Perhaps he was going to give notes.

An hour later they were done. Lili had taken Nina's suggestion and made half a dozen that said *Favored Guest,* in case her sister invited a few more guests at the last minute and still had twenty packets in her basket.

"The wedding is a week from Saturday, so she's still got time to add people, and she can't be trusted." Lili was leaning back against the sofa, holding a glass of wine. Nina had one, too, and they were feeling pretty full of themselves. The finished seed packets looked beautiful, a rainbow of ribbons and flowers.

"Don't they need you to lock numbers at

some point?"

"We overestimated, in case."

"What else are you doing for the wedding? Are there centerpieces?"

Lili shook her head. "No, it's a picnic wedding."

Nina raised her eyebrows. "What if it rains?"

Lili turned up her hands, "We can go inside the conservatory, I guess, where the ceremony is happening, but it's the end of May in Los Angeles. The Internet says the chance of rain is about one percent, and Rachel was happy with those odds. She said she wanted people to sprawl at her wedding, and sprawl they will."

"How will it work?" Nina enjoyed the concept of weddings, although she was getting seriously sick of going to other people's.

Lili stretched. "We rented a load of big rugs, all different kinds, from a prop house, and we're going to lay them out on the grass and surround them with the few hundred assorted pillows we also rented." She looked at Nina. "You really are interested in organization."

Nina shrugged. "I like pinning things down. I like to know in advance; I like to prepare."

Lili looked at the younger woman, and

her smile was warm. "You know, you can't always be ready. Life tends toward chaos, sadly. I thought I had my life all planned out nicely, and then my husband died in a car accident and everything changed completely. It's all very well to have a plan — it's a good idea — but you have to be able to walk away from it if you need to."

"And you walked away from yours?"

Lili finished her wine. "I'm not sure 'walk' is the right verb, but I left it behind. That version of it, anyway. More wine?"

She got up and went into the kitchen.

When she came back, she was clearly ready to change the subject.

"So, why does Annabel hold such a poor opinion of your flirting?" She handed Nina her refilled wineglass and sat back down on the floor.

Nina blushed. "She and the other girls saw a friend of mine come to the store and decided we were flirting."

"You weren't?"

Nina sighed. "Not successfully."

"But this is someone you like?"

"I don't know him at all." Nina paused. "But yes, he's attractive. I'm not sure he's very smart; he seems to know a lot about sports but nothing about books."

Lili frowned. "And that matters? Is book smart the only smart that counts?"

Nina shrugged. "To me, I guess, which I realize isn't very open-minded. I love books; they're my job, my main interest . . . I'm not very sporty."

Lili looked skeptical. "So is the issue that he's not bookish, or that you're not sporty? Maybe there's something you're both interested in. Movies? Animals? Entomology?"

Nina sighed and stretched out on the floor, gazing at the ceiling. There was a clump of something pink up there. "Is that Play-Doh?"

Lili didn't even look. "Probably. You're going to have to go out with him, I guess, to find out whether or not you're compatible." She paused. "Do you young people actually date anymore, or do you run algorithms to see if it's going to work?"

Nina smiled. "Yeah, we have our phones talk to each other and see if our operating systems are compatible. Saves so much time and effort." She added, "And why you're calling me 'you young people,' when you're probably all of three or four years older than me, I'm not sure."

Lili smiled. "Yeah but those are mom years; they're like dog years, seven for every one. Chronologically, I'm thirty-four, but in mom years, I'm ninety-four."

"Well . . . then you look great for ninety-four."

"Thanks. Can't you stalk him online? I thought you guys all did that."

"I guess. I don't know his last name."

Lili laughed and dragged her laptop over. "Well, what do you know about him?"

"I know he's on a trivia team that beat my team the week before last. With a question on horse racing, for crying out loud. Did you know that all racehorses have the same birthday?"

Lili nodded absently. "Yes, January first."

Nina threw up her hands. "Does everyone know this fact except me?"

Lili ignored her. "Here we go. There's a site that lists all the trivia teams in the East Los Angeles Pub League. Is that your league?"

Nina nodded.

"And what's his team name?"

"You're a Quizzard, Harry."

Lili looked over at her and made a face. "Really? And you think he's not bookish?"

"Oh," said Nina, "good point. Not sure that being a *Potter* fan makes you bookish, per se, but I suppose it does mean he can read."

"Are you criticizing *Harry Potter*?"

"Never. I'm a Ravenclaw."

"A bookworm like you? What a surprise." Lili was scrolling down a page of some kind, the screen hidden from view. "Here it is. Team members . . ." She paused and frowned suddenly. "Thomas Byrnes."

"Burns like Edward or Byrnes like David Byrne?"

"The latter. With a Y." Lili was still frowning. "That's bizarre."

"Why?"

Lili didn't answer and then looked up and smiled suddenly. "Nothing, I got distracted." She closed the computer. "So now that you know his name you can stalk him to your heart's content."

"I don't know if that's really my scene."

"You're lying." Lili grabbed one of the blank seed packets and started working on it.

"Yes, I'm lying," Nina said. "But I'm not in the market for dating right now. Things are pretty tight, time wise, and I have my life together and organized, and I think a boyfriend might be too much." She started babbling. "Besides, I don't know if I can manage the Instagram-worthy relationship, with its photo opportunities and matching sweaters and public declarations. I find it hard enough to relate to people in private;

177

having to do that while also creating an effective online presence as a couple . . ."

Lili looked at her, her hand still for a moment. "You do realize it isn't mandatory to live your life online, right? For thousands of years we managed to be miserable or joyful in private. You can still do it."

Nina shrugged. "Sure. But even in private, being with someone else feels like . . ." She trailed off. "It feels intrusive." She thought of something else. "Besides, I have this whole other thing going on." She told Lili about her family, about her dad, while Lili drew and said, "Mm-hmm," every so often. Eventually Nina said, "Besides, even if I didn't have a new cast of thousands to deal with, what would that guy and I talk about once we'd finished discussing *Harry Potter*? He's probably only seen the movies, anyway."

"You're a snob; there's nothing wrong with the movies, and I think that whole thing is an excuse to avoid dealing with it," replied Lili, turning the seed packet over and looking at it. She held it up to Nina. "How's this one?"

The packet had the name *Nina* on it, written in vines, surrounded by amber poppies. "It's beautiful."

"Good," said Lili, "because it's for you.

You're coming to the wedding."

"I'm not invited."

"You are now. Clare invited you. And she doesn't like to be crossed."

"That's true," said a voice from the doorway. Clare was standing there, holding several sheets of paper, with her editor, Frank. "I finished my book and I'm ready for bed." Then she looked at Nina. "You can come to the wedding, but you can't sit with me until after the ceremony, because I am a flower girl, and that is a Series of Responsibilities."

Nina opened her mouth but closed it again.

"Thanks very much," she said.

"You can thank me after," said Lili, getting to her feet. "Assuming you have a good time."

Nina laughed, getting up, too, and dusting herself off. She seemed to have acquired a pretty thick layer of dog fur, lying on the floor. Oh well, it was a chilly night.

"Besides," added Lili, walking her to the door, "weddings are great places to meet people."

Then she and Clare stood at the door and waved good-bye to Nina.

today is the day

DATE _Tuesday 14th May_   M T W Th F S Su
◇ ◇ ◇ ◇ ◇ ◇ ◇ ◇

SCHEDULE

7>8	
8>9	
9>10	work
10>11	↓
11>12	
12>13	
13>14	
14>15	
15>16	
16>17	
17>18	
18>19	
19>20	Trivia
20>21	

TO DO LIST

- ☐ my
- ☐ brain
- ☐ is
- ☐ a
- ☐ blank
- ☐
- ☐ Cat fd
- ☐
- ☐
- ☐
- ☐

GOALS

Wedding!
- dress?
- gift?
- xanax?

NOTES

Bill Murray Marathon

✚ **BREAKFAST**
Coffee

✚ **LUNCH**
Coffee

✚ **DINNER**
Coffee Ice Cream?

✚ **WORKOUT**
please...

ELEVEN

*In which Nina meets more family, and
wishes she hadn't.*

The next morning, Nina got a text message:
*Danger, Will Robinson. Expect call from Sarky.
See you later.* It was from Peter Reynolds,
and it made her frown. She was having her
morning planner time when the text came
in, and she looked over her day carefully.
Was there space for a legal assault? Not
really. And if there wasn't space, it wasn't
going to happen. A schedule was a schedule,
people, and without a proper schedule, the
day would descend into madness, anarchy,
dogs and cats living together, etc. The *Ghost-
busters* reference reminded her of another
Bill Murray movie, *Stripes,* where he begs
his girlfriend not to leave, because "all the
plants are gonna die." She grinned and
flipped ahead to schedule a Bill Murray
movie marathon. See? Even in the most

organized life there is room for whimsy. It just needs scheduling. As her heroine Monica Geller would say, *Rules help control the fun.*

The call from Sarkassian came in a few minutes after the store opened, which was considerate at least. The lawyer sounded somewhat apologetic.

"I'm afraid to say your niece, Lydia, has raised the specter of legal action against you. She's asked for a face-to-face meeting at our offices today. Would you consider attending?" He did sound like he was asking, rather than ordering, so Nina considered it.

"Legal action for what?"

Sarkassian coughed. "Fraud. She thinks maybe you're not actually a Reynolds."

Nina laughed. "And did you tell her that I don't care at all about being a Reynolds, and in fact would have been totally fine never knowing who my father was?"

"Yes, but there is the matter of the will."

"Cut me out of it, then. I really don't care."

Sarkassian sounded horrified. "You can't simply cut someone out of someone else's will. Besides, it might be a great deal of money."

"Or it might be a giant inflatable middle finger. Let me be completely clear: I. Don't.

183

Care. My life is fine as it is. I don't need any complications."

There was a moment's silence. Then, "Well, I know that, and you know that, but perhaps you could tell Lydia that in person? Please, Ms. Hill, it would be enormously helpful if you could attend the meeting. The rest of your immediate family will be there."

So that was why Peter had given her the heads-up. He already knew about the meeting.

"I'll see you later."

"Thank you." The lawyer did sound relieved, and Nina wondered what he was scared of. "My assistant will contact you with details."

Dammit. Now she was going to have to change her planner. Nina hated changing her planner.

The lawyer's office was in a glintingly tall glass and granite building on the corner of Wilshire and Crescent Heights. While not exactly forbidding and Borg-like, it was dark enough that should a battalion of Stormtroopers have emerged from the parking lot, Nina wouldn't have been surprised. Well, she would have been surprised by the Stormtroopers per se, obviously, but it would have made sense they were coming from that building. The point is, the lawyer's building was intimidating and Nina was intimidated.

While the firm didn't have their name on the outside of the building, a quick glance at the lobby directory showed they had three floors all to themselves, which meant this was no Podunk operation, no, sir. The receptionist was clearly on top of her game, because when Nina walked up to her, she rose and said, "Right this way, Ms. Hill."

"How did you know who I was?" Nina asked. She should have shrugged it off, but she was rattled; see earlier comment re: Stormtroopers.

The receptionist smiled at her as they headed down a long and plushly carpeted corridor. "I have a list of people attending your meeting, which is the only one involving clients right now, and I signed everyone else in already."

"Oh," Nina said. "So, professionalism and logic."

The woman nodded.

"Well played, madam," Nina said, and then wished her head had exploded instead. Why did she say these things? Why did her mouth open and this stuff come out? AIs like Siri and Alexa sounded more relaxed and human than she did.

The woman opened a door, but as the sound of many conversations rolled out, Nina hesitated.

"I think there might be a mistake. Mr. Sarkassian said it was immediate family only." The room was filled with people. Enough food had been laid out on a deep shelf on one end of the room to feed a football team. *After* the game.

The receptionist shook her head. "No mistake. This *is* the immediate family." She moved her head slightly to indicate Nina should go in because she was holding the door and it was heavy, so Nina stepped into the room.

Nina had always been comfortable with the fact that she was not gregarious. Not every interaction needed to be a party, right? Her Room 101, for those Orwell fans among you, would simply contain a couple of people whose names she couldn't remember. Walking into a room full of strangers was about as comfortable for her as putting on a hat full of wasps and tugging it down firmly. But in she went.

"Nina!" Peter stood and came over to her. He took her hand and leaned in close. "Don't pay any attention to this; let it wash over you." He pulled back a bit and looked at her, smiling. "Lydia is not speaking for

186

most of us."

Nina nodded and caught sight of Archie over his shoulder. He was also smiling at her, so maybe this wouldn't be so bad. She took a seat in the total silence that had fallen and felt several pairs of eyes trained on her. She tried the *in through the nose, out through the mouth* breathing a long-ago therapist had suggested. The table was very nice, so she looked at that. Spruce, if she wasn't mistaken.

"Would you like a glass of wine?" asked Peter. "It's terrible, but there's alcohol in it."

Nina nodded, and he got her a glass that, as he had warned, was pretty bad. Nina wasn't a wine snob or anything, but she was a millennial, and as you've probably heard, they drink more wine than any generation in history. This would probably be disputed by the ancient Romans, but the Internet doesn't check sources very thoroughly. Nina had a policy of treating the Internet the way she might treat a guy in a bar, one who's wavering gently on his stool and holding a honey mustard pretzel nugget. He *might* be an expert in international arbitrage or arms dealing or the history of Catholicism, but it's more likely he isn't. But anyway, she did drink wine, so the Internet nailed that one.

Sarkassian arrived and threw a haunch of dead lamb on the table, and the lion feeding began. The haunch came in the form of a pile of documents, but still.

"Thank you all for coming," he said, in time-honored style. "I'd like to take a minute now to introduce everyone to Nina Hill." He indicated her, and she looked around and smiled the smallest, tightest smile in the history of smiles, which, when you consider geopolitical world history, is saying quite a lot. *I am not happy,* said the smile, *but I am willing to be polite for as long as you all are.* What it also said, if you knew Nina well, was, *I am starting to have a panic attack, so please can we move this along before I throw up on the table?* But no one there knew her well, so her secret was safe.

The lawyer went around the table. "Let's start with your siblings. This is Becky Oliver; she was William Reynolds's first child." The woman was maybe in her late fifties. She looked a lot like her son, Peter, and her smile was like his, too. She held up her hand in a peace sign, which Nina took to be a gesture of, well, peace. "The woman on her right is your sister Katherine, and on her left is their mother, Alice."

Alice's eyes were fixed on Nina, but she might have been stuffed for all the animation she showed. She had one of those hairstyles that looked like it could be removed in one piece, possibly in order to replace it with an identical one in a different color. She favored statement jewelry, but what her statement was, it was difficult to say, unless it was simply, *I am a hollow shell of a person, which is fine with me, because my shell is shinier than yours.* That statement came across loud and clear. Nina remembered Peter's warning about Alice and tried not to look directly at her.

Katherine was different. She wore zero makeup and clearly gave less than zero fucks about her appearance. Her hair was messy, her clothes were untidy, but her eyes were as sharp and penetrating as a robin getting ready to ambush a worm. Nina was painfully aware she was the worm in this situation.

The lawyer swallowed and moved on. "To their right is Archie, who I think you've already met, and his wife, Becca. He is the son of Rosie, William's second wife, sadly deceased."

"Hello again," said Archie. "Sorry about this."

"Shut up, Archie," said a younger woman who was sitting exactly across from Nina. "Don't be such a quisling." She switch-bladed a glance at him, then looked back at Nina, unblinking. She was in her midthirties, maybe, wearing a violet pants suit with one of those blouses that have a bow for a tie. Possibly she thought she was attending a meeting in 1986, or interviewing for a job as a minor character on *L.A. Law.*

Wow, thought Nina, quisling, eh? Bringing out the fifty-cent insults already. Respect. Although if the woman didn't blink soon, her shiny little eyes were going to drop out of their sockets and roll across the table like marbles.

The lawyer sped up his introductions. "Your youngest sibling, Millie, isn't here, but sitting next to Becca is Eliza, who is Millie's mother and William's widow."

Eliza smiled tightly at her, but whether the tightness was for her or a general default setting, Nina had no idea.

Alice suddenly leaned forward and pointed at Eliza. "She killed him, you know, so I suggest you watch yourself. Come between her and the gold she's been digging, and you might not live to regret it."

Eliza snorted. "You're mistaken, Alice. And possibly senile."

"I'm not," replied Alice. "I'm simply too old to make nice if I don't want to. You killed William so you could take his money."

190

Sarkassian interrupted. "Please, Alice, that's slander and completely baseless."

Alice looked at Eliza. "Murdering whore."

"Emasculating harpy," replied Eliza, calmly.

"Ladies, ladies," muttered the lawyer, clearly used to this level of familial invective. He frowned at them, cleared his throat, and continued. "OK, now we come to nieces and nephews. Peter you already know, and sitting next to him is his sister, Jennifer." Jennifer looked like Peter and waved a friendly hand. "Jennifer has children who are your great-nieces and great-nephew, but they're younger and not legally required to be here."

"Am I legally required to be here?" Nina looked at Sarkassian. "I thought it was just an invitation."

"It was," he replied quickly. "I simply meant that they are legally still minors, and therefore not party to any action."

Nina frowned at him, but before she could ask anything else, the woman across from her snapped, "And I'm your niece Lydia, your sister Katherine's daughter, although I doubt we're actually related at all." She looked aggressively at Nina. "What proof do you have that my grandfather was your father and that you're not a con artist?"

Nina gazed at her for a beat or two, then slowly raised one eyebrow, a skill she was rightly proud of. If this woman thought she could intimidate her by being rude she was about to be disappointed. Nina might battle crippling anxiety once or twice a week, but she also worked in retail, and rudeness is the special sauce on the burger that is the Los Angeles shopping public.

"Oh, I don't know. My birth certificate? His own word? My mother's word?"

Lydia smiled like the meanest girl in school about to comment on some underling's shoe choice. "Well, that's hardly sufficient, is it?"

"Legally it is," said Sarkassian, briskly. "William Reynolds is listed on her birth certificate; he made provision for her in his will, proving he was aware of her existence, and her mother has confirmed he was her father. As far as the law is concerned, we're good."

"Well, who's to say she is actually who she says she is?" Lydia looked scornful. "She might be some grifter pretending to be Nina Hill to get her hands on our money. She may have kidnapped the real Nina Hill and be keeping her in a basement somewhere."

At this, the last remnants of Nina's anxiety peeled away, revealing a cold center of anger. This wasn't necessarily a good thing. Sometimes when her social anxiety got pushed too far, a strange confident madness would take over her mouth, which had led to some very unfortunate outcomes.

"Well," she said, apparently completely nonchalant, "if I am a grifter, I've been playing a very long con, seeing as I went to school as Nina Hill, went to college as Nina Hill, got a job as Nina Hill, and have been working at it for six years, still pretending to be a totally unimportant and regular person. Presumably in case someone I'd never heard of dropped dead and left me a mysterious something." She turned up her palms. "It's a lovely blend of cynicism and optimism, but as a con it seems a little high intensity, don't you think?"

Several people laughed, but Lydia didn't seem amused.

"Also," continued Nina, "I didn't approach you guys; you came to me. I had no idea who my father was. He could have been anyone."

"Is your mother a prostitute?" Lydia asked.

Nina paused. "No," she replied evenly, "I didn't mean it that way. She's a news photographer. She won a Pulitzer."

"Lois Lane won a Pulitzer, and she's a

fictional character."

Nina happened to know that was true, and for a split second recognized that Lydia, for all her assholery, was a kindred trivia spirit. However, any fellow feeling quickly dissipated when Lydia kept talking.

"Where is your slutty single mother now?"

"She's in China."

"Convenient."

"Not if you want to hand her something."

Eliza spoke up from the end of the table. "This whole thing is ridiculous. If William left this woman something, isn't that an end to it? He could have left anything to anyone, right?" She turned and looked at Nina. "I didn't kill him, by the way. He died of a heart attack after years of smoking, drinking, and eating red meat with almost every meal." She shrugged. "He stopped all that when we met, but the damage was done."

"You brainwashed him," said Lydia. "He became a vegetarian. He tried to talk me into doing a juice cleanse. It was horrible."

Nina raised her eyebrows and looked at Sarkassian. "Is there any question about my father's death?"

"Yes, the question is whether he was your father or not," spat Lydia.

"No," said Sarkassian, rolling his eyes. "There is no question. As Eliza correctly says, he was in his seventies and died of a heart attack."

Eliza was staring at Lydia. "You barely knew your grandfather, Lydia. I'm not sure how you think you know anything about his health. When was the last time you visited him?" She was elegant in every way, this woman: pale blond hair, gray cashmere wrap over charcoal cashmere sweater, layers of gold necklaces and bracelets; but she was also irritated in a very human and somewhat ruffled way. Possibly because she was having to confront an insane ex-wife and a stepdaughter who was at least half basilisk.

"You wouldn't let any of us visit him. You kept him hidden away so you could poison his mind against us." It was remarkable how much anger Lydia was cramming into every syllable, while at the same time keeping a pretty even tone.

Peter finally joined the conversation. "Lydia, darling, this isn't a telenovela. It's amazing William lasted that long, to be honest, and attacking his widow is both tasteless and unattractive. Eliza loved William."

Lydia whipped around. "Peter, you have no idea what's attractive in a woman, so keep your nose out of it."

"Really?" said Archie. "Now you're attacking Peter?"

Lydia pointed her finger angrily at him. "Archie, stay out of this. You shouldn't even be here. You get more money than any of us. Why do you care?"

Archie flushed. "You mean because my mother is dead? Yeah, it's a great trade. You might be happy to exchange your mother for cold, hard cash, but Becca and I . . ."

And suddenly everyone was talking at once, and none of it was very nice.

"Oh for God's sake," said Nina loudly, bringing the argument to a sudden halt. "You're all mad. I'm not coming to the will reading, I don't want anything he left me, and good-bye."

Lydia looked smug. The lawyer looked worried. Everyone else looked embarrassed.

Nina got up and left the room, making it out into the fresh air before she ran out of oxygen completely. She leaned against the building and slowly slid down until she was sitting on the sidewalk. She put her head between her knees and waited until normal service was resumed. She was going to go home and have a brandy, and change her phone number, and possibly her name, in order to be done with the Reynolds family.

She just fervently hoped they were done with her.

TWELVE

In which Nina gets another chance to act
like a human being.

Once Nina got home, however, she found
herself putting all thoughts of her dumb
family aside. It was Tuesday, which meant it
was Trivia Night, and this evening was
particularly significant because it was another chance to qualify for the regional Quiz
Bowl semifinals. And why was winning the
Quiz Bowl so important? Well, there were
the prizes: $10K to the charity of your
choice, and T-shirts that said, *I had all the
answers and all I got was this lousy T-shirt.*
Second prize was, in true movie-buff fashion, a set of steak knives. Third prize? No
third prize. There was the winning team,
there was the team who came in second,
also known as the losing team, and that was
it. Nina's team had come in third the previous year, and it had awakened a competi-

tive spirit that had yet to be quenched. This was their year.

Nina had devoted considerable time to reading the last six months of *Sports Illustrated* and several books about the history of baseball (America's Pastime), football (America's Sport), and, just in case, ice hockey (Canada's Thing). She read Wikipedia entries on as many athletes as she could, and felt — if not actually competitive in this category — at least less likely to have to crawl out of the bar on her belly.

Tonight's venue was in Los Feliz, at a bar called Arcade. Nina looked around and saw the whole story: Someone had come across fifty of those tables that used to be so popular, with video game consoles sunk into their surfaces, and had gotten them cheap. Having been carried away in the moment, they then realized they had to do something with them, and opening a bar sounded like a good idea at the time.

The rest of Book 'Em were already there, seated at a *Galaga* table that actually worked. Lauren was playing while Carter and Leah heckled from the side.

"Ladies," said Nina, as she settled herself down. Leah handed her a glass of wine, which she immediately started drinking. She must be more nervous than she thought.

"Thanks," said Carter. "I realize I am a sensitive guy, but I'm not actually a lady."

Nina shrugged. "How's she doing?"

Leah looked up from the game. "Well, if the fate of the planet were in Lauren's hands, we'd all be doomed."

"Just as well it isn't, then," said Lauren, throwing her hands up in frustration as her rocket was utterly destroyed.

"My turn," said Carter, reaching down to put in some coins.

Nina looked casually around the bar. She'd finished her wine already and reached across the table to steal Carter's half glass.

"They're not here yet," said Leah.

"Who isn't?" Nina asked innocently.

"Don't pretend. Quizzard. They're not here yet, but they are on the board. We're up against them in the second round, assuming we can beat Menace to Sobriety."

"Which we presumably can?"

"No clue; new team."

"Where are they?"

Leah pointed to a group of guys on the other side of the bar. "*Ms. Pac-Man* table."

Nina looked and grinned. "Oh, we're totally good. That guy used to be in Tequila Mockingbird. He's half-drunk already; let's send over a round of shots."

"That's cheating."

Nina looked scandalized. "That's not cheating. That's being supportive." Then she looked at the door and Leah whacked her on the arm.

"Stop obsessing over that guy. It's going to weaken your attack. Stay focused, Hill. We win this, we advance to the semis."

"I'm not obsessing."

"Sure."

Carter suddenly let out a whoop. "I'm on the leaderboard!" He stood and shimmied around the table, kissing everyone extravagantly, which is of course exactly when Tom walked into the bar. He was with the girl from the movie theater, Lisa. She went off to find a table, and Tom headed to the bar. Not that Nina was keeping track or anything.

"You can go order your round of sabotage shots now," said Leah. She looked at Nina. "Go say hi to your little friend."

"My little friend? Are you referencing *WarGames* or *Scarface*?"

Leah made a face at her. "Neither. Most people are able to use language without it being a movie or book reference. You're the one who lives her real life in a fictional universe."

"You say that like it's a bad thing," said Nina, getting up. She walked across the bar,

200

surreptitiously tugging her dress out of any potential folds it might have settled into. She was a real person; when she sat, she folded. Fortunately, her dark green dress was vintage, and made of sterner stuff than its modern counterparts, so she was able to pull it back into sleekness with no problem. God bless natural fibers and cutting on the bias.

She squeezed up to the bar, next to Tom. "Uh, hi there."

Tom had actually been watching Nina approach in the mirror behind the bar, having spotted her instantly when he came in through the door. He'd watched her straighten her dress and immediately wanted to unstraighten it again. He was clearly losing his mind.

"Hi," he said, and smiled at her, glad the lights in the bar were dim so she couldn't see him blushing. "Ready for battle?"

She nodded, also secretly blushing. "Hopefully. You?"

He shrugged. "Hopefully. Lisa, who you met the other night, has allergies, so she's being whiny. The other two aren't here yet."

"Is she your girlfriend?" *Oh. My. GOD. What is wrong with you?*

He paused, and a tiny frown creased his eyebrows. "No, she's a friend. We've known each other since high school."

"Oh." Nina flailed around for a comment. "Cool beans." At this her brain threw up its metaphorical hands and curled up on its stem like a pissed-off hen. *I'm not playing anymore,* it said. *If the mouth isn't going to wait for my advice, I'm done.*

Nina ordered a round of shots. Tom feigned horror. "Aren't you taking a risk, doing shots before the contest? What about your laser focus and impressive recall?"

She made a face at him. "Are you mocking me? You beat us last time."

"That was luck. I've seen you play a hundred times, and that was the first time I've seen you beaten." He paused. "Well, apart from the semifinal last year."

"Oh, you saw that?"

He blushed deeper. "Yeah. We got knocked out in the semis, too. By the Spanish In-quiz-ition." He grinned. "Nobody expected it."

She grinned back at him. Monty Python *and* Harry Potter; Not just a sports nerd after all. Her shots arrived, and she was about to tell him they were for the other team, but suddenly it did seem like cheating. Dammit.

He shifted his feet, so he was facing her more completely. Her head came up to his shoulder, and she had to tip her head back a little. They were very close; she could smell sawdust and soap. "Enjoy your shots," he said. "I'm ordering a proprietary blend of caffeine, omega-6 oils, cinnamon, and ginseng. I have it shipped directly to the bars so my team is in tip-top form."

"Really?"

He shook his head. "Nah, not really. It's a bucket of beer and a bowl of pistachios."

"I love pistachios."

"Me too."

"They're chock-full of fat-soluble vitamins."

Here the conversation faltered, unsurprisingly. The phrase "chock-full" might have been the killer. Nina picked up her tray of shots and pivoted to go.

"Well, it's nice to see you again," she said, lamely.

He nodded. "I look forward to beating you." He paused. "That sounded weird."

Nina frowned up at him. "Good luck with that. We're on fire this evening. We've been warming up with *Galaga* and have successfully defended our planet for a solid hour."

He laughed. "If you've been here for a while and now you're doing shots, it's going to be an easy win for my team of highly trained, entirely sober intellectual giants."

"Want to bet?"

"Sure."

"Twenty dollars?"

"Dinner."

Nina studied his face, but he wasn't joking. "Dinner it is. If I win, you can take me to Denny's."

"Really?"

She nodded. "I love Denny's."

"Moons Over My Hammy?"

"Every time. And if you win?"

"Chicken and waffles."

She laughed. "We're a classy pair."

He nodded. "I wonder what else we have in common apart from lowbrow tastes?" He smiled slowly at her, and she had no comeback at all. She swallowed.

Suddenly, Howard's voice filled the bar. "Good evening, brave competitors and cowardly observers. It's time for tonight's challenge. In the first round we have Book 'Em, Danno up against Menace to Sobriety, and if last week's performance is anything to go by, Menace has nothing to worry about."

"Gotta go," said Nina, and hurried back to her table.

Tom watched her go, noticing the way she curved herself through the crowd, small and deft. Denny's had never seemed more appealing.

In most pub trivia leagues, or quiz leagues, or whatever they're called in your neck of the woods, teams are given written lists of questions and a limited time to complete them. Cheating is strongly discouraged, but of course it happens, especially now that you can search the Internet from your phone. In response to this, the organizers had changed things up for the Quiz Bowl qualifiers. Competing teams sent single members up to battle face-to-face, like on a TV game show. Questions were posed, buzzers were pressed, and points were awarded. If the first one to answer was correct, she got two points. If not, and the other competitor knew the answer, she would get one point.

Teams were invited to bring their own buzzers, which had led to some very strange noises. Tonight, Leah had been in charge of the buzzer, and she'd brought a vintage train whistle she'd found on eBay. Its action was a little sticky, and questions were raised about her judgment until Lauren revealed she had a miniature can of WD-40 in her purse and the problem was solved. Then questions were raised about why Lauren was carrying aerosolized hydrocarbons in her purse, and then questions were raised about why Nina used that phrase to describe it. The whole discussion took nearly thirty seconds of time, which, fortunately, was how long Howard was taking to describe the rules, so it was fine.

"Category one: World Geography. Teams, please choose your champions."

This one was easy for Book 'Em, because Leah was scarily good at geography. She had been homeschooled by a mom who believed in memorization as a form of relaxation, and she could still recite all the states (with capitals, state birds and flowers, major rivers and landmarks), countries in the world (including all the African ones, even though they changed a lot), books of the Bible, presidents and first ladies (and pets, including Coolidge's raccoon), and every actor who'd played Doctor Who since the beginning. That last one she'd done on her own.

"But wait," said Nina, concerned. "What if history comes up next and we can't play her then?"

Leah shrugged. "Play Lauren instead; she's pretty good at geography."

"I'm not," said Lauren, in a furious whisper. "Last time I got confused and said the longest river in the world was the Mississippi and then spelled it like a five-year-old at the Scholastic Spelling Bee. I even repeated it at the end."

"You spelled it correctly."

"Yes, but that's not the point. I got the question wrong, *and* I can never go back to that bar."

Nina conceded. "Leah, you go."

Howard had recently taken things a notch further in his quest to create a trivia league YouTube channel, and had built a podium. Leah and a guy from Menace approached it.

"Don't touch the podium," Howard hissed. "It's still wet."

"From what?" asked Leah, stopping immediately.

"From being painted, of course. I added the glitter too soon and it slowed it down."

"That's what she said," said the guy from Menace, and guffawed.

Leah rolled her eyes and clutched her whistle.

Howard looked at his friend, Don, who was live-streaming the contest. "Ready, Don?"

"Ready when you are, Mr. DeMille." Don was a jokester who enjoyed old movies, poetry slams, and pretending to be a cinematographer.

Howard cleared his throat. "Here we go: Ladies and Gentlemen, welcome to the Southern California Quiz Bowl Qualifier. Tonight, competing for glory and a chance to go forward to the next round, Book 'Em, Danno; Menace to Sobriety; You're a Quizzard, Harry; and Olivia Neutron Bomb. One team will make it through the night; the other three will be buried in ignominy. Our first contest is Book 'Em versus Menace." He turned to Leah and grinned. "And what's your name, little lady?"

Leah raised her eyebrows at him. "My name is Death to Sexism, little man."

Howard ignored her and turned to the guy from Menace. "And you, sir?"

"I'm Al. You can call me Al."

Howard faced front and grinned at the phone Don was holding up. "Let the battle commence." He got serious. "How many stripes are on the United States flag?"

"Thirteen," snapped out Leah.

"Contestants must use their buzzers first. Sorry, Book 'Em. Menace, do you have an answer?"

"Uh, thirteen?"

"That's correct. Two points to Menace."

Nina, Carter, and Lauren howled a protest, but Howard held up his hand. "Heckling won't help you, Book 'Em. You know the rules."

Leah looked apologetically over at her team.

"OK, next question: Montevideo is the capital city of which South American country?"

The guy from Menace squeezed his rubber chicken, which squawked.

"Uh . . ."

Howard waited.

"Uh . . ."

"Would you care to make a guess?"

"Hey," said Leah, "no fair. If he clucked too soon, it's my turn."

"All right, your turn."

"Uruguay."

"Correct. Two points to Book 'Em. Next question: What is the official language of Greenland?"

A brief pause, then Leah slid up her whistle. "Greenlandic."

"No way," said the guy from Menace. "You made that up." He squeezed his chicken in protest, multiple times.

"Google it, idiot," said Leah. "Or ask Howard; he has the answers."

"It's true. She's right," said Howard. "For a bonus point, name the other language spoken in Greenland."

"Danish," said Leah.

Howard stared at her. He had fallen in love with Leah the first time she'd competed in one of his tournaments and had totally aced World Religions, followed by Royal History of England, and then Animals of the Serengeti. He loved her for her mind. And her curves.

"Is there anything you don't know?" he asked, forgetting his microphone was on.

"Yes," replied Leah. "I don't know why you aren't giving me that point."

The bar erupted in laughter, and Howard frowned. "No lip, contestants. Bonus point withdrawn."

Leah bit her tongue and tried to smile at Howard, but couldn't make herself do it.

"Next question: What is the capital city of Canada's Yukon territory?"

Squawk!

"Whitehorse." The guy from Menace grinned at Leah. "I'm Canadian."

She stared at him blankly. "Congratulations."

Howard cleared his throat. "Last question of this section: Which sea separates the East African coast and the Saudi Arabian peninsula?"

Whistle!

"The Red Sea." Leah was totally confident

on this one and returned to the table in triumph: Book 'Em, six points; Menace, four.

"After a short break for refreshments, we will return with a little category I like to call . . . Books." Howard grinned around, but no one was really listening. "And remember, folks, it's two-for-one shots tonight, so get yourselves to the bar and become inebriated." Don counted down, 3 . . . 2 . . . 1, on his fingers and then indicated he'd stopped filming. Howard dropped his smile and leaped forward to look at the footage.

Nina looked at Howard thoughtfully. "It's his gift for witty repartee that sets Howard apart as a host."

"He's a poet, really," agreed Leah.

"Let's do these shots," said Carter. "There are sober children in Africa who'd kill for these. We can't waste them."

So they did.

Nina stood at the podium — not touching it — and faced a different guy from Menace. He was good looking and cocky, and Nina could hardly wait to hand him his hat, metaphorically speaking.

Don had started filming, and Howard was channeling his quiz show host. "OK, folks, time for Books, or Literature as some people like to call it."

"Stuck-up people," said the guy from Menace.

"Literate people," replied Nina.

"No bickering, please. Let's keep it civilized." Howard looked reprovingly at them. " 'Call me Ishmael' is the opening line from . . ."

Nina whistled. *Moby-Dick."*

Howard nodded, but said, "Please wait for the complete question before answering."

"Sorry."

He frowned at her. "Who wrote *Don Quixote*?"

She whistled. "Cervantes."

"Full name?"

Nina narrowed her eyes at him. Such a dick. "Miguel de Cervantes."

"In the children's books about a twenty-five-foot-tall red dog, what is the name of the dog?"

Squawk!

"Clifford!" Handsome was 100 percent confident on this one.

Howard snapped out, "Bonus question: Why did he grow so much?"

The guy suddenly looked sappy. "Because Emily loved him." He paused. "Her love made Clifford grow so big that the Howards had to leave their home."

Howard nodded, very serious. "Yes. Yes, it did."

Nina was vexed. "That's from the TV show theme song, not the books."

"Are you sure it isn't in the books?" Howard tutted at her. "No, you aren't, so keep your opinions to yourself. Next question: *Being and Time* is an ontological treatise written by which German philosopher?"

There was a long silence.

"Wait, we went from *Clifford the Big Red Dog* to *that*? Does philosophy even count as Literature?" asked Nina. She was feeling a little punchy. She really shouldn't drink at these things.

Howard shrugged. "Well, a) that's a very philosophical question, and b) the category is books. Nice try, Book 'Em." He looked at them both. "No?" They shook their heads. "Anyone from either team?" Silence. "Anyone in the bar?" Deeper silence. Howard sighed patronizingly, because of course he had the answer in his hand. "It was Martin Heidegger."

"Good to know," said Nina. "Do you think Emily's love would have done anything for him?"

Howard ignored her. "What are the four

houses at Hogwarts School of Witchcraft and Wizardry?"

Whistle! Squawk!

Nina and the guy from Menace glared at each other. *Whistle! Squawk! Whistle! Squawk!*

Howard held up his hand. "Rock–Paper–Scissors."

Nina threw rock. Menace threw paper. Crowing, he yelled: "Hufflepuff! Slytherin! Ravenclaw! Gryffindor!"

"Keep your hair on," muttered Nina, annoyed at herself for throwing rock. Scissors is always the better choice.

"OK, the scores are Menace, five; Book 'Em, four. Last question: Who wrote *The Metamorphosis,* first published in 1915?"

Nina confidently blew the whistle. "Kafka." Howard hesitated. "Franz Kafka," she said, irritated at him. He hesitated again. "Franz Ferdinand Kafka." She was totally winging the middle name, but she was willing to bet Howard knew even less about Kafka than she did.

He nodded, then said, "And for a bonus point, name the creepy movie where Jeff Goldblum turns into a fly."

"The Fly," shouted the Menace guy.

"That's correct. The teams stand level at six each."

There was an uproar. "Wait!" said Nina. "That's totally unfair! That film isn't even based on Kafka's book. The guy turns into a cockroach, not a fly; it's a movie, not a book; and besides . . ."

"Sorry, my decision is final." Howard was firm, although he was backing away slightly from Nina's pointing finger. Then, as Leah and Lauren turned up to join the fray, he took another step back and suddenly sat in the lap of a woman who couldn't get out of the way fast enough. Drinks were spilled. Shells were split as pistachios skittered across the floor. People leaped to their feet and skidded on the nuts. There was falling. There was cursing. Menace to Sobriety showed up in force, and, twenty seconds later, so did security.

Half a minute later, standing outside the bar, Carter sighed. "Nina, why is it always you that gets us banned?"

She looked at him, still mad. "It wasn't even a book question!" She shook beer from her sleeve and several pistachios flew out. "It's the principle! If you don't stand for something . . ."

"You'll fall for anything?"

She turned around. Tom was standing there, shrugging on his jacket. "I thought you might need a ride home." He grinned.

"You seemed a little . . . heated."

"Well," said Nina, "I'm supposed to be getting a ride with Leah . . ." She looked around. Down the street, she could see Leah and the others disappearing around a corner. "Oh."

THIRTEEN

In which we learn a little more about Tom.

Nina sat next to Tom as he drove her home, and, again, she smelled sawdust.

"Are you a carpenter?" she asked, the alcohol making her a little unguarded. "You smell of wood." She leaned toward him and sniffed theatrically.

He laughed. "Sort of."

Nina frowned at him. "Well, do you carpent, or not?"

"I don't think that's even a verb."

"It should be. Why isn't it?" She threw herself back in the seat. "I carpent, you carpent, he or she carpents . . ."

He shot her a glance, then went back to looking at the road. "Do you drink a lot?"

She shook her head. "No. I really shouldn't drink at all; I'm hopeless at it. I get drunk right away, then hungover two hours later. I don't do it well."

He laughed. "So, not a boozer, then, that's what you're saying?"

She shook her head. "I usually end up crying."

"Wow. Then yeah, you should stick to soda." He flicked on the indicator, and Nina tapped her toes in time to the click.

"Soda makes me fart." Then she closed her mouth tightly and promised herself she wouldn't say anything else. Possibly ever.

"Well, plain water it is, then." He looked sideways at her. "Not that there's anything wrong with farting."

She kept her promise and said nothing. Instead, she stared out of the window, noticing the usual things: homeless people waking up after a day of sleeping in order to be alert during the more dangerous night. Hipsters who dressed like the homeless people but with better shoes, crowding around doorways, or waiting for ride-share cars, looking up and down from their phones, reading license plates with more attention than they ever had in their lives before. Bodegas and liquor stores lit up like Christmas, their lights pooling on the damp and sticky sidewalks out front. Then they entered the residential part of Larchmont, where the streetlights were desirably vintage, but few and far between.

They pulled up outside the guesthouse. She'd left the reading light on next to her armchair, and the glow was inviting. Part of her wished she'd stayed home tonight, because now her head hurt and she hadn't even won the trivia contest. She sighed.

"Nice pad," said Tom.

"Thanks." She was fumbling with the door handle, something that normally didn't give her any trouble. Tom leaned across and opened it for her, pushing the door all the way open.

"Do you need help finding your keys?" He was teasing her.

She looked at him and shook her head. "I think not." Something occurred to her. "Wait, did you desert your team? Weren't you up in the next round?"

"Yeah." Tom shrugged. "Without your team to play against, all the challenge was gone."

She frowned. "And did your teammates see it that way?"

He nodded. "They don't take it very seriously." It had been Lisa who'd pushed him out the door to see if Nina needed a ride home, but he didn't think he needed to mention that. "Besides, I'm sure QuizDick will reschedule it."

"OK then." She told her legs to swing

around and get out of the car, but they weren't having it. She frowned and made them do it — jeez, who was in charge of this bus, anyway? Once out and standing, she swayed a little, and then Tom got out and was right there, holding her arm.

"You really aren't good at drinking, are you?" he said, smiling.

She looked up at him. "Do you read books?"

He frowned. "Sure. Occasionally."

"Good books?"

"Well, books I think are good."

"Have you read Jane Austen?"

"No."

"Kurt Vonnegut?"

"No."

"Truman Capote?"

"No." His face was blank, but she could see he was getting vaguely irritated by this line of questioning.

Harry Potter?" She was desperate.

"When I was a kid, of course."

"Do you know which house you're in?"

"No. I'm not a total nerd."

She swayed again, and suddenly leaned up into him, turning her face up, so there was really nothing he could do except kiss her.

Which he did. Lightly, but properly.

"Do you want to come in?" she said, once they'd separated.

"Are you sure I'm welcome? I haven't done the required reading."

She nodded and stretched up on her toes again, pulling him back down. His arm was tight around her waist, he was kissing her deeply, but then he pulled away and shook his head.

"No. I don't take advantage of tipsy book snobs. It's a rule."

"It is?" Nina was confused. "Who said?"

"Me." He turned her gently around and pointed her toward the house. "Go on, I'll make sure you get there in one piece."

She walked into her house, managing the stairs pretty well, actually, and once inside went to the window and opened it. He was still in the driveway.

"Hi," she said.

He grinned up at her. "Hello."

"Shall I let down my hair?"

He shook his head. "It's not long enough to reach me, for one thing, and secondly, I never understood why that was a good idea. Why not cut the hair into lengths, braid them into ropes, and create an actual ladder? It wouldn't be that hard."

"But it would be less romantic. And a much shorter story."

He shrugged. "Yeah, but it would be pretty hard core of what's-her-name to create a hair ladder and escape, right?"

"Rapunzel?"

"If you say so." He turned to leave but paused and looked back up at her, haloed in the reading light. "I'd like to see you again."

Nina inclined her head regally. "I'm prepared to consider it."

"Don't overwhelm me with enthusiasm."

"OK."

"Bye, then." He climbed into the car and pulled away, waving out of the window.

"Bye, then," said Nina, watching his lights fade away. Then she went inside and closed the window.

"Phil," she said to the cat, who was back-and-forthing on the floor, waiting to be fed, "I think I met someone."

"That's fantastic," said the cat. "I'm hungry."

As Tom drove away, he pulled out his phone and called his older brother, Richard.

"I think I met someone," he said, as soon as he heard his brother answer.

"Hi, Tom," replied his brother, wryly. "How are you? It's nighttime — did you notice?"

"I'm freaking out," Tom said. "That's why I'm calling."

"If you only met someone, why freak out yet? Keep your powder dry for when you've slept with her a few times and she reveals herself to be a total lunatic and you have to work out how to get away from her. Then you can freak out."

Tom said, "Look, you and I are not the same person. I try to find out their mental status before I sleep with them."

His brother's voice was sarcastic. "Really? What about Annika?"

"That was an exception. Every rule needs an exception."

"But not every woman requires a restraining order."

"She had beautiful hair."

"She did. Until she shaved it off and mailed it to you."

Tom realized he wasn't paying attention to driving at all and pulled over. "This girl is different."

He could hear his brother sigh. "Tell me."

"She works in a bookstore."

"Employed is good. Literate is good."

"She is small and has hair the color of a chestnut."

"Oh dear, you're already waxing lyrical. So, she's a redhead?"

"No, a brunette, but with reddish hints. Like when Amelia used to henna her hair."

"And does this girl henna her hair?"

"No, that's the color it is."

"Amelia used to say it was her natural hair color, too."

Tom frowned. "Look, what our sister did is irrelevant. Nina has reddy-browny hair, and her eyes are hazel, and she's gorgeous and small."

"You already said small. Is she under four feet?" He paused. "Are you preparing me for someone who'll need a booster seat at dinner?"

"No, but she's smaller than, say, Rachel."

Rachel was Richard's fiancée. "Rachel's five foot nine; she's not small at all." Richard's voice was amused. "Not that there would be anything wrong with you dating someone who needed a booster seat as long as they weren't an actual child. Good things come in small packages, right?"

Tom made a frustrated noise. "Richard, she's regular height, she's pretty, and I don't really know why I'm even telling you about her. She's really smart, probably too smart for me."

"That's good. You've had a tendency to date women who are too nice." He coughed. "Or totally insane."

"Her name is Nina."

"You told me that. Did you sleep together?"

"No. We kissed, she invited me in, but I said no."

"Why?"

"She was a little bit drunk. Not a lot, but a bit."

"Oh yeah. I remember your ridiculously firm stance on that. So, what are you going to do now?"

"I'll go see her at work and ask her out." He hadn't realized he had a plan, but apparently he did.

His brother laughed. "Great. Are you coming to dinner this weekend? I want you to meet Rachel's family. It's ridiculous you guys haven't met yet."

"I agree. But seeing as you met Rachel and decided to marry her in the space of, like, a month, we're all scrambling to keep up."

"I guess instant attraction is a family failing."

"Better than a cleft palate."

"Is that genetic?"

"No idea. Google it. I'll see if I can come this weekend. I'll try."

"All right. Good luck with the girl. I hope she isn't an insane stalker like the last one."

"You're hilarious."

"So my future wife tells me."

"Presumably only when you take your pants off."

"And now you're a comedian. Bye, Tom."

Tom said good-bye and hung up, smiling. Then he noticed he'd pulled over in front of a donut place, so he went in and got himself a cruller. He was, after all, a man of action.

today is the day

DATE Wednesday 15th May   M T W Th F S Su

◇ ◇ ◇ ◇ ◇ ◇ ◇ ◇

SCHEDULE

7>8	
8>9	
9>10	
10>11	Work
11>12	
12>13	
13>14	
14>15	
15>16	
16>17	
17>18	
18>19	yoga
19>20	
20>21	Book Club

▷▷ ▷ ▶ ▶ ▷ ▷ ▶ ▷▷ ▷ ▶

TO DO LIST

- ☐ Clean fridge
- ☐ BUY CAT FOOD OR
- ☐ HE'S GOING TO EAT
- ☐ YOU IN YOUR SLEEP
- ☐
- ☐
- ☐
- ☐
- ☐

GOALS

Boyfriend?

NOTES

DO MORE yoga

Read more poetry

✚ BREAKFAST

✚ LUNCH

✚ DINNER

✚ WORKOUT

FOURTEEN

In which Nina learns even more
about her family.

Despite Nina's fervent hope that the Reynolds family was going away, never to return, she was pleased when Peter reached out to her again.

"You don't have to like all of us," he said. "But I think you and I should be friends, even if it's only because we each need someone to talk about paper goods with." He cleared his throat. "Or is that, 'We need someone with whom to discuss paper goods'?"

Nina grinned. He'd called her while she was on her way to work the morning after the trivia debacle, and she'd been happy to see his name pop up on her phone.

"I don't think it matters. I know you're not supposed to end a sentence with a preposition, but I think it's acceptable between friends."

"Or relatives?"

"Or relatives. I will even allow split infinitives."

He laughed. "To actually permit the laws of grammar to literally be suspended?"

She winced. "Ouch, that's enough. It hurts more than I thought it would."

Peter's tone changed. "I'm sorry about Lydia. After you left the meeting, Sarky basically told her she can't force you to take a paternity test, and that as far as the law was concerned, she didn't have a leg to stand on. She didn't have anyone on her side except her mom and Grandma Alice, so in the end she stormed out." He sighed. "Your existence was a bit of a shock, but I thought Archie was the one who was going to get upset."

"He seemed somewhat irritated when we met, but a cheese sandwich made it all better."

"It usually does. Anyway, Archie is pretty distracted right now, what with the baby."

"He has a baby?"

"Not yet. You didn't notice how pregnant Becca was? I guess she didn't stand up. Their little boy is two, and the new one is due any minute. I don't think he's thinking all that much about his father."

But Peter was wrong.

When Nina came out of work at the end of the day, Archie Reynolds was standing in the street waiting for her. Even after only meeting him twice, it was a pleasure to see his face. Her brother. Her older brother. Better late than never, she supposed.

He half smiled at her. "Hi, sis."

She went to shake his hand and then realized that was dumb and hugged him. This was a benefit of family she'd never thought of: more hugging. Once her nanny Louise had moved away, there wasn't really anyone around she could just, you know, hug on to. Her friends hugged her when they said hello or good-bye, but it wasn't like she could scooch up next to Polly in the store and lean on her for twenty minutes. She stepped away from Archie and realized she was related to someone she wouldn't have picked out of a lineup two weeks earlier. Presumably, she would get used to it. Most commonplace things started out strange: Electric light! Running water! Watching ALL the episodes one after the other!

In turn, Archie looked at her closely, seeing elements of his father's face in hers, wondering if it would ever not seem strange that he'd actually been in this bookstore many times without noticing those same similarities. He must have seen Nina before; there had been a stretch in his son's early life when they'd come to Knight's once or twice a month, after the weekend farmers' market. He may have talked to her, certainly smiled at her, purchased books from her, without ever even thinking about her for more than a moment or two. How many people do we encounter every day who might be related to us, or simply people who might have become the best friends we ever had, or our second spouses, or the agents of our destruction, if we only spent more than seconds with them? He realized he was staring.

"It's weird, right?" Nina had been staring at him, too. "This whole thing is really a bit upsetting."

Archie nodded. "It is. I wanted to talk to you. Are you rushing off somewhere?"

She had been on her way to yoga class, but any excuse not to feel inflexible and clumsy was welcome. And to be fair, she was only going so when she got to book club later on she could say she'd been to yoga and feel OK eating as many cookies or cupcakes as she wanted. She shook her head. "No, not at all. Do you want to get coffee?" She pointed across the street. "We could go back to our usual spot."

"Excellent." Archie turned to cross the street. He pulled open the door of the café and said, "By the way, our whole family should be bowing our heads in shame for letting Lydia bully you like that yesterday." He held the door for her. "I'm sorry."

"It's OK," said Nina. "Is Lydia always like that?"

"Aggressive and ridiculous?" He laughed. "Yeah, pretty much. She's not mellowing with age, that's for sure."

They sat down at the same table.

Vanessa wasn't working that day, but Nina waved at Andi, another waitress she liked a lot. Andi grinned at her and brought over a menu.

"You don't need this, obviously, as you probably know it better than I do, but maybe your friend . . . ?"

"I think just coffee, thanks." Archie was still finding it hard not to stare at Nina.

"Me too," said Nina.

Archie cleared his throat. "You know, if things had been different, we would have grown up together. You're only a couple of months younger than me. Why didn't your mother want us to know each other?"

Nina was surprised. "I don't think she thought about it that way, to be honest."

She shrugged. "It's hard to know, with her; she's not super forthcoming about her motivations. She said, when I asked her essentially the same thing, that she didn't think your dad would have been a good father."

"He was your dad, too."

"So you all keep telling me. I'm not sure that simple biology makes someone a father, though. Don't you have to do some actual fathering? I mean, yeah, he provided a sperm, but after that nothing. I always thought parenting was more active than that."

Archie paused while Andi put down their coffees. "You said your mom was away a lot when you were a kid."

"She still is."

"But you consider her your mother, even though someone else did most of the mothering."

"Yeah, true." Nina shrugged. "I guess there are as many ways to mother someone as there are mothers. Mine wasn't there physically, but she sent a lot of cool postcards." The postcards had been a regular feature of Nina's childhood she'd mostly forgotten. They would show up once or twice a month, with a brief message (*You'd hate it here,* or *Everything smells of cheese,* or *Been throwing up for days, weather's good, though*), and signed *Mum* in big, loopy handwriting. Louise and she would examine the stamps, look at the photo, and stick the cards to the fridge. She wondered where they were now, then remembered she'd cut off all the stamps and given them to a fifteen-year-old boy she'd had a crush on. Epic fail in terms of dating strategy; he'd looked at her strangely, thanked her, and never spoken to her again, and now she couldn't remember what she'd done with the cards themselves. She dragged her attention back to Archie.

"But your . . . our . . . father wasn't even heard from until two weeks ago. For a serial cheater, he was a man of his word." She smiled ruefully.

Archie didn't. "I'm really struggling to get my head around it, but I'm also finding it hard to understand why I'm struggling to get my head around it, if you can follow that. He cheated on his first wife . . . Why would I think he wouldn't cheat on my mother?"

Nina made a face. "Because he loved her?"

Archie shrugged. "I don't think his cheating was actually anything to do with his wives, or how he felt about them. I think he liked other women and was selfish about it.

234

We talked about it once, when I was older and about to get married myself. My wife is . . ." He blushed, suddenly. "Very beautiful, as you saw the other day. I was deeply in love with her when we got married, still am, actually. But my dad took me out to dinner and told me that I would cheat on her one day."

"How did he know that?"

Archie's mouth twisted. "He didn't. He genuinely thought every husband cheated, maybe every wife, too. He said the lure of fresh flesh was too strong. He implied it was pointless to resist it."

"That seems to be kind of an overstatement. What made him so certain?"

"I'm not sure. He had this central belief in the importance of sex, I think. He thought it was the driving force behind every great story, every great event."

"You disagree?"

"I don't know. I think it was *his* driving force." Archie looked at her. "Mind you, he had lots of them: sex, women, cigarettes, money, booze. He drank a lot — you know that, right? He was an alcoholic. I didn't realize it when I was a kid, but it was obvious looking back. He was very anxious in the mornings; he woke up shaking and would hide in the bathroom a lot. My mother said he had low blood sugar and would bring him orange juice and treat him like a baby." He drank his coffee. "But actually, he was hungover, and waiting until he could get to the office and have a drink."

"Great," said Nina. "It's probably just as well I don't drink very much then." A sudden flash of the kiss with Tom crossed her mind.

Archie nodded. "I think Becky and Katherine both stopped drinking pretty young; not sure about the others." He finished his coffee and looked around for Andi. "It's genetic, you know."

Nina nodded. "And did you?"

Archie frowned. "Did I what?"

"Did you cheat? On your wife?"

He shook his head. "Not yet. But now that I know about you, I worry that it's predetermined, like the drinking. If he couldn't control himself, maybe it will be the same for me. I didn't think so, but you kind of messed up a lot of what I took for granted." He caught Andi's eye and mimed a request for more coffee for both of them. "Sorry, I know it's not your fault."

Nina shrugged and pressed on. "But you thought he didn't cheat on your mother. You thought there could be exceptions."

"Yeah, because she died pretty young,

right? I thought maybe he'd managed to keep it in his pants long enough. But he didn't, not at all. He cheated on her with your mom, and who knows who else, and that was years before she got sick."

"Yeah, but look at me. My mom can't stay in one place for more than a month, and I've barely left the state. Just because he was a jerk doesn't mean you have to be."

"Maybe not."

Nina tried changing the subject. "When is your baby due?"

"Next month." He pulled out his phone and flipped through some photos. "This is my son, Henry, and there's Becca." The photo showed an adorable little boy with tiny glasses on, and the beautiful blond woman she'd seen at the lawyer's office, both grinning at the camera like idiots.

"They look happy," said Nina.

"They are," replied Archie. "Long may they stay that way." He put his phone away and rubbed his face with his hand. "Do you ever worry that you are going to mess things up?"

"What kind of things? I mean, yes, of course, all the time, but what specifically?"

"I worry I'm going to lose control of my life, that I'm going to make a massive mistake and it's all going away. I don't know why, but things have been hard, with Becca pregnant and Henry being only two and work . . ." He put his hands on the tabletop, but not quickly enough to prevent Nina from seeing that they were shaking.

"Do you get anxiety?" she asked.

He nodded. "I do. I used to get it worse, but I take medication for it now. You?"

She nodded. "Yeah. I have Xanax for when it's really bad, and sometimes it does get really bad. As long as I keep on top of things, it's manageable, but I don't do well with surprises." She took a breath. "I'm easily thrown; I guess you could put it like that. I feel like I don't have a deep well of calm. I feel like I was lightly misted with calm, and it doesn't take a lot for it to evaporate." She grinned. "Not sure this metaphor is going to last all that much longer, either."

He smiled at her. "My wife has the deep well of calm in our house. She's like Lake Calm, in fact. I'm more like you." He shrugged. "Dad was not in any way calm; he revved very high indeed, and then his blood, mixed with the cyanide that runs through Alice's veins, produced Katherine, who is truly horrible, but also Becky, Peter's mom, who is the kindest woman on the planet. One more generation down you get Peter and Jennifer, who are awesome in every way, but also Lydia, who's a total nut-job. Genetics are funny things, right?"

Nina put her hands flat on the tabletop, across from his. "We have similar hands, look."

"Mine are bigger."

She looked up at him. "No shit, Sherlock."

He laughed. "I don't know why I'm even telling you all this."

"I'm your sister?"

"Yeah, I guess. And you can't stop being my sister, even if you know how anxious I get. I . . . I felt like maybe you would understand." He studied the tabletop.

Andi delivered their coffees. Nina took a sip and wiped the foam off her lip with the back of her sleeve. "Understand why you're wigged out about suddenly discovering something upsetting about a guy who, let's face it, had already caused a lot of trouble even before this all came out?"

He nodded.

"Wouldn't anyone understand? A week or so ago I thought I was the child of a brave, creative, brilliant world traveler and never understood why I was shy, nervous, and basically unwilling to travel outside my zip code. Now I know where some of that came from, but I've also inherited potential alcoholism and an inability to remain faithful, so, you know, not exactly a win-win."

Archie grinned suddenly, and anyone watching them would instantly have known they were related. "Yup, that's about the size of it. You've probably inherited money, too, of course."

"Unconfirmed. And not if Lydia has her way."

Archie rolled his eyes. "Lydia's angry all the time; you're just today's focus. It's a pity, because she's really brilliant. Brain like a steel trap but, sadly, she mostly uses it for storing up imaginary insults and injuries."

"That's awesome. What a lovely family you all are." Nina arranged a small pile of sugar packets into a tower.

"*We* all are," said Archie with a grin. "It's your family, too." He stuck out his finger and knocked over her tower of sugar packets.

"Not if I don't want it to be." Nina smacked his hand and started rebuilding.

Archie called for the check. "Good luck sticking that cat back in the bag." He looked at her hands. "You're single?"

"Very much so. I don't have time for a boyfriend right now."

"That's sad."

"Is it?" Nina thought about Tom. "I meet people, but no one I want to give up anything for."

"Your life is so full of excitement and adventure?"

"Are you kidding? I have a weekly book club, a regular movie night, a dedicated physical wellness practice at least one night a week, a cat . . . I am living the dream."

He laughed and signed the check. "You're a lucky woman."

"Yeah. And now I have you lot to contend with. A man would have to be pretty special to squeeze into my life."

Archie got to his feet and stretched the exact same way Nina usually did. "Well, maybe one of us will introduce you to someone worth canceling book club for."

Nina followed him out of the café. "I seriously doubt that. You've heard the phrase fact is stranger than fiction?"

"Of course."

"Well, it's also much less attractive. I'll stick with my fictional love life, thanks. In both senses of the word."

Archie stopped on the sidewalk. "I'm parked up there. Do you want a lift home?"

Nina shook her head. "No, thanks, I like walking."

"Cool, we'll talk later." He hugged her, and in that brief embrace she felt a warm, reassuring acceptance. However mean Lydia might be, Archie and Peter were certainly making up for it. She'd never had brothers, obviously, and had never dated a man long enough to reach the point where she could take him for granted, and hug for no reason beyond affection, and she suddenly felt elated to have it in her life now. *I have a big brother,* she thought again. *I am a little sister.*

She watched her brother disappear up the street, his walk strangely familiar. She flicked a glance at her watch; great, the yoga class was completely over, so now she could go home, feed the cat, get into her are-they-pajamas-or-are-they-just-comfy-pants, and head to her friend's house for book club.

Yup. Nina Hill was living the dream.

today is the day

DATE Thursday 16th May

M T W Th F S Su
◇ ◇ ◇ ◇ ◇ ◇ ◇

SCHEDULE

7 > 8	
8 > 9	
9 > 10	work
10 > 11	
11 > 12	
12 > 13	
13 > 14	
14 > 15	
15 > 16	
16 > 17	
17 > 18	
18 > 19	
19 > 20	NOTHING ♡
20 > 21	

GOALS

Improve handwriting

NOTES

Saroyan

TO DO LIST

- milk
- tuna
- cat fd
- bread
- TP
- shampoo
- body wash

✚ **BREAKFAST** no

✚ **LUNCH** due

✚ **DINNER** at

✚ **WORKOUT** all

FIFTEEN

In which Nina is too organized for her
own good.

Thursdays were Nina's favorite day. After work on Thursdays she had nothing scheduled. Literally, from 6 to 10 P.M. she had written *Nothing* in her planner. Which actually meant reading, because when she had nothing to do, reading is what she did. Sometimes people tried to get her to do something instead, but she was fiercely defensive of her nothing.

So when she looked up from the pile of books she was reshelving and saw Tom entering the store, her first thought was she couldn't go out with him that night, because she had nothing to do. Her second thought was that he hadn't even asked her out, and she had no reason to think he was going to ask her out. Her third thought was that she was apparently getting a little full of herself and needed to pull herself together. And her fourth and final thought in this parade of small thoughts was that he was walking toward her and she should probably say hello.

"Hi there," she said. He was taller than she remembered. Or she had shrunk, one or the other.

He smiled at her. "Hi."

"Are you looking for a book?"

He shook his head. "I'm not a book person, remember? I'm not illiterate; I just don't read much." He turned up his hands. "Sorry."

She raised her eyebrows. "Maybe you haven't found the right kind of book yet."

"I'm not trying very hard," he said, easily. "Anyway, I came in to see if maybe you'd like to go out for dinner?" He was impressed with his relaxed, assured tone. There was absolutely no way she could guess he was as nervous as a shortsighted fly at a spider convention. *Crushed it.*

"Uh . . . sure." *Nice, Nina, way to sound enthusiastic.*

OK, well, she doesn't sound all that interested, but let's press on. "What day works for you?" He remembered the feeling of her in his arms, the kiss, the invitation . . . It didn't look like that girl came to work today.

"Let me get my planner." Nina carried the remaining books back to the counter and dug underneath for her planner.

"Wow," said Tom, once she'd pulled it out. "That is a serious planner." He thought about his own planner, which was a small section of his brain that rarely had anything to do. If he had more than two or three things to remember, he might jot them on a Post-it, but that was about it. This girl might be a little hard-core organized for him. What would she be like in bed? *Two minutes on this nipple, please, then forty seconds of . . .*

Nina looked at her planner as if seeing it for the first time. It was big and heavily accessorized. It had bookmarks sticking out at various points; it had ribbons and tabs; it had a pocket full of special, planner-sized equipment.

"I enjoy being organized," she replied. "It's just . . ." She opened the planner to that week, and Tom frowned when he saw how full the page was.

"Wow," he commented. "You've got a lot going on."

"Yeah." Nina nodded, suddenly a little embarrassed. "Uh, this week isn't good. How about next week?" She flipped over a few pages. "No, that's pretty full, too."

Tom watched her face as she looked

through the planner. Her nose was straight
and delicate, with a speckling of freckles.
Tom had a relatively active love life — he
was an attractive thirty-year-old man in Los
Angeles — but he hadn't fallen for anyone
in several years. He liked the women he
dated, but none of them had captured his
imagination the way this woman had. He
thought about her, wondered how her skin
might feel, how his hand might fit on her
waist, about holding her against himself . . .
He frowned and tried to focus on the actual
person in front of him rather than the adult
version he suddenly had in his head.

Nina looked up at Tom and found him
gazing intently at her. She blushed. "Uh,
how about three weeks from now? I have a
Friday night . . ."

Tom clunked back into reality, hard.
"Three weeks?" He was nonplussed, taken
aback. "Really?"

"Yeah . . ." She looked down at this week.

He craned his head to look at the page.
"What about that?" He poked his finger at
the page. "It literally says you have nothing
to do tonight."

Nina shook her head. "Nothing actually
means something."

He looked at her.

"I mean, it means something to me; it

means reading."

"You have enforced reading?"

"It's my job." *And I'd rather be reading than anything else, but that's not relevant.*

"Wait, what about that?" He pointed to the entry that said *Movie Night.* "We could go to a movie together." He looked triumphant. "You already have a ticket."

"Good point," replied Nina, "but not this weekend. I'm going to see *Aliens* with my friends. It's set up already."

"How about the week after?" Suddenly, Tom was embarrassed. If Nina didn't want to go out with him, he wasn't going to keep pushing it. It wasn't that he expected her to clear her schedule for him completely and immediately, but a little bit of mutual interest would be nice.

She had flipped ahead. "No, I'm going to a Jane Austen movie marathon with Liz, my boss." She looked up and smiled. "*Pride and Prejudice, Emma,* and *Sense and Sensibility.* Awesome, right?"

"Uh, sure." This was maybe not the good idea he had thought it was. Maybe this girl wasn't a good fit for him after all. He hadn't read Jane Austen, hadn't seen any of those movies, didn't like reading, didn't like being organized, didn't like knowing what every minute of every day held for the next week, let alone the next month. Then she moved her head and there was that scent again, honey and lemons, and he knew he still wanted to take her out. Wanted to see if he could get under that organized layer.

Nina was still flipping through the planner. "But I can do the week after. Probably."

Probably? "Do you have a piece of paper?" Tom asked, his smile fading.

Nina found him one and handed it to him, frowning. He took a pen from the pot next to the register and scribbled on the piece of paper. He handed it to her.

"That's my number. If you get a cancellation, text me. I'll see if I can fit you in."

He turned and walked out of the store, trying to cover his disappointment and — at least from where Nina was standing — being completely successful.

"Well, that's a load of balls," said Polly, when Nina told her about it later.

Nina looked dubiously at her. "Is it? Or is it that I'm lame for being too wedded to my schedule."

Polly was nothing if not fair minded. "Well, there's that, too. I mean," she added quickly, "I'm not saying you're lame; I'm saying sometimes you get a little anal about your schedule."

"I do?"

Polly leaned back against the nearest bookcase and nodded. "Do you remember the time the Spin studio flooded and you were completely thrown, because you had scheduled a Spin class and you weren't sure if you could fit anything else in?"

Nina tugged her away from the bookcase, straightened the books, and frowned at her. "Well, Spin takes eighty-two minutes, and that's what I had allotted."

"Exactly. The very fact that you know Spin takes eighty-two minutes . . ." Polly paused. "Wait. Spin class is forty-five minutes long."

Nina nodded. "Yes, but it takes three minutes for me to walk there from here, seven minutes for me to change, a minute to adjust the bike and get a towel, two minutes afterward to cool down enough to leave the gym without dripping on everything, fourteen minutes to walk to Chipotle and get a salad, and then ten minutes to walk home from Chipotle to my place."

"How on earth can you predict that getting dinner will take fourteen minutes? What if there's a long line, or their salad bar catches fire?"

"They don't have a salad bar. Plus, lettuce isn't the engine of combustion you seem to think it is."

Polly looked exasperated. "That's not the point. I'm saying life is unpredictable. Any number of random things could happen."

"Of course," said Nina. "My plan is based on averages and experience. It takes that much time, like, most of the time, so I plan accordingly. I can be flexible. I can roll with the punches."

Polly snorted. "What about when Phil got worms and you had to take him to the vet?"

"That's a great example," replied Nina, starting to be a little stung. "I cleared my schedule completely that day. No hesitation at all."

Polly laughed. "Yeah, because you couldn't work out how to reschedule everything to allow for the vet appointment, so instead of trying, you canceled it all."

"What's your point?"

"My point is that you're inflexible." Polly smiled at Nina. "And that you'd rather blow it all up than spend time fixing things. But it doesn't really matter, unless you care that you missed out on a date because of it."

Nina shook her head. "He wasn't right for me, anyway. He didn't read."

"Reading isn't the only thing in the world, Nina."

"It's one of only five perfect things in the world."

"And the other four are?"

"Cats, dogs, Honeycrisp apples, and coffee."

"Nothing else?"

"Sure, there are other things, even good things, but those five are perfect."

"In your opinion."

"Yes, of course in my opinion. Everyone has a different five perfect things."

Polly thought about it. "I can get behind that. Mine would be movies, *steak frites,* Jude Law in his thirties, clean sheets at night, and indoor plumbing."

"Mine would be making a profit, keeping a bookstore open, books that get shelved, orders that get filled, and employees who don't stand around talking," said Liz as she appeared suddenly behind them.

"See?" said Nina airily, picking up a list of customer orders. "Everybody has five."

252

Sixteen

In which Nina reads, and texts,
and reads again.

There are people who have no time for
books. Nina had met those people; usually
they came into the bookstore to ask for
directions and would then look about con-
fusedly when they realized they were surrounded by these strange paper oblongs.
Maybe they had rich fantasy lives, or maybe
they were raised by starfish who had no ac-
cess to dry printed material, who knows,
but Nina judged them and felt guilty for
doing so.

She had always been a bookworm. There
was a picture hanging on her bathroom wall
that showed her lying on a rug somewhere,
fast asleep, surrounded by books. She had
been around one, maybe. She was still
traveling around with her mom at that
point, going where she went and sleeping

where she slept. But even then, the only constant thing — apart from Candice Hill and her camera, of course — had been books. On her shelves somewhere she had *The Tale of Peter Rabbit* (the single story, not a collection) in English, French, Tagalog, Russian, Greek, Hindi, and Welsh. They hadn't visited *all* those countries together, but once Nina was settled in Los Angeles it became somewhat of a thing for her mom to send her *Peter Rabbit* from wherever she was working. Nina still found herself occasionally hunting online for languages she didn't have, although it felt like cheating to order them all on eBay. Besides, she didn't have the shelf space.

Shelf space was always a problem for the dedicated booklover. Nina had three large floor to ceiling bookcases, a stroke of good fortune that made her friends gasp when they first walked into her apartment. One entire bookcase was Book of the Month selections, which was a problem, because they kept coming — monthly, naturally — but space was running out. Louise had given her a membership when she turned eighteen, and she had tried very hard to restrict herself to only one a month, but that still meant she now had over 120 beautiful, hard-backed books in that one section alone. Another section was books that had been signed by their authors; again, an easy hundred of those. She was strict about only including books she'd had signed in person; buying them already signed didn't count. In a totally separate, smaller, glass-fronted bookcase were rare first editions or interesting printings, which was a much smaller collection, because Nina could only afford those occasionally. One time an elderly customer who'd been coming to Knight's for years brought her a first edition of *The Prophet,* by Kahlil Gibran, and pressed it into her hands.

"I'm too old to read the print now, Nina. You should have it. I was given it when I was not much more than a child, and it was special then. I think my mother bought it when she was young."

Nina had been incredibly touched. "But don't you want to give it to your son?" She'd met him, once, when he came in with his mother, but she couldn't remember much about him.

The lady had smiled and shaken her head. "He would be more impressed that it's worth a little money than by the book itself, and that's not right. You take it, then I know it will be well taken care of."

And it was, carefully covered with an acid-free slipcover and frequently admired. It contained Nina's favorite saying: *You talk when you cease to be at peace with your thoughts.* She wanted to wear it on a T-shirt, embroider it on a pillow, or maybe tattoo it on her wrist. But the trouble with wordy tattoos is that people start reading them, then you have to stand still while they finish, and then they look up at you and frown and you have to explain yourself . . . Way too much human interaction, plus also the needles, the pain, the fear of the needles and pain. So, no tattoo, but an embroidery wasn't out of the question.

Another wall was dedicated to books Nina had already read, which were obviously alphabetized by author and then subordered by date of publication. A few years earlier, while recovering from a broken heart, she had purchased a little stamp kit, library tickets, and library ticket pockets, and spent five weekends in a row organizing her library. It turned out that her heart was only slightly dented and that five weeks is exactly how long you need to spend distracting yourself in order to realize it. Plus, now she could keep track of every time she reread her books or, on the rare occasion she had a friend who could be trusted, when she loaned them out.

Libraries were her favorite places, and when she traveled, she would start out at the local library, thus immediately identifying herself as a total nerd. They say you always remember your first time, and Nina definitely did. Walking into the Los Angeles Central Library to get her first library card, when she was eight or so, was still a memory she treasured. The entry hall of the library was as beautiful as any cathedral, and Nina had looked around and realized she would never run out of things to read, and that certainty filled her with peace and satisfaction. It didn't matter what hit the fan; as long as there were unread books in the world, she would be fine. Being surrounded by books was the closest she'd ever gotten to feeling like the member of a gang. The books had her back, and the nonfiction, at least, was ready to fight if necessary.

So, Thursday night was reading night, the best night. She had a routine: She left work, she picked up dinner, she got home, she ate, she showered, she put on pajamas and special fluffy socks that she preheated in the microwave, and then she curled up in her enormous chair and read until her eyes crossed.

That night she was reading *The Human Comedy* by William Saroyan. Liz had been horrified when Nina had said she'd never read anything by him and insisted she take it home immediately.

"Some people say he's too sentimental, but I think he's one of the few writers brave enough to write about the intense beauty of love and joy and the ugliness and fear they sometimes cause."

Nina had looked at her and raised her eyebrows. Liz had shrugged. "See, that's the kind of statement one makes after reading Saroyan; you can't help it."

Nina was enjoying the book; the writing was beautiful, the characters were real, the situations were bittersweet, but it was after an hour or so of reading that she came across a line that struck her so forcefully she had to close the book for a moment: "I'm lonely," the young character Ulysses said, "and I don't know what I'm lonely for."

Nina knew that double whammy: the emotion itself and the frustration of not being able to put it into words. She'd read somewhere that if you can't put language around an experience or feeling it's because it's from your earliest childhood, before speech, when everything was inexplicable and overwhelming. She often felt that way when she was alone in a crowd of people. She'd look at their faces, and ideas would hover on the edge of her mind just out of sight. If she tried to capture them, they'd dig themselves deeper like sand crabs, glimpsed for a second as the feelings washed over her and then were gone.

Impulsively, she pulled out her phone and tugged the little slip of paper with Tom's number from her pocket. Without giving herself time to think it over and change her mind, she texted him.

"Hi, this is Nina. From the bookstore."

Then she closed her phone and went back to her book. It buzzed. The phone, not the book.

"Hi."

Hmm, not exactly an inspiring response. But then, "I don't know any other Ninas, so you don't need to qualify yourself."

She sat and thought for a moment, then typed, "I'm sorry if I seemed rude today."

"No problem."

She smiled wryly. He wasn't saying, no, you weren't rude, don't worry about it. He was saying, yes, you were rude, but I'm prepared to accept it and move on. "I have a lot going on right now."

"So I could see."

Was he mad at her? It was so difficult in text, and she wondered if her generation's reliance on written communication was making them better writers or simply more confused people. Body language told you so much; text on its own was subject to misinterpretation in every way possible. You'd think they'd all get very good at subtlety and vocabulary, in order to make their brief conversations more precise, but she hadn't noticed that trend.

He texted again. "Between chapters?"

He'd remembered what she was doing that night, but did that mean anything? Only that he had a good enough memory to hold a fact for a few hours; let's not read too much into that, Nina. She pushed down her fluffy sock and scratched where the elastic had been.

"Yes," she replied. "Something I read made me think of you."

Dammit. Why had she said that? Now he was going to ask her what, and she was going to have to come up with something, because if she told him it was a line about loneliness, she would suddenly a) reveal too much about herself and b) look like a loser. A lonely, lonely loser.

"Well, it's nice to hear from you."

Nina sighed. He'd deflected, thank God.

A few miles away, sitting on a barstool and half watching a soccer game on TV, Tom creased his eyebrows. He'd wanted to ask her what she'd read, but then he'd gotten worried that it would develop into yet another conversation where he felt like an illiterate peasant. He'd managed to dodge that bullet. Now what? It was her turn, so he waited.

Nina knew it was her turn, but she wasn't sure what to say. At this point she had two broad options: continue the conversation, or sign off. If she signed off, *Well, just wanted to apologize for today,* she could feel better about herself, but she'd still have to avoid him at quiz night. If she continued the conversation, she . . . wasn't sure what would happen.

She went with a question. "What are you doing?"

"Watching soccer in a bar on my own."

Apparently, he wasn't scared of being seen as a lonely loser, so confidence points to him. "Who's winning?"

"Not me, that's for sure." Even the text looked rueful.

Nina smiled. Tom added, "However, the pistachio farmers of California are gaining ground. I'm surrounded by shells and feel vaguely regretful, despite the fact that I'm chock-full of fat-soluble vitamins."

He was calling back their conversation at

Trivia Night. She blushed, thinking of their kiss.

"Did you know California produces ninety-eight percent of the pistachios in America?"

There was a pause. Then he said, "And they're only one of two nuts mentioned in the Bible." She raised her eyebrows, but then he added, "I have Wikipedia, too."

"I wasn't using Wikipedia. I have a lot of facts in my head I can't get rid of."

"That sounds annoying. And it explains your trivia success."

"Yes." She paused again. Did she want to talk about trivia league? Did she want to talk about the contents of her head? That's one positive thing about texting; you can pause and consider your options, whereas in face-to-face conversation, a silence of three minutes would be weird.

New text from Tom: "What did you have for dinner?"

This she could handle. "Sushi."

"Huh, me too."

"So in a way we did have dinner together."

Again, Nina, not a great response.

"And yet, in another, more literal, factual way, we didn't."

"True." She reviewed the conversation. He was quicker and funnier than she had expected.

Suddenly: "Hey, I have to go. Thanks for reaching out."

And just like that, he was gone. In the bar miles away, Tom stood up to greet the woman who'd said yes to his invitation, while wishing he could be continuing to text Nina instead. He put his phone away, so he wouldn't look at every notification and be rude. It was tough, but he was a grown-up, so he managed.

After a moment or two of waiting in case he came back, Nina shoved her phone down the side of the chair cushion and picked up her book again.

Three hours later, the book finished, her cheeks a little pink because it was so sad and lovely and sad again, Nina stood up and stretched. Coming out of a book was always painful. She was surprised to see things had remained in place while she herself had been roaming other towns, other times. Phil had been asleep the whole time on the end of her bed, and now he raised his head and blinked at her.

"Coming to bed?" he asked silently, yawning until the tips of his whiskers touched.

Nina nodded and padded around for a moment, turning off lights, checking her door, going to brush her teeth and deciding she couldn't be bothered, that kind of thing. Finally, she climbed into bed and then had to get out again because she felt bad about not brushing her teeth and because she needed to find her phone so she could set her alarm. For once remembering where she'd put her phone, she slid it up from under the chair cushion and saw she'd missed a message from Tom.

"Good night, tiny bookworm," it said.

Smiling, she set her alarm and went to sleep.

today is the **day**

DATE *Saturday 18th May*

M T W Th F S Su

⬠ ⬠ ⬠ ⬠ ⬠ ⬠ ⬠

SCHEDULE

7 > 8	
8 > 9	
9 > 10	*Wake*
10 > 11	
11 > 12	
12 > 13	
13 > 14	
14 > 15	
15 > 16	
16 > 17	
17 > 18	
18 > 19	
19 > 20	*aliens!! ✦*
20 > 21	

▷ ▷ ▶ ▷ ▷ ▶ ▷ ▷ ▶

TO DO LIST

- ☐ YOU ARE OUT
- ☐ OF TOILET PAPER
- ☐ YOU HEATHEN.
- ☐
- ☐
- ☐
- ☐
- ☐
- ☐

GOALS

Find Human
Comedy Movie
online

NOTES

✛ BREAKFAST

✛ LUNCH

✛ DINNER ·
more candy

✛ WORKOUT

SEVENTEEN

In which Nina eats dinner
with a new friend.

"One time," said Liz, around a chocolate croissant, "I had to push a guy out of a moving taxi cab. He wouldn't take no for an answer, the cab driver was listening to the radio rather than me, and, in my defense, we weren't going very fast. It was Greenwich Village at eleven on a Friday night. We were crawling along. The guy barely even bounced."

"Was he upset?" asked Nina. It was Saturday afternoon, during one of those 4 P.M. lulls that sometimes happen. Polly and Nina were sitting on the floor behind the counter, sorting books and listening to Liz's stories about Dates That Went Wrong.

"Well, he called the next day and asked if I wanted to go out again, so apparently not very." Liz turned and looked out of the store

266

window, thinking of her twenties and not missing them at all.

"And did you?"

"No. I asked if he was out of his mind and hung up the phone." Liz smiled. "That was back when you called someone on the phone and had to physically lift a receiver to talk to them."

"Weird," said Polly.

"Yeah," said Liz, "you couldn't hide behind a veil of casual, the way you guys all do. But you could slam the phone very loudly, which was satisfying." You could also have a private life, she thought to herself, and not get haunted forever by poor decisions, but decided not to rub it in. It wasn't as though millennials didn't know what they'd lost; they simply weighed it up against everything they'd gained and decided it was probably a wash.

Unaware of her boss's philosophizing, Polly shuddered. "One time I ended up in bed with this guy who was trying to decide whether or not to enter a Catholic seminary, or whatever you call Priest School. I thought I'd provided a pretty convincing four-hour case against celibacy, but the next day he called and said he would pray for me."

"Wow. You tipped someone over into the priesthood?"

Polly shrugged. "Maybe he thought after me it was all downhill, and he might as well devote himself to giving back to the world, after the world had given him one incredible night with me." There was no hint of sarcasm in her voice, no self-deprecation at all.

Liz and Nina stared at her.

Polly was shameless. "Or maybe the whole thing was an elaborate ruse to get me into bed. He didn't realize he could have simply asked. I was in one of my 'say yes to everything' phases." Polly wasn't overconfident; she was simply one of those women who tore up the societal memo about being underconfident. Nina had never envied her more.

"I remember the last one of those," said Nina. "You broke your big toe trying out for Roller Derby."

"Yes. It turns out tiny wheels are not my friends."

"And got food poisoning after eating a grasshopper."

"Yes, although in the grasshopper's defense, I did also have sushi that weekend."

"And slept with a mime."

"Yes," said Polly. "It was great. Quiet, but great." She looked thoughtful. "Once he got out of that imaginary box, he really blew my doors off."

Again, Liz and Nina stared at her, and then Nina said, "Look, as far as I'm concerned, this whole conversation is a firm reminder that I'm better off alone. I'm totally happy, I like my own company, and I already have to integrate a load of new relatives. I'm going back to quiet evenings at home and eating healthy and getting to the gym and cutting out sugar."

"Well that's unfortunate," said Polly, sticking her chin out defiantly, "because I was going to tell you about the fantastic new waffle house I found and now I won't."

Liz laughed. "Tell me instead," she said. "I love waffles."

"Ah, Ms. Quinn."

They all froze, then Polly and Nina got to their feet. Mr. Meffo had somehow crept up on them, and the landlord was now standing there twirling his mustache and getting ready to tie one of them to the railroad tracks.

Actually, he was just standing there, smiling politely. He wasn't a tall man, or imposing in any way, but apparently he had a stealth mode.

Liz gathered herself and smiled back at him. "Ah, how lovely to see you, Mr. Meffo. I'm so sorry I missed you the other day. I was meeting with representatives for J. K. Rowling, who is thinking of launching her next book here." She paused, then doubled down. "It's a surprise new installment of the *Harry Potter* series, so I think it might be good for business."

"Really?" Mr. Meffo was not a big reader, but he wasn't an idiot. "I find that challenging to believe." He paused. "I'm here to collect the rent. I noticed it still hasn't arrived in my checking account."

"But I sent it! I sent it last week, after you visited."

"You did?"

"Yes," Liz said, firmly. "I instructed the bank to make the transfer. I'm so sorry there's been a problem. I'll contact them right away."

Mr. Meffo smiled broadly. "No problem, you can write me a check here and now, and I'll return the transfer if and when it arrives."

Liz looked apologetic. "Oh, I'm sorry. I'm all out of checks. I've ordered more, but they haven't arrived yet." She paused. "I requested the Hello Kitty ones; maybe they take longer."

Mr. Meffo was still smiling, though it was clearly taking an effort. "We could walk to the bank and get a cashier's check."

"It's our policy not to use cashier's checks. Haven't you read about all the scams?"

He looked puzzled. "That applies to sending money to people you don't know, or have only met online. Not to paying your rent to the landlord you've had for over a decade."

"Really?" Liz looked worried. "Better safe than sorry, don't you think?" She turned to Polly, who nodded enthusiastically and leaned closer to Mr. Meffo.

"My aunt lost a fortune sending a cashier's check to cover the bail for an Ethiopian prince who said he'd known her father at college," she said, with an impressive level of commitment. "You can never be too careful these days. If you can't trust an Ethiopian prince, who can you trust?" She smiled at the landlord. "Mr. Meffo, have you read any good books lately?"

Mr. Meffo had a bit of a soft spot for Polly, who he had once seen on a Tide commercial where she went — fully clothed — through a car wash. It had left a favorable impression.

"No, Polly, I haven't." He turned to Liz again, but she had disappeared.

He sighed and looked back at Polly. "Tell your boss she has one week to pay the rent or I'm looking for a new tenant. I'm getting tired of chasing her every month."

Polly smiled at him sweetly, Nina made sympathetic noises, and Liz, who had dropped to the ground behind the counter, made a mental note to install a bell on the front door.

That evening Nina went to see *Aliens* with Leah, Lauren, and Carter. Occasionally, the trivia team went on field trips like this, and did their best not to talk trivia. They usually failed.

"You know, Ripley was nearly played by Meryl Streep," Lauren said, as the lights went down.

"And the alien's saliva is actually K-Y Jelly," replied Carter.

"And the shots where the aliens are scrambling through the air ducts were actually filmed with the actors lowered on cables down a vertical shaft and the camera was at the bottom," added Leah.

"Stop!" said Nina. "I want to actually enjoy the movie." Then, a minute later, "Look, you can see the spear gun Ripley used in the first movie inside the escape pod door, there, on the floor," to which the other three responded with thrown popcorn.

The thing about watching a classic like *Aliens* at the ArcLight in Hollywood is that every single movie fanatic there has seen the movie many, many times already. When Hicks said, "Game over, man!" so did everyone else, and when Newt said, "They come at night . . ." eight hundred people added, "mostly." It was so much fun, and when the four friends came out of the theater after the movie, they were all giddy and giggling.

Despite that, when Nina saw Tom standing there, chatting with his friend Lisa, her first impulse was to panic and consider various avenues of escape. Then her frontal cortex resumed control and she smiled and went over to speak to him. Not a Xenomorph with acid for blood, just an attractive guy she'd already kissed and texted with. You can do this Nina, she told herself.

For his part, Tom had spotted her as soon as she came through the theater doors and couldn't take his eyes off her now as she approached. He spoke first. "Hi there. You mentioned this was playing, and it's one of my favorites, so, you know."

"It's one of my favorites, too," she replied, and grinned at Lisa. "Hi there."

"Hi, Nina," the other woman replied. "Does your trivia team often socialize together?" The rest of Book 'Em had arrived, and Leah answered for them.

"Whenever none of us can find someone

better to hang out with," she said, not re-alizing this might be a sore spot for Nina and Tom. "We're one another's last resort."

"Yeah, if we're all still single at forty, we're going to set up a commune," Lauren said. "And draw straws to see who has to sleep with Carter."

"Wow, that's flattering," said Carter, rais-ing his eyebrows.

"Yeah, short straw takes the honors," added Leah.

Nina smiled but excused herself to run to the bathroom, and when she returned, Tom was standing there on his own.

"What happened?" she asked. "Zombie outbreak?"

Tom grinned and shrugged. "They all suddenly had appointments. It was weirdly coordinated."

"Huh," said Nina.

"Are you hungry?" Tom asked. "Or do you need to go home and read?"

She looked up at him and smiled. "I'm hungry. Besides, I can always read the menu."

"Great," he said, and turned to lead the way outside.

"Did she go for it?" asked Lisa, hiding behind a nearby cardboard cutout of Jabba the Hutt, which was fortunately big enough to conceal them all, although Lauren had to crouch behind the tail.

"Yes," replied Carter, turning and high-fiving the others. "Yahtzee."

Luckily for Nina's anxiety, they found themselves in one of those restaurants where the menu gave the full provenance of every ingredient. Plentiful reading material is so helpful on a first date.

"It says here," said Nina, "that the fresh mint used in the lamb burger was grown in a hand-thrown but unattractive pot on the kitchen windowsill."

"Really?" said Tom. "Did they include a photo?"

Nina shook her head. "Not even a witty little pencil sketch."

"Disappointing." Tom looked at his menu. "Well, it says here that the pomegranate extract used in the salad dressing was hand squeezed by the middle daughter of the farmer who grew it."

"Really?" said Nina, hiding a smile. "Well, if one of us orders the *steak frites,* a young boy named Harold will catch a bus to the the nearest community garden and dig up the potatoes for the *frites* himself."

"Well," said Tom, gravely, "it's getting a little late for Harold to be out alone. Maybe we should choose something else."

"I appreciate your consideration for Harold's welfare," said Nina. "I'll have the burger instead. The lettuce and tomato were picked an hour ago by a willing volunteer, so, you know."

Tom nodded and closed his menu. "I wish more restaurants had backstories for everything."

"We're doing fine on our own," replied Nina. She ran an exploratory systems check and was pleasantly surprised to discover she didn't feel anxious. Maybe she was still a little hyped from the movie.

"Ripley might be my favorite movie heroine," she said. "I love the way she's clearly scared out of her mind and would pretty much give anything not to be there, but she sucks it up and powers through. That's real heroism."

"Yeah," agreed Tom, "my mom always used to say, 'If you're not scared, you're not brave.' " He took a sip of water. "Mind you, she was usually saying it to get me to try something dangerous."

"Isn't that unusual, for a mother?"

"She's unusual," he said, but didn't elaborate. The waitress came over and they placed their orders, falling silent for a moment once they'd cleared that hurdle.

276

"I'm glad we ran into each other," Tom said.

"Me too," replied Nina. "I'm sorry about the other day."

"No big deal," he said, looking down at the table. Nina noticed a tiny scar by the side of his eye and suddenly wanted to touch it. He continued, "Not everyone has as open a calendar as I do."

Nina was interested. "Why is your time so free?"

He laughed. "Because I don't schedule anything. I pretty much work, then take the rest of it as it comes. Not a big planner."

"I like planning."

"I saw that."

"It makes me feel better."

"Better than what?"

"Better than chaos. Better than unpredictability."

"But doesn't that mean you also lose out on serendipity? If everything is planned, nothing is surprising." He regarded her thoughtfully, genuinely interested. While he waited for her answer, he found himself wondering if she was wearing lipstick, wondering what color her cheeks would turn when she was aroused, wondering why he couldn't stop wanting to go to bed with this woman he barely knew. He wasn't a teenager, but she made him feel that way.

Nina sighed. "I still get surprised all the time. You can make whatever plans you want, but life still happens, right?" She looked at his face, the angles and planes growing familiar, his gaze intent but his eyes so, so warm. What was he thinking? "For example, I recently discovered I had a father." She clarified, "Or rather, I knew I must have a father, but I found out he was dead already." That didn't really come out right, but she didn't think she could make it better, so she left it. Bad things sometimes happen to good sentences. What can you do?

Tom took another sip of water. "You thought maybe you were an immaculate conception?"

Nina made a face at him. "Yes. My mother told me I came out of her forehead fully formed." Tom looked at her, his curly mouth turned up in a smile. He waited, and Nina continued. "No, I just never knew who he was. I asked, of course, when I was little, but my mom shrugged and said she didn't know."

"Party girl, your mom?"

"I guess. And apparently also a liar." Nina waited while the waiter poured them both some wine and then raised her glass. "To surprises, hopefully pleasant ones.'"

"Yes," said Tom, clinking his glass against hers. "And to trying new things."

A pause. Then Nina said, "But you do have some scheduled activities, right? The trivia team, for example."

Tom grinned. "It's hardly a full-time occupation. I do it mostly because Lisa needed someone who knew sports."

Nina crowed, "I knew it! You're a jock."

"Nope, an armchair quarterback with a good memory." He raised his eyebrows. "Are you going to tell me more about the whole dad thing, or are you going to move on to something else? That's kind of a big deal, right?"

"I guess so," said Nina. "I'm still not really sure what to think about it. I'm not a little girl anymore, right? And it's not like he's even around to get to know."

"Brothers and sisters?"

Nina nodded. "Several. And nieces and nephews, and great-nieces and great-nephews, even."

"How is that?" Tom asked, so Nina explained. Archie and Peter had been right; it got easier.

Tom smiled. "Well, it sounds like you got at least one good brother and a fabulous nephew out of it, and that's more than most people."

Their food arrived, and Nina continued the conversation around a bite of cheeseburger.

"Do you have a big family?"

"Not like yours. I have a brother and sister."

"Older or younger?"

"One of each. Older brother, younger sister. My brother's getting married soon."

"Are you going to be a bridesmaid?" Nina looked up at him through her eyelashes. "Will you have a pretty frock?"

"Yeah," he said, "if they can find one to fit me. I'm not built like the other girls." He copied her glance-through-the-eyelashes move, pulling it off surprisingly well.

"I can see that," replied Nina, then blushed. She wasn't anxious around Tom, which was unexpected and pleasant, but she was definitely . . . aware. It was there in the air between them, an unspoken expectation of more to come. A whole other conversation was going on, wordless but clear.

"Shall I get the check?" asked Tom, his voice quiet.

"Yes," said Nina. She swallowed. "I should head home."

"Still time for a chapter before bed?" He smiled.

"Maybe," she replied.

It turned out they'd both taken ride share to get to the movies, so they started walking south toward Larchmont.

Tom took a deep breath. "So, I guess your busy schedule doesn't allow for much dating?"

Nina took a similarly deep breath. "Not really." She paused. "And I'm pretty happy being single, honestly. I have plenty of . . ."

"Friends?" finished Tom, and Nina nodded. "Me too. You never wanted anything more?"

Nina didn't reply for a moment, as they crossed Santa Monica Boulevard. "I'm not against it. I'm just not looking for it. Do you know what I mean?"

"Sure," Tom replied, easily. He effected a Garbo-esque accent. "You want to be alone."

"You know, she never actually said that. She said she wanted to be *left* alone, totally different." Nina shook her head. "I get it. I want to be left alone, too." She looked at him quickly. "Not by everyone. Just by most people. I like a quiet life."

He snorted. "Have you thought about leaving LA? It's not exactly a Trappist monastery." A chorus of horns underscored his point.

"I noticed that," she replied. "But I grew up here; traffic is the rumble of the ocean to me." They crossed Melrose. "What about you? Do you date a lot?"

He shrugged. "On and off. I had a girl-friend for a while. We broke up a few months ago."

"Oh yeah?" Why did that make her frown, wondered Nina. Maybe because a few months didn't seem very long.

"Yeah. It ended badly, so I've been enjoying my own company." He sounded fine, but she wondered if he was still getting over it.

"You're not friends?"

He shook his head. "No." He was silent for a moment, navigating a busy cross street. "My brother says I'm a sucker for difficult women. He says I like a challenge."

"You disagree?"

Another shrug. "I don't think it's conscious. I'm a fairly boring person, I think."

"Not to me. Not yet, at least." Nina was glad she wasn't looking at him, because she felt herself blushing yet again. Her cheeks were such traitors.

"Well, thanks. Maybe 'boring' is the wrong word. I'm calm. I kind of take things as they come. Do you know what I mean?"

"I guess," said Nina, laughing. "I'm not like that, but I've heard people like you exist. Like unicorns."

"I'm pretty sure we're more common than that." He stepped around a crowd of teenagers and found himself more closely at her side once they were reunited. Their sleeves brushed, and neither of them moved apart. "Maybe that's why I'm attracted to people who have some kind of spark, you know? Sometimes that ends up being not such a good thing, but it's true of my friends, too. Lisa, for example. We've been friends since high school, and she was always the brightest star in our group. Interesting. Different."

"She seems very nice."

He laughed. "Well, I don't know if 'nice' is the right word, but she's definitely her own person, and I like that." They walked in silence for a while, and Tom was thinking about reaching out to take Nina's hand when suddenly she said, "This is me," and stopped.

He looked up at the guesthouse. "So it is," he said. "Do you know that cat?"

Phil was perched on top of the gate, watching them.

Nina nodded. "I do. He's mine."

"What's his name? He's judging me."

"His name is Phil, and actually," said Nina, "he's judging me." She looked up at Tom. "I'm really glad we ran into each other. I feel pretty good we didn't send Harold out for potatoes."

"Me too," said Tom, and stepped closer to her. She looked at him, then stepped closer still, tugging at his coat and pulling him into a kiss. After a few moments they stepped apart, and Nina opened her mouth to invite him in.

"Well, good night, Nina," said Tom. "Maybe we can do this again soon?" He leaned down and kissed her again, then smiled against her lips and turned away to leave. "I'll text you, OK?"

"OK," she replied, watching him go with a little crease between her eyebrows. Crap, she thought. What went wrong there?

But when she went inside her phone buzzed.

"I wanted to come in," he texted, "very, very much. But you were planning to be Garbo tonight, and I decided not to push my luck. Besides, as another actress said, tomorrow is another day."

She smiled and picked up a surprised Phil and hugged him.

"Watch the whiskers, lady," he said. "They don't stay gorgeous on their own."

today is the day

DATE _Sunday 19th May_   M T W Th F S Su

◇ ◇ ◇ ◇ ◇ ◇ ◇

SCHEDULE

7 > 8	
8 > 9	
9 > 10	
10 > 11	Clean
11 > 12	
12 > 13	apartment
13 > 14	
14 > 15	
15 > 16	
16 > 17	
17 > 18	
18 > 19	
19 > 20	
20 > 21	

▷▷▶▷▷▶▷▷▶

TO DO LIST

- ☐ Change Sheets
- ☐ Make gyno apt.
- ☐ WAX EVERYTHING
- ☐ white wine
- ☐ chocolate
- ☐ berries
- ☐ whipped cream
- ☐ condoms

GOALS

NOTES

new undies?

✚ BREAKFAST

✚ LUNCH

✚ DINNER

✚ WORKOUT

EIGHTEEN

In which Nina fulfills her first
family obligation.

Sunday was usually Nina's extravaganza of planning. She would sort out clothes for the week, plan her meals, make sure she'd read whatever she needed to for work and for the book club, make a proper shopping list and shop for groceries . . . It was her reset and recommit day, and she always felt like she'd crushed it by the time the evening rolled around.

However, on this day, things were already out of whack by 10 A.M., and it was all Peter Reynolds's fault. For the first time in her life Nina had a family obligation, and she wasn't entirely sure she liked it.

Peter had texted her at nine, an hour he said was the earliest acceptable time to contact someone on a Sunday.

Nina had still been asleep. Somewhat

acerbically, she suggested he recalibrate and set *her* earliest acceptable time to eleven.

"No," said her nephew, "if I make an exception for you, I'll need to customize my entire system, and that won't work at all."

"You have a system?"

"Of course. There is a standard weekday wake-up time, and a different weekend time. There is a time in the evening after which one cannot call anyone except good friends or lovers, and a time after which one can only call if there is an emergency."

Nina's phone was lying on her pillow, on speaker. "I assume there's a booty call exception to that rule."

"You assume correctly. See? It's a good system. If I have individual wake-up times attached to everyone I'll mess it up. I like to keep it simple."

"Well, I guess we all better bend to your will then." Nina might have been a little cranky, still, and she was definitely under-caffeinated.

"It would be best. Besides, you had to wake up in order to answer your phone, so no harm, no foul." Nina could tell from his tone of voice that her new nephew was a morning person, that despicable breed. She said nothing, but turned her head and pressed it into the pillow so her phone slid down and rested in her little ear divot.

Peter was still chirping at her. "So, I was wondering if you wanted to come with me today to visit my mom? She lives in Culver City, and I need to get my dog's claws trimmed."

Nina opened her eyes and looked at the ceiling. Nope, she had to ask: "What do those two things have in common?"

"My mom's a vet. She taught me a lot, but not how to cut dog claws without messing it up and making them bleed. The last time I tried, the house looked like a Quentin Tarantino movie for days."

So, here she was, at ten on a Sunday morning, sitting in the front seat of Peter's car, with the world's smallest greyhound resting on her lap. Neither she nor the dog were entirely sure this was a good idea.

"So," said Peter. "Something about your face tells me you had a good night last night."

She turned and looked at him incredulously. "How on earth can you tell that?"

"I have mad skills." He grinned at her. "I learned that phrase from one of my students, and I'm afraid it's become a habit."

"I'm not sure anyone even says that anymore."

Peter shrugged. "And yet I still do. You

might conclude I don't care what other people think of my vernacular, and you would be correct."

Nina and the greyhound rolled their eyes at each other. Then Nina said, "Well, I did, as it happens. I met this guy and at first I didn't like him and then I did and we kissed and then I messed up and then I got another chance and this time went better."

Peter laughed. "Well, that sounds good, I think. Can I ask a round of rapid-fire questions?"

"Sure."

The greyhound swallowed nervously.

"What's his name?"

"Tom."

"What does he do?"

"I think he's a carpenter, but it's unconfirmed. He smells of sawdust, but for all I know he's homeless and sleeps in a sawmill."

"Is he cute?"

"Yes."

"Is he sexy?"

"Very."

"Is he funny?"

"Yes."

"And, I'm sorry, did you sleep with him already?"

Nina shook her head. "I would have, to be

honest, but the first time I invited him in he said no, and last night he left before I had a chance to invite him again."

"Hmm."

Nina looked over at him. "Do you think that's a problem?"

"No." Peter slowed the car to let someone cross. "Just interesting. My observation of young men in Los Angeles — admittedly, I have a different cross section than you do, probably — is that they're all 'sex first, talk later.' Maybe he's from out of town."

"Not really. Pasadena."

Peter made a left and started looking for a parking space. "Ah well. Pasadenans are weird."

"They are?"

"Yeah. Caltech is there. And the Jet Propulsion Lab. And CalArts, where all the great animators study. It's a strange intersection of pocket protectors and Miyazaki movies." He found a space and parked deftly. "Let's go."

Peter's mom, Becky, lived in a part of Culver City that Nina hadn't visited in a while, and she was surprised to find it had become totally gentrified, with the requisite chain coffee place named for a whale hunter, a juice place, a frozen gluten-free yogurt store, and an organic grocery store where the carrots were priced individually. Peter rang the doorbell and apparently his mother released a pack of hellhounds, who dashed themselves against the wood with the fury of a thousand wolves who hadn't eaten in some time. Once the door opened, they were revealed to be three small mutts with enthusiastic tails and hanging tongues, whose only goal appeared to be declaring their undying love for Peter's dog, whom they'd clearly met before.

Becky was the woman who'd waved a peace sign at Nina back in the lawyer's office, and she greeted her now with a lazy smile. "Hey, you brought my newest sister," she said, kissing her son. "Ignore the mess."

Most of the time this is something people say when their houses are immaculate, and the idea is you say, 'Oh, you should see mine,' or something similar. In this case it really was a mess, and Nina found it enormously relaxing. She counted two more dogs, older and less enthusiastic, who nonetheless waved their tails at her from their sleeping stations on the sofa and floor. Several cats were watching her cautiously, or sarcastically — it's always hard to tell with cats — and the whole place was covered with a fine patina of fur. There was a vague smell of woodsmoke and the inside of dogs' ears.

Nina and Peter followed Becky through the living room into what turned out to be the kitchen, which was marginally cleaner, at least in places. An older man was sitting at the table, deseeding an acorn squash.

"Hi there," he said. "I'm John. I'm Peter's stepdad." He waved his sticky hands at her. "Welcome to chaos central."

Becky clicked on a kettle and turned to face Nina.

"Do you want a cup of tea? Coffee?"

Nina nodded. "Whatever you're having." She looked around. Peter had launched into a conversation with his stepdad, and the dog pack had headed outside in order to run in giant circles and wrestle over a stuffed margarita dog toy. Why a margarita? thought Nina. Are dogs such big cocktail drinkers?

Becky's phone rang, and she made a face but answered it. She listened, smiled, then said, "Sure, but only for tonight." She listened some more. "I'm not promising anything. Bring him over." She hung up and shook her head, putting tea bags in cups and eyeing the kettle, which was made of glass. Bubbles, but not boiling yet.

"John, you having tea?" she asked, and then with the next breath, "Do you like animals, Nina?"

"Yes, very much. I have a cat called Phil, and I'm always wondering if I could handle a dog."

Becky nodded. "Cats are good. I have three or four dotted around the place. Or is it five? I can't remember." She looked a question at Nina as she held a teaspoon of sugar over her own cup, and Nina nodded. Becky gave John and Peter their tea, and sat down at the table with a sigh. "I'm not an animal rescuer, but I take animals from animal rescuers when they need to park them in a safe place. It's not really fostering, because they usually move them somewhere longer term pretty quickly, but it takes the pressure off. I love them all, even the difficult ones."

"I think you especially love the difficult ones," said John, smiling. He looked at Nina. "What you see in front of you is one of the softest hearts on the planet."

Nina asked, "And was that call another animal coming?"

"Yes. A dog." Becky motioned out of the kitchen window, which was tall and wide, and Nina looked and saw a large but cluttered yard with a wire-fenced area in one corner. "I can take rabbits and chickens and things like that, too, in the smaller yard. I can't take ducks, though, sadly. No pond."

"Are there a lot of lost ducks in Los Angeles?" Nina asked, surprised.

"Oh God, don't get her started," said Peter, but it was too late.

Becky shrugged. "Lots of lost everything, unfortunately. Do you know several charities airlift small dogs from our shelter system to other parts of the country where they don't have so many? Other areas have lots of large dogs, but no small ones, and we have too many. They get snapped up elsewhere and put to sleep here. Lots of people are working for animals, in this town. It's as big a subculture as any."

John finished with his seed work and went to wash his hands. "So," he said, over his shoulder, "you two are sisters? That's funny." He turned off the faucet. "Bill Reynolds was a pain in the butt, but he sure made pretty kids."

Becky rolled her eyes at Nina. "Ignore him," she said. "I found him on the street with one of the dogs and he followed me home."

Peter laughed. "Are we going to keep him?"

John flicked water at them both. "It was the luckiest day of your life."

"That's right," said Becky. "Best dog I ever had." She smiled at Nina. "It's weird to think we share a father, right? How old are you?"

"Twenty-nine."

"And I'm fifty-nine. He was twenty when he fathered me and fifty when he fathered you. Men keep on trucking, right?" She drank her tea, then leaned forward to call the dogs. "Only claws today, Peter?"

Her son nodded. "Thanks, Mom."

Becky shrugged. "I'm doing it for him, not you, you lazy swine."

All the dogs piled through the door, and Becky grabbed the little greyhound and held him in her lap. She pulled a pair of nail trimmers from her pocket and swiftly clipped his claws as they talked.

"Do you remember your dad very well?" Nina looked at her sister's face, focused on its work and filled with gentleness. She suddenly thought of Tom, whose eyes were equally as kind.

"Sure," said Becky. "Not so much as a child, but from when we were older. He divorced Alice, our mom, and married Rosie when my sister and I were pretty young. But we still saw him a lot, because that's what Dad wanted. He liked the concept of fatherhood, you know, the job description. He just didn't want to do the actual work."

"Was he abusive?"

"No, not physically, never. But he was a bit of a narcissist." Becky grew more thoughtful, putting the greyhound down and watching the pack streak outside again. "You might have liked him of course; he was charming when he wanted to be, or when he'd had a few drinks. He loved to hold forth on his grand philosophies of life, you know, give romantic advice, for example, which is ironic for someone who couldn't stay faithful for twenty minutes."

The doorbell rang, and Becky stood up and nearly got knocked down by the pack as she went to open the door.

John and Peter looked at Nina, who was finding all the noise and activity a little overwhelming.

John smiled. "Like I said, chaos central."

Becky came back with another woman who was carrying a black-and-white collie mix and a handful of papers. The new dog had his tail tucked and his eyes were grave.

The woman was talking. "His shelter name was Boris, but they gave it to him, so who knows, and he's negative for heartworm and neutered and about three." She looked over, "Oh, hey, John."

"Where did they find him?" John asked. "He's gorgeous."

"Someone found him running on the

street and brought him in. No chip, of course."

Becky took the dog from her and plopped him on the kitchen counter, where she could look at him without being swarmed by the other dogs. He stood there patiently, his tail moving very slightly at the end. She looked at his ears, his teeth, his eyes, then moved her hands over his body, feeling for injuries. He waited, and his tail moved a little more when eventually she stopped and cupped his head, tipping it up. "You," she said — and his tail wagged completely now — "are a good boy, and we shall be friends." She kissed him on his nose, and he licked her chin politely. She lifted him down and opened the back door. All the younger dogs bashed their way out to run around and get acquainted. The humans watched, jealous of the ease with which they handled it.

Becky sat down and stroked the head of one of the older dogs, who'd laid his heavy chin on her knee and was gazing up at her. "The problem with dad was that he kept disappearing. He'd promise to do this or that, but there was always a last-minute reason not to show up. Eventually we all stopped expecting anything from him; if you bend something too much it breaks, right?" She looked up at Nina, and her kind eyes had grown cool in memory. "My first husband, Peter and Jennifer's dad, was like that."

Nina looked at Peter and John, who were listening and drinking their tea. They were clearly so comfortable together.

"How old were you when your dad left?" she asked Peter.

His mom answered. "He and Jenny were three and one. They don't remember their dad."

"He's not around?"

"No." There was a slight pause, but nothing further.

"Luckily for all concerned," said John, stretching his arms above his head and then ruffling Peter's hair as if he were still three years old. "I showed up about twenty minutes after he left and made everything better again."

"It was a couple of years, but same difference," said Becky, still petting the dog.

"John's my dad," said Peter, shrugging. "There's never been a better one."

John made a face at him, but Nina could tell he was touched. "It's a lot easier to know you want to take care of a kid who's so cute that old ladies faint in the street," he said, gruffly. He looked at Nina. "The thing about being a stepfather is you know what you're getting into. I saw a beautiful woman with two fantastic kids and a totally ridiculous number of animals. I guess Peter's dad had a different dream in mind, but for me, it was everything I'd ever wanted." He looked at his wife. "I feel sorry for him every day." He paused. "Except when something throws up on me, then I feel sorry for myself."

There was a scratching at the door, and they turned to see the new dog, Boris, standing there. Becky let him in, and the dog docked his smooth head with her hand as if they'd been engineered together. He looked up at her with melted chocolate eyes, and when she spoke she was looking at him but may have been talking to her husband. "It takes a lot to join a family that's broken, but sometimes it turns out you're exactly the glue it needs." Then she looked up at Nina. "Hey, are you sure you don't want a dog? This guy is a total sweetheart."

Peter laughed. "You know you're going to keep him, Mom."

John nodded. "She has a terrible weakness for sheepdogs. Show her something black and white and smart as a whip and she's putty in their paws."

Becky grinned and ruffled the dog's ears. "Well, to be fair, there's always room for one more in the family." She looked up at Nina and grinned. "Even if you're not a dog."

today is the day

DATE Saturday 25th May   M T W Th F S Su
⬡ ⬡ ⬡ ⬡ ⬡ ⬡ ⬡

SCHEDULE

7>8
8>9
9>10
10>11   Work half day
11>12
12>13
13>14
14>15
15>16   wedding !
16>17
17>18
18>19
19>20
20>21

TO DO LIST

☐ Pick up dress from
   leah
☐ shoes ???
☐
☐
☐
☐
☐
☐
☐
☐
☐

GOALS

NOTES

Harriett books
for Becky, check
order.

➕ BREAKFAST

➕ LUNCH

➕ DINNER

➕ WORKOUT

NINETEEN

In which Nina attends a wedding.

As a woman in her late twenties, Nina had attended many weddings. Indeed, the last several summers had been a painful forced march of dry chicken breasts and soggy canapés, stilted conversations with relative strangers and clammy dances with people she vaguely remembered from college. However, shortly after arriving at the wedding of Lili's sister, Rachel, Nina realized this wedding wasn't going to be business as usual.

The camel was her first clue. It was standing on one side of a large expanse of grass, tied to a tree by a long rope, wearing a jeweled, pom-pom-covered, traditional Rajasthani camel outfit of such incredible ornament that a crowd had formed. Admittedly, it was a crowd of children, but still.

Nina wandered over, spotting Annabel.

"Hi there," she said, casually. "Is this your camel?"

Annabel, who was wearing a sparkly dress and cat ears, looked surprised to see Nina. "I thought Clare was making it up, that you were coming," she said. "But I'm really happy you're here. We can talk about books later. I've got questions."

"Great," said Nina. "But the camel?"

Annabel shrugged. "It's not mine. It's here for the wedding."

"Was it invited?"

"No," said a voice behind her, and Nina turned to see Lili, looking resigned and amused. "It was sent in place of someone who was invited, but what I'm supposed to feed it, I have no idea. It came with a guy who backed it out of a horse box, handed me the rope, and said, 'I'll be back in three hours.'" She looked at Nina. "You saw the invite; the RSVP was yes or no, not yes, no, or send a camel."

The camel turned and regarded them thoughtfully, found them boring, and turned away again.

"Well," said Nina, looking around at the rugs and cushions. "It sort of goes with the theme. And at least it didn't bring a plus one."

A tall man came over with two buckets of

water, which he placed in front of the camel. Annabel's little sister, Clare, was behind him.

"Hi, Nina," she said. "Did you meet the camel? Isn't he lovely? They didn't tell us his name, but I'm calling him Humpy Bogart. Did you know camels don't actually store water in their humps, that they're just big mounds of fat? Like boobs?" Behind her Lili covered her face and the tall man snorted.

Nina nodded. "And did you know that they can drink up to forty gallons of water in one giant slurp?"

The tall man frowned. "Maybe I should have brought bigger buckets." He had an accent and smiled at Nina. "I'm sorry, my name is Edward. We haven't been introduced."

"This is Nina," said Clare. "She's my guest. I invited her."

Edward nodded. "Lovely, so happy you're here. Clare, you better find out where Nina's sitting and show her to her . . . uh . . . rug."

Clare reached out and took Nina's hand. "Come on, let's look at the chart. The show will be starting soon."

Nina followed her. "But I still don't understand about the camel."

"Me neither," said the little girl, "but my mom said Aunty Rachel knows a lot of strange people all over the world, because she's a smuggler of rare and beautiful things" — she ran that last part all together, so it sounded like rareandbeautifulthings — "and one of those people sent the camel." She glanced up at Nina and made a face. "It's not for keeping, though; it's only for looking at."

"Bummer."

"You said it." Clare paused and lowered her voice. "I'm thinking maybe the camel stays." Nina could see the cogs turning.

They reached the front of the meadow, where Clare tugged Nina up to a large display board. They'd passed dozens of people, all of whom were lolling, exactly as the bride had planned. So far, so good.

Clare studied the board. "Where are you?" Nina, looking over her head, quickly spotted her name.

"I'm on rug fourteen. With . . ." — she read out some names — "Mike and Angie, Eloise and Frances, and Frances and Michael." She smiled at the little girl. "Two Franceses?"

Clare nodded. "They're easy to tell apart. One is bigger than the other."

"But if they're both called Frances then I

can use the same name for both, right?"

"Yes," she said. "Because they're easy to tell apart."

There comes a point with young children, Nina had learned, where it was best to say OK and walk away.

"It's a good rug," said Clare, like a maître d' leading a guest to a special table. "They're garden club people, apart from the other Frances, who's a friend of my mom's."

Nina arranged her features in a friendly expression, getting ready to be introduced to strangers. For some reason, she wasn't feeling as anxious about it as usual. There was something about being outside that kind of gave you more room. Perhaps she should move into a tent.

"Hi, Clare," said a larger, older woman who was sitting on the rug Nina and Clare were clearly approaching. "I thought you were a bridesmaid."

"I am," said Clare.

"Well, shouldn't you be getting ready?"

"I am ready."

Both the lady and Nina looked at Clare, who was, Nina realized, wearing Peppa Pig pajamas with a long pink slip over the top. The kind of slip Elizabeth Taylor wore in *Cat on a Hot Tin Roof;* the kind with lacy bits and straps.

"And very nice you look, too," said another woman, who looked vaguely familiar. "I bet that's your favorite dress."

"It is," beamed Clare, glad someone was on the ball this evening. She turned back to Nina. "These are the Franceseses." She stumbled over the pronunciation, and tried again. "Francesssess. Franceses." She sighed. "They have the same name."

Both women smiled. The older one reached up a hand. "I'm Frances from Gardening Club," she said. "This is my wife, Eloise." Another lady who looked pretty similar to her waved lazily.

"And I'm Frances from school," said the other one. "Don't you work at Knight's, on Larchmont?"

"Yes," said Nina, "I'm Nina Hill," and she reached out and carefully shook both their hands.

Frances-from-school beamed. "I've seen you there lots of times, of course. I live around the corner, and my kids and I are there at least once a week."

Nina recognized her now. In Nina's head she was "nonfiction and parenting" because those were the books she bought, and her kids were (she thought hard, and placed them) young adult, early chapter and picture books, respectively. This Frances was the kind of woman who made you feel welcome, even if you were both in a strange situation. She was wearing jeans and a hooded sweatshirt, which was an odd choice for a wedding, but the invitation had said "wear whatever you want." Frances caught her looking and grinned.

"I don't know Rachel, the bride, very well, but I know Lili, and she assured me Rachel really didn't give a fig what people wore. So I went with a clean version of what I wear every day, because it makes me comfortable." She looked around. "And I guess I'm not the only one."

It was true. People were dressed in everything from cocktail dresses and black tie to, in at least one case Nina could see, footie pajamas. On an adult.

Clare had already run off to do her bridesmaid thing, and presently a voice could be heard over a loudspeaker.

"OK, people." It was Lili. "We're going to do this thing, so try and find a rug, yours preferably, but any is fine, and let's get these folks married. Rachel has insisted that everyone stay on their butts while she walks through, because she says she intends to dawdle."

Frances leaned over. "Isn't this fun? The

camel was a lovely touch."

"I heard they spit," muttered the other Frances. "Ten dollars someone gets it in the eye before the evening is out."

"I'll take that bet," said a man who was lounging on the other side of the rug, presumably Frances's husband, Michael.

But Nina wasn't listening. She was looking at Rachel the bride, who was incredibly beautiful, wearing a vintage '70s cream linen suit, and looking like a million bucks. She was making her way across the meadow, with Clare and Annabel behind her, wearing their favorite outfits and no shoes. Nina realized the haphazard arrangement of rugs was actually a way for Rachel to pass by each one on her way to the front, and people were handing her single flowers to make up into her bouquet. She was thanking them, greeting them, and even occasionally bending down to kiss people. It wasn't the most formal wedding ceremony Nina had ever been to, but it was already memorable for its friendliness. At one point Rachel looked toward the front, where the bridegroom and best man were waiting.

"I'm getting there, babe," she called. "I just want to say hi before I'm too drunk to recognize anyone."

The bridegroom, who looked like he

might already have had a few, waved his hand at her. "Take your time, Rach. We've got the rest of our lives." Then he grinned at her, like an idiot.

Next to him, the best man was talking to Lili, who was wiping tears from her cheeks and watching her sister and her daughters make their way across the grass. Then the best man turned to look at Rachel, too, and that was when Nina realized this wedding really wasn't going to be business as usual, and not just because of the camel.

The best man was Tom.

The vows took quite a while, because they were wide-ranging. Nina's favorite was a promise to always set up the coffee maker the night before, followed by a paired promise to never let them run out of half-and-half.

Finally, the officiate said, "For their last vows, Rachel and Richard have asked to read the lyrics of their favorite song."

Rachel said, "Richard, we wrote our vows together, and they mean a lot to us. But we also know when someone else has put it better, so here goes."

She cleared her throat. "I'm never going to give you up."

He replied, "Never going to let you down."

She said, "Never going to run around and desert you."

Nina turned to Frances and raised an eyebrow.

Frances shrugged. "It is a classic song of their childhood, I suppose." They both watched as the happy couple finished up by promising never to tell lies or hurt each other, then Frances added, "The great philosopher Richard Astley knew a thing or two about commitment."

"He's in the *Guinness Book of World Records,*" said Nina, unable to help herself. "His first eight singles reached the top ten in the UK; he's the only male singer to do that. As far as I know, the record still stands."

Frances patted her arm. "Good to know."

Nina peered into the picnic basket and pulled out a packet of Pocky, those little biscuit sticks with chocolate on them. Again, a big improvement over chicken breast or mushroom vol-au-vents. There were sandwiches in the basket, and bread rolls, and cheese and fruit and enormous bars of chocolate. Tiny pastries in a tin. Meringues shaped like flowers.

"What's in the other basket?" she asked Frances.

Frances lifted the lid, then turned and

grinned at Nina. "It's a cooler pretending to be a basket. It's full of ice cream bars."

Every so often a waiter would come around with fresh drinks, and although Nina had switched to fizzy water after the toasts, she was feeling as buoyant as everyone else. The sun had gone down, strings of lights had come on, and it really was magical.

Lili appeared and sat down on the rug next to her. "Is it the right Tom?" she asked, getting to the point.

"Yes." Nina nodded. "But I don't really understand."

Lili hugged herself. "Well, when I looked up the team, I saw his name and thought it was entirely possible there was more than one Tom Byrnes in Los Angeles, right? I knew Richard had a brother named Tom, but he and I had never met, and you and I had never really met properly before that night. It was a long shot."

"Yeah," said Nina. "Kind of unbelievable."

"And yet these things happen," said Lili. "In my experience they happen more than you'd think. So I invited you to the wedding, and if it was supposed to be, then he would be the right one." She shrugged and looked around. "Besides, there are lots of single men here because most of the people who work for Rachel are young guys who lift stuff, so if Tom wasn't the right Tom then you still might meet someone nice."

"Clare said your sister was a smuggler?"

Lili laughed. "She's an importer of art and artifacts. She works with museums and private collectors, but one time when Clare was visiting her at work, Rach told her she was a smuggler, and then it was funnier to leave it like that."

"Let's hope Clare doesn't grow up to work for the IRS."

"Wash out your mouth," said Lili, and got to her feet. "Have fun tonight. Tom seems very nice, and Richard is fantastic. We're definitely improving the gene pool in the family by adding him." She looked around. "Wait . . . where's the camel?"

It turned out Clare had the camel and was trying to persuade it to climb into the back of her mother's car. It further turned out that camels are not easily persuaded, particularly if you want to fold them up like umbrellas and squeeze them into small spaces, so Clare wasn't getting very far.

Once she was separated from Humpy, under duress and with a lot of heated tears, she revealed she'd had four ice cream bars and two bags of gummy worms, and then threw up all over the back seat of the car. Nina offered to go hunt down a damp cloth and a roll of paper towels and headed off. While she was talking to a helpful waiter, Tom came up behind her.

"Hey, Nina, fancy meeting you here." He'd spotted her after the ceremony, but he'd had to go and pose for fifty thousand wedding photos, and it had taken him until now to come find her. "I'm not sure *how* you are here, I'll be honest." He blushed slightly. "I mean, I'm really glad to see you." Smooth move, ex-lax, he thought.

Nina had her arms full of paper towels, which was good because she could hand him a roll and explain the Clare–camel–gummy worm situation as an opening conversational topic. That way maybe he wouldn't notice how flushed her cheeks were.

"So, let me get this straight," he said, as they crossed the grass. "You're here at the invitation of Clare, my new sister-in-law's niece, who has been overcome by sugar and attempted camel-napping, and we're on our way to provide assistance."

"That's about the size of it," replied Nina. "Her older sister is one of the girls who was staring at you last week at the bookstore. She's in my elementary book club."

"Wow, it's a small world."

"No," said Nina, spotting Lili and Clare still sitting on the ground by their car, the camel chomping the grass nearby. "It's a very big world, but Larchmont is very small."

Clare was looking much better, so Tom led the camel back to its original spot while Nina helped clean up and Lili explained to Clare that no, she couldn't have more ice cream now that she felt better. No, even though she'd made room by throwing up. No, even if it was probably the gummy worms that had caused the trouble. And no, she couldn't have a camel.

Tom and Nina decided it was probably best to back slowly away. Lili clearly had this under control.

"Congratulations, by the way," said Nina, as they meandered across the grass. People had started dancing now, in an area near the front, and many of the rugs were empty.

He looked at her, puzzled.

"On your brother's wedding. Congratulations on your new sister. I don't know her, but Lili is really nice. And her nieces, as you saw, are great."

Tom grinned. "I only met them myself very recently."

"Oh? Richard and Rachel haven't known each other very long?"

Tom shook his head. "No, they met last summer, although apparently Richard had seen her before and kind of fell in love at first sight. Then, when he spotted her again, he went for it."

"Wow. That's . . . bold."

Tom shrugged. "That's the Byrnes family for you. Overconfident. We'd rather try hard and fall on our faces than not try. It's my mom's fault; she's insane."

Nina paused. "Actually insane, as in mentally ill, or mad as a hatter insane?"

Tom laughed. "Well, I'm not a psychiatrist, but she's definitely mad as a hatter. She likes to try lots of new things and get out there and do stuff. She skis, she sky-dives, she rides horses, she runs marathons."

Nina smiled but said, "She sounds exhausting."

Tom nodded. "She can be. Richard is like her, my sister, Amelia, is even more like her, and I'm a little bit like her. I'm not so adventurous."

Nina looked up at him. "And your dad?"

Tom was watching where he walked, trying not to trip over any of the rugs. "I'm more like him. He's . . . normal. He likes to watch my mom do all this stuff, and cheer her on, but not actually break his leg falling off things."

"Does she break her leg a lot?"

Tom shook his head. "Not lately."

They had wandered across the whole meadow now and stood watching the dancers.

Tom turned to her. "Would you like to dance?"

Nina shook her head. "I'm not a good dancer. I love music, but I get nervous and then I mess up." As if I needed to underscore my lack of adventurousness, she thought.

A slow song came on. "Girl Talk," by Julie London.

Tom smiled. "You can't mess up a slow dance. Come on."

Nina shook her head but let herself be tugged onto the dance floor. "This is the most sexist song ever," she said.

"Yes," said Tom, pulling her close and starting to dance. "It is, but follow me and don't think about it."

"I can't *not* think about it," said Nina, although she was following his steps and enjoying the feeling of his arms around her waist. She'd had to put her arms around his waist, too, as he was too tall for her to hold him around his neck. "*We chew the fat about*

317

our tresses and the neighbours' fight . . .
honestly."

"But her voice," said Tom, bending his
head so she could hear him over the music.
"Her voice is the most beautiful thing in
the world."

Nina smiled and looked up at him. "It is.
She really did have the most . . ."

And then he kissed her. Properly. And it
was just as well he was holding her, because
otherwise she might have lost her balance.

Over on the side of the dance floor, Clare
turned to her mom and held out her hand.
"Told you!"

Lili sighed and pulled a gummy worm
from her pocket. "You win."

Clare chewed and watched Nina and Tom,
who were still kissing. "I knew they were
going to kiss. I could tell."

"How could you tell? You're six."

"I watched you and Edward. People who
are going to kiss do it with their eyes first."
Clare shrugged. "You can see it coming a
mile off."

Tom and Nina pulled apart and looked at
each other silently, and Clare held out her
hand. "See, still kissing. Worm me."

Lili slapped another worm in her daughter's palm.

Clare chewed. "And now the lips again."

318

TWENTY

In which Nina shares more of herself.

"Wow," said Tom, walking into Nina's apartment. "Those are some serious bookshelves."

Nina held back, watching him enter her space, seeing what he looked like in her home. She hardly ever brought men back to her apartment. She preferred to go to theirs so she could leave if she needed to. Nothing worse than a date going wrong and having to throw someone out in the middle of the night or pretend everything is fine until the next morning. A shiver of anxiety crossed her stomach, but then Tom turned and smiled at her, and it faded.

"These must have been here since the guesthouse was built. They don't make them this way anymore." He ran his hands along the edges of the shelves.

Nina smiled. "I don't think I've ever had

anyone compliment the actual shelves before. People are usually more focused on the books."

"Yeah, there are a lot of them." But he was still looking at the shelves.

"Would you like a drink?" Nina went to see if she had any wine or beer, but she didn't.

"No, I'm fine," he said, coming up behind her, sliding his hands around her waist. She was small, this woman, but strong. He could feel her muscles moving under his palms as she twisted around and kissed him again. There was nothing hesitant in her reaction to him, not on the dance floor, not at the wedding, not in the car on the way here, not now. He leaned into her, wrapped his arms tightly around her, and half lifted her higher against him. Suddenly, he felt a sharp pain in his ankle and pulled away, exclaiming.

Nina laughed as she looked down. "Oh, sorry. That's Phil." A small cat was standing on the kitchen floor, his tail lashing, his ears back. "He's hungry."

Tom bent to stroke the cat, who hissed at him. "I don't think it's hunger; I think it's hatred."

Nina was filling a small silver dish with cat kibble and shook her head. "No, he's a lover not a fighter." She put the dish on the floor, and Phil started to eat. "See? Just hungry." Tom went to step around Phil, but Phil whirled around and sank his teeth into his ankle again. "Huh," said Nina. "I was wrong. He hates you."

Eventually, Phil allowed Tom to pass, and they headed into the sitting room area. Tom sat on the giant armchair and pulled Nina onto his lap. "Is this where you spend all your time?" he asked, between kisses.

"Yes," she said, "it's my favorite place in the world." She was straddling him in the chair, and as she tugged her dress over her head, Tom smelled lemon and honey again, and pressed his lips against her stomach. "Although," she said, undoing the buttons on his shirt, "I've never done . . . this . . . here before." She finished with his shirt and started on his belt, loosening the buckle and tugging it out of his waistband.

"You surprise me," said Tom, standing and lifting her in order to step out of his pants, her legs around his waist, then turning and setting her down in the chair again, kneeling on the rug in front of her. "It's so perfect for it."

He bent his head to her stomach again, then began to work his way down.

"Oh," said Nina, closing her eyes and

leaning her head back. "You're right. It's . . ." — her voice faltered for a second — "perfect."

The next morning, Nina woke and through her sticky contact lenses saw Tom moving around in the kitchen. She smiled, remembering the way it had been. For once, she didn't want to leave, or get him to leave, or do anything other than everything all over again.

He looked over and saw her watching him. "Good morning, beautiful," he said. "Coffee?"

She nodded.

"I went out already and got breakfast," he said. "And I made peace with your insanely jealous cat."

Nina realized Phil was standing on the kitchen counter, eating something. "How did you do that?"

"Old-fashioned bribery," replied Tom, carrying two mugs of coffee over to her. "It turns out he's happy to share you in return for organic smoked salmon." He sat on the floor next to the bed and leaned forward to kiss her. "How are you?"

She sipped her coffee and smiled at him. "I'm good. You?"

"Very good." He smiled back. "Last night

322

was amazing. You're amazing."

She handed him back the coffee cup and lifted the duvet. "Come back to bed," she said. "I thought of a few more amazing things."

He grinned and slid under the sheet.

A few hours later, they managed to make it out of the apartment, and wandered hand in hand to Larchmont Boulevard, which was wearing its Sunday best. Sunday was not Nina's favorite day in the neighborhood, because the Farmer's Market brought what felt like a million visitors to the hood, all of them vying for limited parking and carrying ethically sourced string bags they filled with overpriced produce.

Tom turned to Nina. "Are you hungry?" he asked.

"Not really," she replied. "But I can always have ice cream."

He smiled and kissed her softly on the lips. "You don't think you're sweet enough already?"

She made a face at him. "I might be sweet, but do I contain an interesting variety of carefully curated ingredients? I don't think so."

"It's a good point," he said. "Besides, what if you collapsed from vanilla deficiency?"

"Exactly," she said. "Only the rapid application of ice cream will prevent disaster."

They turned into one of the two, yes, two, artisanal ice cream stores on the Boulevard. Sometimes Nina imagined their workers, late at night, coming out onto the street, scoopers at the ready, or maybe with a giant ice cream trebuchet, throwing enormous balls of frosty death at one another, competing to be the Ice Cream Monarch of Larchmont Village. An Ennio Morricone version of an ice cream truck jingle would hang in the air, and in the middle of August, the ice cream would melt on the hot street and cream would run in the gutters.

Nina told Tom about her theory as they waited in an impossibly long line, and he listened to her very carefully, nodding at the trebuchet part and pursing his lips in consideration of the street-cleaning ramifications. Then he sighed and kissed her so deeply that conversation in the line stopped while people admired his technique. Finally, he let her go and said, "You are a complete lunatic, Nina Hill, and I doubt I will ever have any idea what's going on in your head."

Nina caught her breath and nodded. "It's probably just as well," she said, although right at the moment, he was the only thing

324

in her head. No need to tell him that, of course.

Then she ordered a scoop of salted peanut butter with chocolate flecks and Tom ordered Brambleberry Crisp and they went outside to sit on a bench silently licking and watching people go by, enjoying that incredible feeling after you've finally slept with someone you wanted to and it turned out to be even better than you hoped it would be.

People walked by with the joie de vivre all Angelenos have, at least in that neighborhood. People were fit, healthy, attractive, and living their dream, or at least trying to live their dream. It was Sunday, and they were busy working up their enthusiasm for the coming week. Each morning they would face possible disappointment (no callbacks, no job interviews, no call from the Academy) but would march themselves to lunchtime yoga and drink a green juice and look forward to the next opportunity to Break In or Go Big or Make It Work. Maybe this week they would meet The One. Los Angeles runs on youthful optimism, endorphins, and Capital Letters.

Tom licked his cone in silence, which Nina appreciated. First, because the ice cream deserved respect, and second, because her favorite sound was no sound at all. It couldn't last, however, and Tom broke it.

"I really like your name," he said. "Are you named after someone in the family?"

Nina laughed. "Well, until three and a half weeks ago, the only family I had was my mom and the nanny that raised me, but no, I'm named after a girl in a photo."

"A photo?" He looked quizzically at her, and Nina explained.

"My mom's a photographer. There's a girl in a famous Ruth Orkin photo called *American Girl in Italy* whose name was Ninalee, and she always loved that name." Nina shrugged. "She also likes those drawings by Hirschfeld, you know, where he hid the name Nina somewhere in the picture . . . ?" She ground to a halt. Her ice cream was dripping and Tom was staring at her and maybe she was being boring.

Tom was indeed gazing at her. He had been thinking her voice sounded like a bell, much lower than most women's voices, imagining the sound waves of it bouncing off his skin, remembering how it had sounded saying his name, and suddenly all he wanted to do was go back to the apartment.

He blushed. "Did you ask me something?"

He coughed. "I'm sorry, I lost track of what you were saying."

Nina's mouth twisted. "Wow, I guess it wasn't really that interesting."

He sputtered. "No, it was. It was about photography, and about your name . . . I got distracted by your voice . . ." He reached for her hand. "I'll be honest, looking at you makes me lose my mind. Can we go back to your place?" He lowered his voice. "Please?"

Nina laughed at him and stood up. "Yes," she said. "I think we've had quite enough of the great outdoors for one day."

"How did your father die?" It was early evening now, and Tom was gazing up at the ceiling, Nina's head on his shoulder. They hadn't said very much for several hours, but now they were tired and ready to talk.

Nina shrugged against him, her hair tickling his neck. "Heart attack."

"And you really never knew him, or knew anything about him?"

"No. It seems weird now, but at the time it was just the way it was."

"So, you were kind of an orphan."

"No, not really. My mom was away, working, but we heard from her a lot, and she came to visit. I had no dad, but I did have a nanny who was as good — if not better —

than any biological mom might have been. I wasn't raised in a box."

"Really?"

"Actually," said Nina, "that's not true. I was lucky. I had a Carnation Condensed Milk carton for the first few years, then upgraded to a refrigerator box once I got too tall to stand up in the first one."

"Those refrigerator boxes are sturdy." Tom knew she was dodging the question, but he didn't want to push her. "And it explains how you're so comfortable in this single bed." He'd found the lack of space challenging, but he'd worked around it.

Nina nodded, liking the way Tom was always ready to be silly. Silly is a highly underrated quality. "Mine was European, too, so it was reinforced for export."

"Fancy."

She shook her head. "It wasn't fancy, but it was home, you know?" She paused. "Actually, I grew up here, right in the neighborhood. I've barely left the East side of LA my whole life."

He laughed. "Maybe you're the one who needs to be reinforced for export."

Nina smiled. "Do you travel a lot?"

He shook his head. "No. I grew up in Pasadena, went to college there, then moved all of sixteen miles to Los Angeles. I drove across country with some friends after graduation, like everyone does. But then I got on a plane and came right back."

"I never did that."

"You still could."

"No car. And I have a cat." She laughed. "A jealous, ferocious cat. Plus, I don't want to go anywhere." She was starting to feel hungry and wondered idly if they should get up and get dinner. "What's *your* dad like?"

Tom replied, "He's pretty typical. Like I said, he's quieter than my mom."

"But what was he *like,* your dad? How was he when you were a kid?"

Tom frowned and thought about it. "He was a good dad, I think. I only had the one, right? So I can't really compare him properly to anyone else's. One time he saved my sister's life."

Nina raised her eyebrows. "Sucking out snake venom?"

He grinned. "No, Heimlich in a Mc-Donald's. The story is that she choked on a chicken nugget and when he gave her the Heimlich the piece of nugget hit my older brother in the eye so hard they had to take him to the emergency room. The crumb coating scratched his cornea. He had to wear an eye patch to school."

"That's a good story."

He nodded. "Yes, and fairly typical. There was always a lot going on at our house. It was a happy childhood, for the most part. I saw my parents bicker a lot, but they always made up and never stopped loving each other, so, you know. It was . . . committed."

"And your brother and sister?"

"They're great. Richard got married, obviously, you were there."

"That's right," said Nina.

"Hey," said Tom, suddenly. "That means their anniversary will be ours, too!" There was a pause.

"Assuming we last long enough," said Nina, lightly.

"Right," said Tom. "You may get bored of me."

Nina looked at the side of her own hand where it rested on his chest. She curled the fingers under. "Or you might get bored of me. I don't do much."

Tom looked fixedly at the ceiling, trying to backtrack. "Maybe we'll have one glorious Sunday and then both be killed by a falling piano."

"At the same time?"

"No, two separate pianos, separate places, total coincidence."

Nina considered this, feeling the wave of

330

anxiety that had threatened to crest slowly losing power. "I've always wanted to die that way. Or under a safe. One of those Acme safes from *Road Runner.*"

"Any of those *Road Runner* deaths would be fine with me. Running off a cliff while still running, then pausing in midair, holding up a sign that says, *Whoops,* and then plummeting to my death . . ."

"Running into a hole painted on the side of a rock and then getting hit by a train that shouldn't be there in the first place."

"Watching a bird eat a lot of explosive birdseed and being fine and then trying a single one and exploding."

"Yeah, any of those would be OK."

"And a fitting end to our grand romance." Tom could feel her relaxing under his arm. She was so touchy, this one. Hard to navigate, although in bed they were so easy together, so relaxed and in tune. It was only the afterglow that held land mines.

He squeezed her shoulder. "Getting hungry?"

She nodded, wondering at the way his presence was somehow canceling out her anxiety. Each time she started to panic, the feelings just washed up against this big, solid wall of . . . him. He wasn't doing it consciously, or at least she didn't think he was, but he was 100 percent real, and her anxiety — which was, after all, made of smoke and mirrors — was no match for him.

"I need to work up a tiny bit more appetite," she said, sliding her hand under the sheet.

He smiled and caught her hand before it reached its target. "No," he said. "Let's leave room for dessert." He swung his legs out of bed. "I don't want you to get a blood sugar crash and have a fight on our first day." He tugged her to her feet. "Let me take care of you."

She sighed, nodded, and got up.

today is the day

DATE _Monday 27th May_   M T W Th F S Su
◊ ◊ ◊ ◊ ◊ ◊ ◊

SCHEDULE

7 > 8	
8 > 9	
9 > 10	
10 > 11	
11 > 12	_work_
12 > 13	
13 > 14	
14 > 15	
15 > 16	
16 > 17	
17 > 18	
18 > 19	
19 > 20	
20 > 21	

GOALS

Don't. Freak. Out !!

NOTES

new sheets !

TO DO LIST

- [ ] _Cat fd - salmon flavor !_
- [ ] _more condoms_
- [ ] _body lotion_
- [ ] _razors_
- [ ]
- [ ]
- [ ]
- [ ]

+ BREAKFAST _tom_

+ LUNCH _tom_

+ DINNER _tom_

+ WORKOUT _tom_ ☺

TWENTY-ONE

In which Nina proves useful.

Polly was thrilled for her, but then again, Polly's default state was thrilled.

"It's all very romantic," she said. "Enemies first, then a kiss and an epic fail on your part . . ."

"Hey," said Nina.

"Then coming together at a wedding, the fates aligning . . ."

Nina frowned. "I think it's stars that align, not fates."

Polly frowned at her. "Does it matter?"

"I suppose not."

"Are you going to see him again?"

Nina nodded. Then shook her head. Then nodded again. "I imagine so. We got on pretty well to not see each other again." She thought about it. "Of course, he is a guy, so who knows. I may never hear from him again. Or he might send me a picture of his penis any minute."

"Well then," said Polly, "keep checking your phone."

Nina's phone buzzed, obligingly. She picked it up but shook her head. "It's not him; it's Archie."

"Oh, now, his penis I'd be totally open to seeing." Polly leaned over to look, but Nina held the phone away.

"Excuse me, that's my married brother you're salivating over." She looked at the text. "And it would be pretty weird of him to send his sister a dick pic."

"Good point."

"He's wondering if I'm around for lunch. He says he's bringing a friend he wants me to meet. Do you want to come? Maybe the friend is single."

"How can I join you? Liz isn't here. Are you suggesting we close the store?"

"Oh yeah." Nina laughed. "Who knew you would turn out to be so responsible?"

"Not me." Polly walked away. "I think it's your terrible influence. I used to be carefree and disorganized, and you've ruined me. The other day I was able to put my hand directly on something I was looking for. It threw me off for the rest of the day."

"Sorry," said Nina.

"You should be," Polly replied, heading

into the office to grab some paperwork.

Archie's friend was nothing like Nina had expected. She was only four feet tall, for a start.

"This is Millie," said Archie. "She's your sister." He paused. "Mine, too."

Millie wasn't a redhead, but there was still something familiar about her. She looked more like her mom, Eliza, the woman who had attempted to stop Lydia's tirade the other day, but there was still plenty of her dad in her bone structure.

She stuck out her hand. "Hi, Nina. It's nice to meet you."

Nina shook her hand. What a formal child. "I didn't realize you two hung out," she said.

The three of them found a table at the back of the restaurant, and Vanessa came over to take their order.

"More family?" she asked. She looked at Millie. "Do you want a kids' menu?"

Millie looked up at her, thoughtfully. "Is there coloring on it?"

"Yes, and a word search."

"Well then, yes, please." She looked at Nina. "I love a word search."

"Who doesn't?" said Nina. "And Mad Libs."

"Yeah!" said Millie, clearly tickled to have

336

found a kindred spirit. Word geeks love to discover one another. Come upon. Identify. Recognize. Etc.

Archie cleared his throat. "Actually, we don't usually hang out. Eliza reached out to me after the meeting at the lawyer's a couple of weeks ago, and we decided it might be fun." He looked at Millie and then back at Nina. "I brought her to lunch because I can't talk about books anymore. I'm exhausted. I thought you could take over."

Millie smiled at him and patted his hand. "It's OK, you knew quite a lot about *Harry Potter.*"

"And if you'd read *The Hunger Games,* I would have been able to talk about that, too." He grinned. "But your mother is a sensible woman."

Nina said, "*The Hunger Games* is great, but maybe a little bloody for a . . ."

"Ten-year-old," said Millie. She took a sip of the lemonade Vanessa had delivered. "But I wanted to talk to you about Daddy, anyway."

Nina's smile faded a little. "You know I never met him, right? I didn't know him at all."

Millie frowned. "You didn't?"

Nina looked at Archie, who shrugged. "No

337

one even knew I was alive before your dad died. He was never my dad, really."

Millie was silent, processing this. "He wasn't married to your mom at all?"

Nina shook her head. "You know the other families, though?"

Millie turned the lemonade glass around slowly on the table. "A bit. I've met Archie before, at the holidays, but I wasn't paying all that much attention, honestly." She looked up at Nina, her eyes clear. "I mean, I'm a kid; it was Christmas."

"I came to see you in the hospital when you were born," said Archie.

Millie smiled. "You did?"

Archie nodded. "I was a teenager, so I was pretending to be really cool about it, but you were deeply ugly as a baby."

Millie giggled.

"Your mom kept asking if I wanted to hold you, and I kept saying no. I was worried you would suddenly attack."

Millie giggled harder, then stopped. "I miss my dad," she said.

Nina nodded. "I bet you do. What was he like?"

Millie smiled. "He was amazing. He played with me all the time. He was pretty old, but he came up with the best games. He watched my favorite shows with me, that kind of thing. We would read together every single day. He sat with me at night when I went to sleep, because sometimes I get scared of the dark." She looked at Nina quickly but found no judgment there. "And sometimes he would set up my toys in funny ways. Long lines of Littlest Pet Shop animals marching across the floor, dinosaurs dressed in Barbie clothes, you know? That kind of thing."

Nina smiled. "That must have taken some effort."

"Yeah, dinosaurs have shorter arms than Barbie."

"Everyone has shorter arms than Barbie."

Millie nodded. "He rolled up the sleeves. My mom works a lot, but he was kind of retired, so he picked me up from school. Now my babysitter does it. She's OK." A little lemonade had spilled on the table, and she drew a starfish. "It's been over a month now, but I'm always sad to see her car."

Nina wasn't sure what to say. She was surprised by Millie's description of her dad. Their dad. For the first time, she wished she'd met him and impulsively reached across the table and squeezed Millie's hand.

"He sounds great. I'm really sorry I didn't know him."

Millie looked up, her eyes shiny. "Yeah,

you would have liked him, I expect." She took a breath. "Lots of people did. He was my best friend, outside of school."

"Who's your best friend in school?" Nina was curious.

"Oh, you know, it changes." Millie looked at the table. There was a sudden stillness to her shoulders, and Nina looked at Archie.

"Do you like school?"

Millie shook her head, and suddenly burst out, "Not really. I have friends, sometimes, but most of the time no one talks to me. Which is fine, honestly, because I'm happy on my own; it's totally fine. Really fine. And no one wants to talk about books, except sometimes *Harry Potter* because they've read it, but honestly, I don't know if they really read properly because they don't know *anything,* and if I say, well, what about *The Candymakers,* or *Calpurnia Tate,* or *Penderwicks,* and they're like, what's that, then I feel bad." She subsided.

"Bad for them because they haven't read those books, which, by the way, are all awesome, awesome books? I love all of those." Nina felt herself relaxing further; this was her favorite topic. She wished she didn't feel so much identification with Millie, though; it was giving her flashbacks to her own school years. Recess and lunch, finding a spot to be alone, and then half wishing someone would find you.

"Bad that I can't think of anything to say if it isn't about books." Millie looked crestfallen. "They want to talk about Pokémon or whatever, and I like Pokémon, but I don't know all about them like I do about books." She looked at Nina somewhat pleadingly. "It's hard to find stuff to talk about sometimes. It gives me a tummy ache."

"Well, we can talk about books whenever you like," Nina said. "Do you think your mom would let you join a book club at the store? I have a whole group of girls your age who love all those books and lots more." She remembered that Millie and Eliza lived in Malibu. "It's a long way to come."

Millie looked hopeful. "I can ask her."

Archie added, "You can also ask the other kids questions; that's what my mom told me, and I think it was good advice. Ask people if they have a dog, or if they like birds, or if they're allergic to anything, or if they still believe in Santa Claus, or whatever pops into your head."

"The only thing that pops into my head is books," said Millie, worriedly. "And if I ask them a load of questions, they'll think I'm even stranger than they already think I am. Last week a boy at school said I was weird,

341

and nobody else said I wasn't. Nobody said anything." Her voice broke a little on the last word, and suddenly Nina was furious.

Trying to keep her voice calm, she asked, "What did he mean, weird?" She looked at Archie and saw he felt the same way.

Millie shrugged. "I don't know. Weird. We had been talking about Aragog — you know, the spider?" Both Archie and Nina nodded. "And then I started talking about Charlotte from *Charlotte's Web,* and all the bugs in *James and the Giant Peach,* and this other book about a boy and a beetle at the Metropolitan Museum of Art . . . ."

"Masterpiece," interjected Nina.

"Yes, and the cockroaches in the *Gregor* books, and I said bugs are interesting because they're smaller than kids, right, and the way characters treat them is like how we get treated by grown-ups, and then he stared at me and said I was weird." She looked at the table. "I thought it was a reasonable theory."

Archie took a drink of water. "Well, I'll be honest, Millie. That's not what I would call weird, it's what I would call smart, but ten-year-old boys aren't famous for their insights into literature." He put his glass down. "Or their manners."

Nina was gazing at her little sister and

wasn't prepared for the rush of affection she felt for a girl she'd met only half an hour earlier. She reached across the table, again. "Listen, I'll call your mom myself. You have to come to my book club, and then we can go have dinner afterward and talk about all this stuff."

"How often is the book club?"

Nina frowned. "Once a month."

"Oh," Millie said. "That's not very much."

"But maybe your mom will let me pick you up after school sometimes, and we can hang out and chat. I don't mind coming out to Malibu." She almost choked on the sentence, but found it was actually true.

Millie looked happier. "That would be awesome. I don't really have anyone to talk to, now."

"Well then," said Nina. "I'll make it happen. We can do it on Thursdays," she added impulsively. "I have nothing planned on Thursdays."

"Really?" said Millie, squeezing her hand.

"Yes, really," said Nina, confidently. "Thursdays can be our night."

today is the day

DATE Saturday 1st June M T W Th F S Su

SCHEDULE

7 > 8
8 > 9
9 > 10
10 > 11
11 > 12
12 > 13
13 > 14 festival
14 > 15
15 > 16
16 > 17
17 > 18
18 > 19
19 > 20
20 > 21 movie?

TO DO LIST

☐ pepto !!
☐
☐
☐
☐
☐
☐
☐
☐
☐

GOALS

Summer festival

NOTES

+ BREAKFAST
coffee

+ LUNCH
sno-cones

+ DINNER
funnel cake !

+ WORKOUT

TWENTY-TWO

In which Nina gets a shock.

The Larchmont Spring Festival was, as you might expect, an annual affair. There was cotton candy and sno-cones, there were hot dogs and burgers, and the scent of burning onions blended beautifully with Los Angeles's signature perfume: sunscreen and money. There were even ponies to ride, though it was hard to reach them through the animal rights protesters complaining that there were ponies to ride.

Knight's was closed for the day, but Nina, Polly, and Liz always went to the Festival and mingled with the punters, as Liz put it.

"It's a community event," she said. "Get out there and commune."

This year, Nina invited Tom to meet her by the carousel and tried not to be filled with childish glee when she saw him. But it was hard; she was a smitten kitten, and she was starting to be OK with that.

He pulled her into a hug and kissed her firmly. Polly, who was tagging along, grinned and demanded a hug, too.

"I've heard a lot about you," she said, but thankfully, didn't elaborate.

"What do you want to do first?" he asked them. "Pony ride? Corn dog on a stick?"

"I want to go in a giant floaty ball," said Polly, confidently.

A major draw for the children of Larchmont was a vast paddling pool of water in which floated maybe a dozen large, clear inflatable balls. You climbed into one, they blew it up around you, and then you rolled yourself into the water and wobbled about and got wet and overheated, and thirty seconds after you realized sunstroke and suffocation were distinct possibilities, your time was up. The kids loved it, but Nina rarely saw adults in there, because, you know, wisdom.

Polly was ready to embrace it, though.

"I think it looks like fun, and every year I want to do it and every year I talk myself out of it, but not this year." She took a breath. "This year I'm going to ignore my inner voice and go for it." She looked defiantly at Nina and Tom, but they just shrugged.

"Honestly, you're overthinking it. Go, be your best self, and get into a smelly ball of plastic," said Nina.

Polly went off to do that, and Nina and Tom wandered over to the sno-cone stand.

"Sno-cones don't really make a lot of sense," said Nina. "They're only ice and sugar water, yet they're deeply pleasing." She sucked on a mouthful of shavings. "They started in Baltimore, you know."

Tom smiled at her. "I didn't know that. What else do you know about the humble sno-cone?"

"Well, they're regionally distinct, of course."

Tom nodded.

"And they became widely popular during the Second World War because all the ice cream was sent to the soldiers."

"It was?" Tom frowned.

"Oh yes," said Nina, warming to her theme. "Ice cream is the frosty treat of choice for the military industrial complex."

Tom stared at her. "You know, I've never met a woman who throws the phrase 'military industrial complex' around with such confidence. It's very sexy."

Nina flicked ice at him. "You should look it up; it's fascinating."

"I'd rather you explained it to me. You're

348

much nicer to look at than Wikipedia."

"Wash out your mouth," she said, and then turned as someone called her name.

"Nina!" It was Millie Reynolds, clutching the hand of her mother, Eliza.

"Hey!" Nina was thrilled and bent down to hug her little sister. "Tom, this is my sister, Millie."

"Is this your boyfriend?" asked the little girl.

"Yes," replied Tom, shooting Nina a sideways glance. "I think it's acceptable to say that, isn't it?"

Nina nodded, feeling unusually relaxed. Maybe it was the sno-cone; maybe it was the sunshine.

"You know, Archie's here somewhere with his little boy, Henry . . ." Millie giggled. "He's my nephew."

"I'll let him know we found you," said Eliza. She smiled at Nina. "Millie told me about your book club. I think it sounds like a good idea. I'll see if I can make it work."

"Great," said Nina. She grinned at Millie, who gave her a quick thumbs-up.

Suddenly, Liz appeared, moving quickly.

"Hide me," she said. "Meffo's here. He's cornering people left and right. He just trapped the toy store owner in front of the funnel cake stand."

Everyone but Nina frowned in confusion, and Nina started looking around for an escape route. She spotted their landlord moving slowly up the street, scanning the crowd left and right like a cop car cruising a shady neighborhood.

She had an idea. "Look, Polly's about to get into a giant inflatable ball. Go take her place." Nina pushed Liz toward the long line to get into the attraction. "Go on!"

Liz scrambled over to where Polly literally had one foot in a ball and rapidly explained the situation. The blower guy was harder to convince, and the line of parents was muttering darkly, but Liz's panic communicated itself, and Polly stepped aside. Liz was launched just in time; Meffo was among them.

"Hi, Nina," he said, smiling politely at everyone. "Is Liz at the Festival? I've been looking for her."

"I don't see her right now," said Nina, which was true.

The landlord sighed. "Can I speak to you privately?" he said, drawing her to one side. "Please tell your boss that time is up. I'm going to rent the store."

Nina frowned. "Surely, we're not that late on the rent, Mr. Meffo?" She'd always kind of assumed the dance about the rent was

350

just one of those things, a normal part of business. Liz certainly never seemed all that worried, not that she discussed business with her. "It's the first of June, I get that, but May just ended yesterday."

Mr. Meffo looked at her curiously. "The rent for May isn't the issue, Nina. It's the rent for last December I'm looking for." He looked sad. "Knight's hasn't made rent in over six months."

Nina stared at him and shook her head. "But we've been busier than usual. I thought . . ."

Meffo shook his head. "I'm sorry, Nina, but the store is barely staying afloat. I have a lot of affection for Knight's, but at a certain point I have to be realistic." He walked away, and Nina watched him, the sounds of the Festival drowned out by the pounding of her own heart. Then she turned and studied her boss paddling around in circles, barely staying afloat herself.

A little while later, Liz, Polly, and Nina sat in the darkened store, talking quietly.

Liz was uncharacteristically somber. "It's true, I'm afraid," she said. "Despite everyone declaring the death of books, business is really good, just not quite good enough." She smiled at her employees. "Your genera-

351

tion is filled with awesome book readers. But the rent has gone up and up and I can't get ahead. I'm sorry. I had to keep the lights on, and I didn't want to fire either of you." She hung her head. "I kept hoping something would turn up."

Polly said, "Maybe Nina will inherit a zillion dollars and she can save the store. Isn't that what happens in movies? Miraculous inheritance?" She looked at Nina. "When is that will reading? It could happen, right?"

Nina shrugged. "It's next week, but I don't know if I inherited anything or, if I did, whether my crazy niece will let me have it without a fight. Mr. Meffo sounded pretty definite." She looked at Liz, not wanting to criticize, but needing to know. "Did you ask the bank for a loan?"

Liz laughed. "Of course, that's how I paid the rent two years ago. Last year I mortgaged my house for a third time, so we were good until December. I tried to find a buyer for my kidneys, but I'm too old."

"You can have one of my kidneys!" said Polly, clearly meaning it. "I only need one, right?"

"Yes," said Nina. "The other kidney gets larger to compensate. In fact . . . ."

"I'm not taking your kidneys or your money," interrupted Liz, firmly. "This is my business, not yours, and it's mine to lose, unfortunately."

"I could do porn! We could buy lotto tickets!" Polly was starting to cry. "I love this job."

Nina was surprised. She knew *she* loved her work, loved the store as the safest place she'd ever been, but she hadn't realized how much it meant to Polly. She thought about the customers, about Jim hanging out in the natural history section, about the reading hour and the bookmarks, and suddenly she was crying, too.

When Nina emerged from the bookstore, she found several members of her new family standing nearby, talking and laughing with Tom. Peter saw her first and came to meet her. Nina was trying to hold it together, but she needed to go home and think about things in peace. The crowd in the street was overwhelming, and the smell of burning sugar was making her head swim.

Peter hugged her tightly. "Hey there, I heard you had to step into work for a bit. Everything OK?"

Nina nodded. "Yeah, it'll be fine." She looked up at him, resplendent in a summer suit. "I didn't even know you were here."

Peter looked shocked. "Miss the Larchmont Festival? Are you mad? Last year there was a near riot over the ponies, as the competing forces of nostalgia and progress went to war over childish ignorant bliss versus animal rights. It was a rich vein, anthropologically speaking." He looked around. "This whole Festival is fieldwork for me, plus I get to eat funnel cake."

Nina leaned over and brushed powdered sugar from his lapel. "You do seem to be entering into the spirit. Powdered sugar is hard to get out of seersucker, though. It gets into the tiny little dimples."

"Ain't that the truth." He lowered his voice. "I like your boyfriend, by the way, very nice."

"He's not my boyfriend," said Nina. "We're just beginning to date."

Peter frowned at her. "He introduced himself as your boyfriend. What's the big whoop?"

Nina nodded, then shook her head. "I don't know, I just . . ." Tom and the others joined them, and she stopped.

"Is everything OK?" asked Tom.

Nina nodded again, unsure of what she was even trying to say, but then Polly ran out of the store, weeping. She came up to them and threw herself on Nina.

"What are we going to do?" she wailed.

"Everything is ruined; it's all going wrong. I'll end up destitute and working in community theater, and what will I do for Christmas presents now?" People passing by slowed down; in common with all actresses, Polly was good at projection.

Nina patted her shoulder awkwardly and looked around at all the surprised faces trying to parse Polly's sorrow and catch up.

"It's all going to be fine," she said. "There's nothing to worry about. Honestly."

"Well, that sounds pretty serious . . ." Peter began, but Nina interrupted him.

"No, it's fine. Polly's just feeling emotional, aren't you, Pol?"

Polly gazed at her with red-rimmed eyes. "Aren't you upset? Don't you care?" She stepped back. "You told me once the store was the only place you ever really felt safe."

Nina felt herself starting to breathe more shallowly, her vision narrowing. She had said that to Polly lightly, of course, but it was true. Embarrassing to have it broadcast to everyone, but still true. "Of course I care, but it's not over yet. Liz will think of something. We'll have a bake sale." She tried to laugh but was finding it hard to catch her breath. She looked at Archie. "I need to go home," she said.

He nodded, seeing from her face what was

going on. "No problem. Let's go," he said, turning to Eliza. "Can you mind Henry for twenty minutes while I get Nina home in one piece? I'll be right back." Eliza nodded and took the toddler, who immediately started crying.

"I can take Nina," said Tom. He stepped forward, but Nina shook her head. He stopped and frowned. "What's the matter?"

"I need to leave right now. I'll text you later, OK?" She was overwhelmed with nausea, starting to lose feeling in her hands.

"I can take you home, Nina." Tom looked almost angrily at Archie.

"It's fine," said Archie, firmly. "We're family."

"Wait . . ." said Nina, her head starting to swim. The bookstore was going to close. She would lose her apartment. Polly was staring at her. Tom was staring at her. There were people all around who needed things from her, who expected things of her, things she almost certainly couldn't give. She reached out blindly, and it was Tom who stepped forward in time to catch her as she crumpled to the ground.

TWENTY-THREE

In which Nina lets herself down.

Nina sat on the floor of the bathroom and laid her head against the side of the bathtub. The back of her neck was sweaty; her palms slipped on the tile floor. She hadn't thrown up, but when Tom had carried her through the door, she'd whispered that he should put her in the bathroom. There was nothing she wanted more than to be alone, but he was moving around in the apartment, doing things. She needed him to leave; she needed to pull her apartment around her shoulders like the cloak of invisibility.

She hated herself. At least today she knew why she was losing her mind; other days her anxiety would suddenly flower inside her, set off by a word. A look. A song on the radio she didn't even remember hearing before. Her anxiety lurked inside like a parasite that occasionally threatened to kill

357

its host; sometimes she could hear it breathing.

Of course, being scared of having a panic attack meant she was permanently on edge, which increased the chance she would have one, so she would berate herself for getting anxious . . . and so it goes, as Vonnegut would say.

She stood and ran cold water on the inside of her wrists, then threw more water on her face and rubbed it with a towel. Time to face the music.

Tom was sitting in her comfy chair, waiting for her. He'd closed the curtains, turned on the little bedside light, made the bed, and turned it down. A cup of tea sat on her bedside table, still steaming a little. It was everything she would have done for herself, and she was touched. She still needed to be alone, but she was touched.

"I didn't know if you wanted tea, but I made it anyway."

Nina nodded. She always felt so drained after an episode like this one, so emotionally hungover, every nerve in her body desperate to shut down and reboot later, when hopefully the storm would have passed.

"Thanks," she said. "I feel better now."

"I can stay," Tom said.

"No, I'm OK."

"But I'm happy to."

"Thanks, but I'm fine. Honestly."

"Are you sure? You can go to bed; I could read to you." He stayed in the chair, even though he wanted very badly to go to her, to put his arms around her and hold her until she relaxed. As it was, she was standing in the bathroom doorway slightly crouched, looking wary and pale.

Nina smiled despite the twist in her gut. He didn't get it. "That's nice of you, but I need to sleep."

He frowned. "So go to sleep. I won't wake you up. I just want to make sure you're OK."

Nina took a breath, praying the panic would stay away for a few seconds more. "Please leave, Tom. I need you to go away."

It hung in the air, the simple request.

He was confused. "I really like you, Nina. I care about you."

"Tom, this isn't about you. This is about me. I get anxiety; I told you. When I get overwhelmed like this, I need to be left alone to recover."

"I want to help."

Nina started to get a little ticked off. "Tom, you're not listening to me. In order to feel better, I need to be alone. For as long as possible."

He looked at her. "Like . . ."

Nina decided to risk leaving the bathroom doorway. She sat on the edge of her bed and picked up her tea. It was good, sweet and hot.

"Thank you for all this, for bringing me home and making the tea and everything."

Tom crossed his legs. "You're not answering my question."

Nina was exhausted. "Which was?"

"How long do you need to be alone?"

Nina couldn't sit anymore; she lay down and pulled the quilt over herself and closed her eyes. "Can I call you in a week or so? It's all too much; the family, and now work is terrible . . . I need a few days to think and sort it all out."

His voice was clear. "You're not sure if I fit into your life right now?"

Nina shook her head, unable to find the right words.

She must have drifted off, because when she opened her eyes again, he was gone and Phil was sitting in the chair instead.

"Rough day?" asked the cat.

"Terrible," she replied.

"I can catch you a mouse if you like," he offered. "Protein is good for you."

"I'm good," she said, closing her eyes again.

The cat watched her face and yawned.

"Liar," he said.

Much later, Nina woke again and lay there in the dark for a while, trying to sort out the inside of her own head. She reached for her phone and dialed a familiar number.

"Hey, Lou."

Her nanny's sleepy voice answered, "Hey, you." Their traditional greeting, a rhyming couplet that always made Nina feel loved.

Louise murmured, "It's late, baby. What's going on?"

Nina looked at the time. "Sorry."

"Doesn't matter. You all right?"

"Not really."

Nina heard a sigh, then a rustle of sheets. "Hold on, let me wake up properly, get myself some tea, and call you back. Gimme five."

"Thanks."

Nina sat up and rubbed her face. She piled her pillow behind her head and scratched the sheet until Phil stretched and made his way up to her side. He curled around her hand and kicked her with his bunny back feet. The phone rang.

Louise's voice was much clearer. Nina

could imagine her soft gray hair, her lined but still lovely face. Her yellow mug of tea. "OK, baby, let me have it."

Nina took a deep breath. "Well, the first piece of news is that I have a dad."

Louise said nothing for a moment. Then, "Well, I never reckoned your mom was the Virgin Mary type, so that makes sense."

"She never said anything about him to you?"

"She never said. I never asked."

"Oh. Well, he's dead."

Louise laughed. "Easy come, easy go. You found this out when?"

"A month ago, maybe. Something like that. I have a brother and three sisters and nieces and nephews and cousins."

"Well, shoot," said Louise. "That might have been nice to know. Just think of all the birthday presents you could have got." Nina smiled. Louise continued, "But you must be freaking out. All those people."

"Yeah, though they're mostly really nice."

"Great." Louise waited. "So . . . ?"

"There's something else. I met this guy."

A low laugh. "I knew there was a guy in here somewhere."

Nina started babbling. "And I really like him but it's too much. There's problems at work, then there's all these new people I need to get used to, so I sort of broke up with the guy, I mean, not really broke up, but kind of, and that's fine, but he was really wonderful so maybe I should have . . ." Her voice faltered. "I don't know. It used to work to close it all off, but it's not working so well anymore."

Louise sighed, and Nina heard her take a long sip of tea. She waited.

"Well, honey, you can't expect the same tricks to work your whole life. When you were little and things got to be too much, you'd put your hands over your ears and sing, but if you do that now you'd get some funny looks, plus you'd know that when you dropped your hands the problem would still be there. Magical thinking only works for children. And politicians, maybe."

Nina's voice was small. "So what do I do?"

"I don't know, baby. The first thing you should always do is . . ." Louise waited.

"Nothing. The first thing you should always do is nothing." Nina supplied the answer Louise had often provided over the years.

"That's right. Wait a day or two and see what happens. Life needs space, just like you. Give it room." The older woman paused. "How's your anxiety?"

Nina shrugged, not that Louise could see

her. "Bad."

"It's only doing its job, poor, overenthusiastic thing. I still remember what that therapist said: Anxiety is what kept us alive, back in the day. It helps us know when things are wrong, when situations are dangerous or people mean us harm. It's just sometimes it gets ahead of itself, right?"

Nina nodded. "I know."

"So, do nothing, let yourself calm down, take some deep breaths, and wait. Your anxiety will pass; things will get clearer. If this guy is meant to happen, he'll happen."

"What if he can't handle my anxiety?"

Louise sounded firm. "His loss."

"He doesn't make me feel anxious. He makes me feel good, actually."

Louise laughed. "Then don't borrow trouble from tomorrow, baby. Don't worry about how it might go wrong; just let yourself be happy."

"Easier said than done."

"Most things are."

"Does everyone else feel like this?"

"Like what? Worried? Uncertain? Hopeful and cynical at the same time?"

"Yeah."

"Sure they do, baby. That's how it feels to be alive."

"It's not a good feeling."

"Well, who knows what a fish feels; it might be even worse."

"And definitely wetter."

"Right." Louise's voice was soft. "Get some sleep now, and call me tomorrow. You like being on your own, Nina, but you've never been alone. You know that, right?"

Nina nodded, holding the phone tightly. "I know. I love you."

"I love you more. Kiss Phil for me. We'll talk tomorrow."

"Bye, Lou."

"Bye, you."

today *is the day*

DATE Monday 3rd June   M T W Th F S Su
                                  ○ ○ ○ ○ ○ ○ ○

SCHEDULE

7 > 8	
8 > 9	
9 > 10	
10 > 11	work
11 > 12	
12 > 13	
13 > 14	
14 > 15	
15 > 16	
16 > 17	
17 > 18	
18 > 19	yoga
19 > 20	
20 > 21	

TO DO LIST

- ☐ Sort laundry
- ☐ clean bookshelves
- ☐ wash towels
- ☐ clean kitchen
- ☐ clean bathroom
- ☐ 2 minute plank!
- ☐ 50 x sit ups
- ☐
- ☐
- ☐

GOALS

Drink water
Get in shape
Find Therapist
Be productive

NOTES

new shower curtain

Hand weights

BREAKFAST
Eggs

LUNCH
Salad

DINNER
Salad

WORKOUT
at home

TWENTY-FOUR

In which Nina becomes an object of pity.

It's hard to keep a secret in Larchmont. After Polly's outburst at the Festival, it took approximately three hours for every single person in a ten-block radius to know that Knight's was in danger of shutting down. Someone started crowdfunding. Someone else posted on social media that the forces of evil were triumphing and that the existence of literacy was under attack. Someone else made soup for Liz, and on Monday morning brought it to the store.

Liz was disgusted by this outpouring of support.

"It's just a bookstore," she said, having spent twenty minutes calming down the soup-giver, who'd been coming to the store for a decade and considered it central to her children's middle-class experience. "I mean, it's adorable, and I'm always glad to take free food, but all we need is more people to buy more books."

Nina looked at her. "I think we need more than that, don't we? We need to pay six months of back rent, un-triple-mortgage your house, and buy back the kidney Polly already sold on Craigslist."

Liz made a face. "She only sold the promise of a kidney. I think she may have discovered a new financial vehicle, actually. If I had early-stage kidney disease, I might be open to taking out a rent-to-buy option on someone else's organ."

"Organ sale is illegal in the United States, although it is legal in Iran."

Liz snorted. "Of course you know that."

Nina shrugged. "I'm shocked you don't."

Polly had called earlier to say she was going on a job hunt in the Valley, which Nina and Liz took to mean scouting for a porn job. They talked her out of that, and she appeared a little before lunch, dressed head to toe in black.

"Did someone die, or are you auditioning for a role as an elderly Italian grandmother?" asked Liz.

"I'm in mourning for the store," said Polly, bowing her head, although probably just to show off the elaborate French braid she had going on. She had incorporated black ribbon, and Nina was reminded of the horses that pull hearses at state funerals. This may not have been what Polly was going for, but that's the law of unintended consequences for you.

Liz snorted. "Get to work, you two. Make the books look pretty. Smile, but look pitiful. When people ask if we're closing, shake your head softly and suggest they buy a boxed set."

"You want us to prey upon the pity of our customers?"

"Yes. Exactly that."

Liz disappeared into her office and reappeared a moment later shrugging on a jacket.

"Where are you going?"

Liz headed for the door. "I'm going to go home and change into something a little more ragged."

Over the next few days, business did pick up quite a lot, particularly as several local celebrities posted on social media and people showed up hoping to see them in the store. Failing that, they bought books and took selfies. Nina didn't think it would be enough, but it was nice to be busy. It helped distract her from the deafening silence from Tom.

She had texted him a day or two after the Festival, just to say hi, she hoped he was OK, she was feeling better, and had he seen that the final for the Quiz Bowl had been scheduled . . . ? Bupkes. Sound of crickets. She couldn't blame him; she'd been pretty specific that she wanted to be left alone, and she could hardly complain he was taking her at her word. But she missed him.

Polly had calmed down and was accenting her black with the occasional pop of color. She'd also been auditioning a ton and was waiting to hear back from a national commercial for flea prevention (for once, she wasn't up for either the part of the cat or the flea, so this was progress) and a web series about a young woman taken over by the spirit of an old Jewish guy called Morty (the series was called *Mortyfied,* and probably shouldn't have made it past the stoner joke it had clearly once been). Liz had been uncharacteristically quiet and spent most of her time in the back room, clearing out papers.

On the Saturday morning after the Festival, Nina did something she rarely did: She headed west. There was so little traffic in the early morning that she was in Malibu before ten, and as she rounded a corner and saw the ocean for the first time, even she could feel her spirits lift.

Eliza and Millie lived in one of those houses that didn't seem all that impressive from the front but that kept going once you were inside. Rooms opened up, hallways turned corners, and eventually Millie led Nina to her room at the top of the house.

"Nice view," said Nina, somewhat unnecessarily. The bedroom had one glass wall, and the floor-to-ceiling view was of the Pacific Ocean across a canyon dotted with olive trees and native California oaks.

"Yeah," said Millie, clearly over it. "It's pretty."

Then Nina turned from the view and realized the entire back wall of the room was filled with shelves. It was like walking into a smaller version of her apartment; the same organization, the same careful lining up of spines. In many cases, the same books, just less heavily read.

"That's an even better view," she said, walking over and tilting her head to read titles. "Le Guin, excellent; Susan Cooper, yes; Ruth Plumly Thompson, nice . . ."

"I've read all of them," said Millie. "The ones I haven't read yet are by the bed." She looked rueful. "Mom made a rule that I can only have six 'to be read' books at one time, otherwise she says it gets out of hand."

"Six is a good number. And presumably once you've read one you can get another?"

Millie nodded. "Is that how you do it? Six at a time?"

"Basically." Nina nodded back, although she meant shelves, rather than individual books. "Do you read books in order?"

"Yes, if there is an order. If there isn't an order, I read them in the order of publication." The child paused. "Sometimes, of course, the first one I read isn't the first one they wrote, and then I feel a bit bad."

Nina laughed. "I've met lots of authors at the bookstore, and I've never met one who cares which book of theirs you read first. They're just glad you read one."

"Really?"

"Definitely."

"Do you have a favorite book?" Millie plonked herself down on the rug. There was a beanbag that had seen a lot of leaning, and a floppy rabbit that had seen a lot of coreading. Nina suddenly thought of Lili's daughter Clare, and her dog. Maybe reading alongside someone was more comforting than she'd considered. She thought of her mom, who'd never read with her, and of Lou, who'd read with her every night. She thought of Tom. She stopped thinking.

"I have lots of favorite books, because I have lots of moods and I have a favorite book for every mood."

"What do you like when you're happy?"

"I like the Jeeves and Wooster books, by P. G. Wodehouse. Jeeves is a valet, and he works for this guy who's an idiot. They're funny."

"What about when you're sad?"

"It depends if I want to stay sad or cheer myself up."

"Cheer up."

"Mysteries. Everything always works out."

"My dad liked mysteries, too," Millie said.

Nina sat down next to Millie and pulled over a pillow for her elbows. "Really?"

Millie shrugged. "Yeah. But he liked all kinds of books." She paused, then got to her feet. "Come on, I'll show you his library."

Millie's room was one half of the upper story of the house; the other, right next door, was her father's library. Or office. Or something. Again with the shelves, and a comfy chair overlooking the ocean that was almost more impressive than Nina's.

Unlike Nina's, these shelves were not organized.

"I was always asking if I could at least put them in alphabetical order," said Millie, almost apologetically, as Nina made her way along the books. "But he said he liked to drift along like a cloud and pick something that leaped out at him."

"Hopefully not literally."

Millie giggled. "Yeah, and he didn't really look like a cloud, but that was what he always said."

It was an extraordinary mix. Austen was there, as was Trollope, and Dickens, and Stephen King, and S. J. Perelman. Dorothy Parker squeezed up next to Joan Didion, and Chinua Achebe made room for John Grisham. Lots of mysteries, and so-called popular fiction, and nonfiction on topics ranging from mountaineering to working at Denny's. Many she had read; others she hadn't. She thought of her own shelves and what the titles might tell someone about her, realizing that she now knew more about her late father than she might ever have known, even if she'd met him.

Millie was watching her. "He loved books, like we do."

Nina nodded.

"You would have liked him."

Nina ran her fingers along the spines of her father's books, pausing at a well-worn copy of *The Human Comedy*, by Saroyan.

She smiled. "Well, I like his books, which

is essentially the same thing."

Millie hugged her, suddenly, and Nina hugged her back.

"I miss my dad all the time," said the little girl, her voice muffled in Nina's sweater. "But I'm glad I got to find you."

"Me too," said Nina. "Very glad."

Later, after lunch, Millie wandered off to work on some project involving a tree, a plastic rabbit, and a dollhouse chandelier, and Nina found herself alone with Eliza. She swallowed and asked the question she'd been dying to ask.

"Did you know about me? Before, I mean?" She pushed her hair behind her ears, nervously.

Eliza looked surprised and a little sad. "No, I didn't. If I had, we would have met years ago." She drank some water and moved the glass around on the tabletop, making lines of half circles like the tracks of a snake across sand. "It was a shock, because I thought William told me everything."

Nina looked at her. "Everyone describes him so differently." She paused, unsure. "He was one guy, but there's no consensus about what he was like. For Peter's mom, he was a blowhard who drank too much; for Millie, he was the kindest man in the world who made endless time for her."

Eliza shrugged. "People change. There's forty years between the William that Peter's mom knew and the William that Millie knew. Parents get stuck in the amber of childhood, right? Whenever my parents visit, I feel myself becoming a cranky fourteen-year-old. I saw William through the lens of being his wife; I look at Millie only as her mother . . . You see what I mean?"

"Sure. So I'll never see my dad properly, only through the filter of other people's opinions."

"Or maybe it'll average out and you'll be the only one who sees the real him."

Nina laughed. "Maybe there is no real thing for anyone. Maybe all of us change depending on where we are and who we're with."

"And that's why you like to be alone." Eliza looked at her and smiled.

"How do you mean?"

"Because you prefer who you are when you're alone."

Nina shrugged. "It takes a lot of energy to be with other people. It's easier to be myself when there's no one else there."

"Some people take energy; some people give energy . . . Occasionally, you get lucky and find someone whose energy balances your own and brings you into neutral." She paused. "My God, I've been in Malibu too long. I said that completely without irony."

Nina laughed. "It was really convincing. I think I even heard a tiny temple bell ringing somewhere . . ."

Eliza made a face at herself. "Your dad used to say being with me was as good as being alone." Eliza laughed. "I think he meant it as a compliment." The two women looked at each other. "I think we're over-thinking this," said Eliza. "More wine?"

today is the day

DATE Monday June 10th

M T W Th F S Su

◊ ◊ ◊ ◊ ◊ ◊ ◊

SCHEDULE

7 > 8	
8 > 9	
9 > 10	Will reading
10 > 11	
11 > 12	
12 > 13	
13 > 14	
14 > 15	work
15 > 16	
16 > 17	
17 > 18	
18 > 19	
19 > 20	
20 > 21	

TO DO LIST

- ☐ bread
- ☐ jelly
- ☐ peanut butter
- ☐ cotton wool
- ☐ mascara
- ☐ raisins
- ☐ broccoli
- ☐ fritos
- ☐
- ☐
- ☐

GOALS

Big
fat
zero

NOTES

Other bookstores?
Back to school?

＋ BREAKFAST

＋ LUNCH

＋ DINNER

＋ WORKOUT

TWENTY-FIVE

In which the will is read, and is surprising.

The following Monday, it was finally time for William Reynolds's will to be read. Nina pushed open the heavy glass doors of Sarkassian's office and saw that the same beautiful receptionist was behind the desk. The woman looked up and smiled.

"Good morning, Miss Hill. The rest of the family is here already. I'll show you to the conference room." She didn't mention the 'well played, madam' from the last time, and it was, of course, possible she didn't even remember it. Nina remembered it, and often thought about it late at night, but let's assume the best, shall we?

"They're here?"

The woman nodded, gesturing to Nina to fall in alongside her. "The meeting began at nine thirty."

Nina shook her head. "No, ten."

"No, it was nine thirty."

"Are you sure?"

The woman shot her a glance, and Nina could literally see her remembering their previous interaction and adjusting her tone. "Yes, I'm sure. I put out the bagels."

"Right." Nina sighed. Maybe this woman and she could once have become friends, but now Nina was permanently cemented in the other woman's mind as a total weirdo and tardy to boot. Plus the cinnamon raisin bagels were probably gone already.

As they approached the conference room, Nina could hear raised voices, but the receptionist never broke stride. Maybe there were frequent full-out brawls in this office. Nina suddenly got an image of the conference room doors flying open and fifteen cowboys tumbling out, saloon doors swinging and spurs jingling. She smiled to herself; it was probably too much to hope for that Sarkassian would be inside with a bright red corset on and yellow feathers in his hair. She'd always wondered how saloon madams in the movies kept their silken outfits so clean when there were always clouds of dust and tumbleweeds blowing about. There were no washing machines, no dry cleaners. It had always bothered her, but then again, so much did.

She and the receptionist did a weirdly awkward thing where she reached for the door handle and so did the receptionist and then they both pulled back to let the other one do it and then both reached forward again, until Nina put her hands up in surrender and the other woman made a noise of triumph and opened the door.

Nina stepped in, and the noise immediately stopped as everyone turned to look at her. No feathers in sight, sadly, although of course Sarkassian could have been wearing anything at all under his suit.

"Good morning, Nina," said the lawyer.

"Good morning," she replied, pulling out the nearest chair and sitting down. Crap, she'd sat directly opposite Lydia again. *Seriously, Nina, take five seconds to look around for sufficient cover next time.*

"Please continue," said Nina, politely. She'd decided on a strategy on the way over: silence, broken only by monosyllabic words and small smiles. No emotions, no drama, nothing to see. She was going to get out of this room alive and cherry-pick the nice relatives and never see the rest of them ever again. She was totally calm and in control.

Lydia leaned forward. "Hello, you money-grubbing millennial pretender."

So much for that plan. "Hello, you crazy,

mercenary sea cow," she replied. Sorry, but you can't call someone a pretender without expecting resistance. She wasn't quite sure where the sea cow part had come from.

"Mercenary?" Lydia snorted. The sea cow insult either didn't register or she didn't care. "There's nothing mercenary about getting one's fair share." She pointed her stubby finger at Nina. "You never even met my grandfather, so any share you get is completely unfair."

Sarkassian cleared his throat. "I'm sorry, Lydia, but you're wrong. William chose to leave his estate in his own way, and we have to abide by his choices. Family relationships don't come into it. He could have left everything to a dog shelter, and there would be nothing you could do about it."

Eliza laughed. "Besides, I don't know what other family she could be part of. She loves books and being left alone, which is one hundred percent like her dad and, I might add, her youngest sister, Millie." She smiled at Nina. "She's very happy you two are becoming friends."

Nina smiled back, touched.

Archie added, "Nina's smart and sarcastic. But at the same time anxious and socially awkward. Quite a lot like me. Plus, of course, the hair."

Peter said, "She's open-minded and well read." He shrugged. "Not to toot my own horn, but . . ."

"And she's obsessed with facts and trivia, which, I'll be blunt, Lydia, is like you." Sarkassian leaned back in his chair. "In fact, she's a lot like all of you, and whether that's genetics or coincidence is kind of irrelevant, but there it is."

Lydia said nothing but fumed.

"So, if no one has any further objections, I think it's time to go ahead and read the will." Sarkassian looked slowly around at everyone over his glasses, but no one spoke. Enjoying the moment, he opened a folder and withdrew a long legal document and cleared his throat.

"William Reynolds was a wealthy man, as you all know, and the estate amounts to a little over forty million dollars in stocks and cash, the house in Malibu, an apartment downtown, and the vacation homes in Mammoth and Palm Springs."

"Holy moly," said Nina.

"Oh, like you didn't know," snapped Lydia.

Sarkassian continued. "Twenty million dollars is to be immediately divided between his four legitimate children, with the adult children receiving their money now and

384

Millie's share being held in trust. His grandchildren each receive a million dollars. Eliza keeps the remaining money, plus all the properties."

He stopped. Everyone looked at Nina, who was looking at the lawyer.

"Nina gets nothing?" asked Peter, clearly surprised.

Lydia laughed. "That is perfect. I guess Grandpa had more brain cells left than I thought."

"No, no, William wrote a very specific section for Nina." The lawyer turned over a page and began reading.

"To my daughter Nina, who has remained unacknowledged by me until now, I leave the contents of the garage at 2224 Cahuenga Boulevard." There was muttering around the table, but when Nina looked at everyone, they didn't appear mad, although Lydia was frowning.

"What's in the garage?" Nina asked. She got a flash of that show where people bid for the unseen contents of a storage container. What was she getting? Several broken table lamps and a stamp album? A severed head in a big glass jar? Nina realized that was from a movie and started trying to place it.

Sarkassian looked slightly embarrassed.

"Well, William was an unusual man, given to somewhat romantic gestures and ideas."

"The garage is full of chocolate?" Nina was totally down for that. "Champagne?"

"No."

"Roses?"

"No."

Nina had a sudden insane surge of hope. "Kittens?" She did realize that wouldn't work; she just always hoped for kittens.

The lawyer coughed. "No. The garage contains a 1982 Pontiac Trans Am."

Nina stared at him blankly, then a fact popped into her head. "Wait, like from *Knight Rider*?"

"Exactly like. A black Pontiac Firebird Trans Am."

"He left me K.I.T.T.?" Nina immediately flashed back to many happy evenings lying on the floor in front of the TV, listening to Louise murmuring about David Hasselhoff's leather pants. "Did he think I was *a lone crusader in a dangerous world*?"

"Good Lord." Lydia's tone was incredulous. "He left you a car?"

"You can have it if you want. I don't want it." Nina really didn't. She didn't care about cars; she barely drove. The movie with the head in a jar was *The Silence of the Lambs,* by the way; it had come back to her.

Lydia shook her head. She was clearly bothered. "An intelligent car is so much more fun than money."

Nina looked at her. "It's not really an intelligent car. It's just a car." She turned to Sarkassian. "Unless it comes with an actual com-link wristwatch thingy, in which case I am totally keeping it."

"I know that," said Lydia, her voice scornful. "But he only left the rest of us money."

There was a pause.

"Maybe he thought you only cared about his money," said Eliza, quietly.

"Well, he would have been wrong. But seeing as he never asked me anything at all about my life, how would he know?" Lydia looked around. "None of you ever ask me anything."

After another awkward silence, Sarkassian coughed and said, "Well, whether Nina takes the car or not, the will makes it quite clear that she has to go drive it at least once before she chooses to sell it or give it away."

Nina frowned at him. "What kind of legal provision is that? What is this, *Brewster's Millions*?"

Clearly, the lawyer had never enjoyed that brand of Hollywood madcap legal comedy, because he looked at her with a tiny wrinkle between his eyebrows. "I don't know what that means. I have the keys here. Please be nice to the mechanic who's been taking excellent care of it for the last twenty years. When I told him about the will, he hoped you would be impossible to find." He slid the keys across the table, and Nina suddenly had a terrible thought.

"I can't drive stick."

He raised his eyebrows, smoothing out that pesky wrinkle. "Well, here's your chance to learn."

As Nina sat in the Lyft heading back home, she checked her phone. Nothing. Impulsively, she sent Tom a text.

"Hi there, I just inherited a car."

No response. Maybe he was working.

"It's a 1982 Pontiac Firebird. Like K.I.T.T. from *Knight Rider*."

Still nothing. Maybe he was busy.

"It doesn't have William Daniels's voice, though, so, you know . . ."

Silence. Maybe he was with someone else.

She looked out of the window, noticing all the couples walking along, holding hands, smiling at each other, or even simply sitting across from each other looking at their phones. She'd always loved the feeling of being separate, of being alone while everyone else clumped together like mold on the inside rim of an old coffee cup. But now she felt lonely.

She leaned forward. "Hey, can I change our destination?"

The driver met her eyes in the mirror. "Sure, but you have to do it in the app."

"I can't tell you? You know, verbally?"

He shook his head. "Well, sure, you can tell me, verbally, or in sign language, or on a piece of parchment carried by a pigeon, but for me to alter my course, you also have to change it in the app." He shrugged, his eyes back on the road. "Despite the fact we're a scant two feet apart, our relationship requires the intermediation of a computer system housed in a server farm neither of us will ever see. Thus technology further separates us, eroding our trust in one another and leading our species down a path to a future where we only know one another on a screen and can only talk to one another in characters, and where ideas are owned by companies run by algorithms."

Nina gazed at the back of his head for a moment.

"So . . . on the app then?"

"Yup."

TWENTY-SIX

In which Nina meets a legendary
Pokémon in human form.

The garage on Cahuenga was part of a larger mechanic's business, with classic car restoration clearly a specialty. There were several old cars parked outside, including a Mercedes, which was the only hood ornament Nina recognized. She was pretty impressed she even remembered they were called hood ornaments, honestly. Cars all looked more or less the same to her, though she sorted them into broad categories like "fancy" and "regular" or "in her way" or "going too fast in a residential neighborhood." They all looked the same from the driver's seat, she reasoned, unless you care about how the people outside the car are looking at you.

The mechanic was an older guy, maybe in his late fifties. Nina couldn't tell; he was covered in a patina of wrinkles and oil that blurred the edges. She'd tracked him down in his "office," which appeared to be the car mechanic's version of the back room at Knight's. Where they had piles of books, this guy had piles of manuals and little bits and pieces of machines that Nina didn't recognize. She had introduced herself, and the temperature had gotten noticeably chillier. She felt bad for the topless garage mechanic — well, she was holding a wrench — on the calendar behind him.

"Oh, you're the new owner?" He looked her over and clearly wasn't happy. "Do you drive a lot?"

"Hardly ever."

"Do you know cars?"

"I know they have wheels."

"Do you understand the inherent beauty of a well-machined engine, the throaty purr of a finely tuned timing?"

Nina frowned at him. "I understand that throaty purr is a cliché, but other than that, no. Look, Mr. . . ."

"Moltres."

She looked at him. "Moltres?"

"Yes. Moltres. M-o-l-t-r-e-s."

"Did you know your name is also the name of a legendary Pokémon?" As was so often the case, Nina immediately regretted saying this. Either he already knew, in which case, duh, or he would have no idea what she was talking about and would consider her possibly dangerous. There should be some kind of twelve-step program for people like her, she thought; Non Sequitur's Anonymous. Then she wondered if maybe that was actually what NSA stood for; they didn't care about national security at all. Then she realized it hadn't, strictly speaking, been a non sequitur, it had just been a stupid question, and that her twelve-step program would more appropriately be named Stupid People Anonymous and that it would be a pretty big group and have the acronym SPA. Then she realized Moltres was still talking to her.

He spoke slowly. "Are you here to take the car?" This didn't help, because now Nina couldn't tell if he did know about the whole Pokémon thing or not, although he clearly realized she needed careful handling.

She shook her head. "No, if that's OK. Do you need me to get it out of here quickly? Is the bill for the garaging . . . ?"

Moltres interrupted her quickly. "The bill is paid through the year, actually. Bill was like that, always paid up front. 'In case I'm hit by a bus,' he used to say." Then he looked annoyed, which might have been his way of showing embarrassment. "Do you want to see it?"

Nina followed him out and through some twisty and utterly filthy corridors until they came to a surprisingly large space out back, where there were several garages with locked doors. He opened the middle one, and there she was: Nina's car.

Nina turned to Moltres. "Did you know that David Hasselhoff holds a Guinness World Record as the most watched man on TV?"

He gazed at her. "No," he said.

"Yes," she continued. "He was already successful from being on a soap opera, but *Knight Rider* was really the beginning for him."

"Is that so?" said Moltres. "How completely uninteresting."

Moltres walked around and opened the driver's side door. "Want to take it out?"

Nina shook her head. "Uh . . . I can't drive stick."

He was disappointed in her already, and that didn't help. Nina realized it was like admitting you can't swim or ride a bike; not really disastrous, just one of those life skills one is supposed to have acquired by nearly thirty. Oh well, she thought, for the record I can both swim *and* ride a bike, so two out of three isn't bad. She could also knit and crochet, so after the apocalypse, he'd be able to drive a manual transmission but she'd have a scarf, so who'd be laughing come winter?

Moltres sat in the driver's seat and turned on the engine. It was loud, really very loud, and Nina could see how *throaty purr* had come into play. She guessed Moltres was willing to drive. She went around and got into the passenger side, and they slowly pulled out of the garage.

Moltres, unsurprisingly, turned out to be not exactly a Chatty Cathy. He did, however, have some questions.

"Your dad never taught you to drive stick?"

"I never met my dad."

Moltres looked over at her, quickly. "Really? And yet he left you his favorite thing?"

"I thought his favorite thing was money."

Moltres shook his head. "No."

Nina shrugged. "Is it that rare not to know how to drive a stick? Aren't the vast majority of cars in this country automatics?"

Moltres shrugged, weaving around a small fender bender in the middle of the intersection. Nina looked at it, as everyone does.

She could tell an experienced LA driver by the speed with which she pulled out her license and proof of insurance, took photos of the mutual damage, if any, and got on her way. Soon, she thought, all you'll have to do is wave your phones at each other, and a drone will appear to photograph everything before the lights have changed. You won't even need to get out of your car, which, by that point, you probably won't even be driving. Then she realized Moltres had asked her something.

"I'm sorry, I didn't hear the question . . ."

He rolled his eyes. "I asked why you didn't know your father."

She looked at him. "Really? You jumped straight from criticizing my driving knowledge to asking me personal questions about my family?"

His mouth twitched. "You're a fascinating mix of spacey and sassy. You totally aren't paying attention and then you whip around and let out a zinger."

"Well, you're very nosy."

He sighed. "Look, I knew your dad for over twenty years. He never mentioned you once. No offense."

"None taken. I never mentioned him, either. Mind you, he knew I existed, and I didn't have that advantage so, you know, reasonable excuse." Nina looked at Moltres. "What did he talk about?"

"Cars," Moltres said. "Always cars." He swung the car around a corner, which it hugged like a long-lost friend. "He was good company." He shot a glance at Nina. "Sorry."

Nina looked at him, then out of the window. "What for?" she said. "It's not like my life would have been better if I'd had more car-related conversation."

Moltres said, "But maybe he would have taught you to drive stick."

"Or maybe he would have deserted me like he did his other kids. I'm the only one he didn't leave, because he was never there in the first place." She looked for a button to lower the window. "Honestly, I think I may have dodged a bullet."

Moltres shook his head as they headed up Laurel Canyon toward the winding roads at the top of the Hollywood Hills. "He was a good guy, Bill was. I'll miss him."

"Story of his life," Nina said, leaning out and letting the wind toss her hair.

Moltres was silent for a while, then abruptly turned left and pulled into a wide-open parking lot that was essentially empty. He stopped the car and turned to Nina.

"I'm going to teach you to drive stick."

■ ■ ■ ■

Moltres began the lesson by introducing Nina to her newest little friend, the clutch pedal.

"Do you understand how a car engine works?"

"Yes and no," replied Nina, who was nervously sitting in the driver's seat. "You press the pedals and the wheels go around."

Moltres sighed. "The power of the engine is transferred to the wheels through the transmission. In order to change gear without tearing apart the transmission, the clutch momentarily disengages it."

"Fascinating," said Nina. Nervousness was making her mean.

Moltres ignored her. "Turn on the car."

She did so.

"There are three pedals underneath your feet: clutch on the left, brake in the middle, accelerator on the right. In order to move in a nonautomatic, you increase the power to the transmission while slowly releasing the clutch to engage the wheels. Get it?"

Nina nodded, not getting it at all.

"As you slowly release the clutch while at the same time pressing on the gas pedal, there comes a point where the car moves, slightly. It's called the biting point, and we're going to practice it now."

Nina looked at him and raised her eyebrows.

"Increase the gas too quickly and you flood the engine and stall the car. Let's go."

She did as he told her, and flooded the engine.

They waited in silence for a moment. Then Moltres said, "So, what do you do for work?"

Nina had put her head down on the steering wheel. "I work in a bookstore."

"Yeah?" said Moltres, interested. "I love reading. I'm a mystery buff."

"You are?" Nina wasn't sure why she sounded surprised. Mystery readers were everywhere, voracious, highly partisan, and passionate. They were among the store's best customers, and unfailingly polite. In private they embraced a bloodthirsty desire for vengeance and the use of arcane poisons and sneaky sleuthing, but in public they were charming and generous. Romance readers tended to be fun and have strong opinions. Nonfiction readers asked a lot of questions and were easily amused. It was the serious novel folks and poetry fans you had to watch out for.

Moltres nodded. "Yeah, since I was a kid.

They're modern fairy tales, right? Good always triumphs over evil."

"Mostly. There are exceptions."

"Sure, but I'm old fashioned. I don't love the newer, edgier, meaner ones, anyway. Your dad and I used to talk about books when we weren't talking about cars."

"Really?" Why was her voice so squeaky?

"Yeah. His favorite thing to do was drive up the coast and find some deserted beach where he could sit and read in peace." He looked at her, patiently. "Now try the car again."

Nina turned the key in the ignition. She went very slowly, and sure enough, there was a moment when she felt the car move under her. She kept working the pedals, and suddenly they moved forward, whereupon she immediately hit the brake without disengaging the clutch and stalled the car again.

"Dammit. This is hard."

Moltres nodded. "You can see why the automatic gearbox took off."

"Why would anyone choose to drive stick?"

"It's more fun," he answered. "You have to concentrate more, pay more attention. You have to work with the engine. Easier isn't always better."

Nina turned the key again, and this time when the car moved she controlled herself and managed to drive forward without incident. "Now, how do I change gears?"

Moltres's voice was calm. "You do the same thing again. Put pressure on the gas until you hear the engine is ready to change up."

"I don't hear it." Nina's voice was less calm.

"Stop the car," Moltres said. "Let's try something else. Don't forget to disengage the clutch when you brake."

Nina managed to stop the car without stalling, and put it in park.

"Let's swap places," Moltres said. He went around the front, Nina went around the back, and then they were looking at each other from the other direction.

Moltres said, "I need you to focus. I'm going to talk you through what I'm doing, and you're going to learn how it sounds." Nina nodded. "Listen, I'm putting it in gear, the clutch is off, I'm adding gas" — the engine note changed — "and now it's in gear and we're moving. More gas, more speed, and can you hear that the engine is starting to work too hard?"

Nina could, kind of. "It sounds too loud. Is that what you mean?"

"If that's all you've got, go with that. Anyway, here I go, disengaging the clutch, changing the gear, reengaging the clutch, second gear."

The engine sounded happier. They sped up again, making swoops across the parking lot. "And now again, second to third. Clutch out, change gear, clutch in, third gear."

Two hours later Nina cracked it.

Three hours later Moltres handed her the keys, declared himself satisfied, and let her drive away. "Keep it for a few days," he said, "then bring it back and I'll fix whatever you broke."

Four hours, two stalls, and much circling later, she found a parking space and remembered why she didn't own a car in Los Angeles.

Back-and-forthing in the space was nerve racking, and Nina kept having to slam the brakes to avoid hitting the car behind her. After one particularly hard brake, the glove box of the car flew open and a pile of envelopes and papers slid out onto the passenger seat and floor.

Nina turned off the car and reached over to pick it all up. She saw her name, then saw *Becky, Katherine, Archie, Millie, Lydia, Peter* . . . There were lots of yellow envelopes, the kind with little metal butterflies on the flap, each addressed to one of William's kids or grandchildren.

Nina frowned; this couldn't possibly be good. She found hers and opened it, still sitting in the car, the engine ticking as it cooled. There was a folded piece of paper, and a very '80s-looking bankbook, with *My First Savings Account* written on it in gold, with an actual rainbow unicorn. Banking used to be so much cuter. She opened it up and goggled at the balance. Over two and a half million dollars. Doubtless there was some mistake. She turned to the letter.

Dear Nina,
I'm going to open this letter in the classic way: If you're reading this, I'm already dead.

Nina made a face at the cliché, but kept reading.

My being dead probably doesn't bother you much, seeing as you didn't find out I was alive until I wasn't. I've wanted to reach out to you many times, and I used to come and watch you get picked up from school, to make sure you were happy. Your mom was quite right to keep me out of your life; looking back,

my biggest regret is how much I hurt
my kids, and you were spared that. But I
did love you, even if it was creepily, and
from a distance.

Nina looked out of the window. It would
be nice to know what her father's voice
sounded like, so she could imagine the letter in voice-over, but as she didn't, she
decided to pretend the car was talking to
her in William Daniels's voice. It had started
raining, which seemed appropriately anom-
alous for this moment.

Anyway, I'm leaving you this car, and
also the savings account. Your mom
refused to take money from me, so I put
it away for you. One hundred dollars
every week you've been alive, plus interest, and it's ended up being an excellent
example of the miracle of compounding.
Spend it on something amusing. If you
want to sell the car, please offer it to
Moltres first; he loves it. Don't be fooled
by his gruff exterior. He's really a pussycat and a good man. I'm not suggesting
you marry him or anything, but he'll
give you a fair price.
Here's the thing, Nina. I have a feeling
you and I are very alike. I know you love

books even more than I do, and I know you enjoy being alone. (Yes, I stalked you a little bit online as you got older. There's nothing you can do about it now that I'm dead. Sorry.) But I made mistakes in my life, and I want to give you some advice.

Oh God, just like Becky had said. Tablets of stone. Advice from beyond the grave.

I was an anxious child, with parents who didn't like me. My father wanted a big, brave boy, and my mother wanted my father to be happy. I learned very early on how to cover up, and cover up well. I was terrified of the other kids at school, even more than the teachers. So I kept my head down, got all A's, didn't make eye contact, and ran home every night to do homework and read. I rode that horse all the way through college. I don't have a single friend from those days, and when my parents died, I didn't know enough about them to write a eulogy. I asked a neighbor to do it.

Eventually, I discovered drinking, and that helped, right up until it didn't. It certainly helped me achieve my primary goal, which was to avoid feeling uncomfortable at all costs. Difficult feelings? Drink and get numb. Painful relationship? Drink and leave. Children who need me, or whose mothers needed me? Drink, leave, and pretend it was for their benefit. I was a real loser, Nina, as I'm sure your brother and sisters have told you.

Ultimately, after Archie's mom, Rosie, died, my life fell apart completely. On the surface it was better than ever. The firm was thriving, my bank account was enormous, I had beautiful girlfriends and lovely cars and no joy at all. I drank myself to sleep and hoped I didn't dream.

Then I got lucky: Eliza walked into the middle of this disaster and pulled me out. She helped me stop drinking, she helped me get into therapy, she helped me start over. There was something about her, a deep reservoir of calm and confidence I could cling to. For the first time it was acceptable to simply be me. But there was nothing she could do to fix the crap I'd left in my wake, and I'll admit it: It was easier for me to walk away than it would have been to go back and make it all right. I could see how much damage I had done, but I told myself it was too late, anyway. The truth is I was scared of my own kids, and how angry they were, so I hid on the other side of town.

I'm not saying you shouldn't enjoy being alone; there's a lot to be said for it. But if you're choosing to be alone because you're scared of other people, resist that fear. Trust people with your truth, and bravely tell them you're not brave at all.

Finally, hold on to the family you've suddenly acquired; they're my real gift to you. And you, dear Nina, are my gift to them.

He signed it,

Love, Dad

Well, damn, thought Nina. I guess I left the window open; there's rain all over my face.

today *is the day*

DATE _Tuesday June 11th_   M T W Th F S Su

◇ ◇ ◇ ◇ ◇ ◇ ◇ ◇

SCHEDULE

7 > 8	
8 > 9	
9 > 10	
10 > 11	_Deliver letters_
11 > 12	
12 > 13	
13 > 14	
14 > 15	
15 > 16	
16 > 17	
17 > 18	
18 > 19	
19 > 20	~~TRIVIA FINALS~~
20 > 21	

TO DO LIST

- [ ] _Lydia_
- [ ] _Millie_
- [ ] _Archie_
- [ ] _Betty_
- [ ] _Peter_
- [ ]
- [ ]
- [ ]
- [ ]
- [ ]

GOALS

Move on!

NOTES

Trans-am Club?

Knight Rider
Streaming?

✚ **BREAKFAST**

✚ **LUNCH**

✚ **DINNER**

✚ **WORKOUT**

TWENTY-SEVEN

In which Nina delivers a letter.

Lydia lived in Santa Monica, which would normally be enough reason to avoid her all on its own. But now Nina had a mission, so the next day she crossed the 405 for the second time in a week, and made her glacial way down Olympic Boulevard.

Santa Monica is literally a separate city from Los Angeles, albeit one with no perceptible border or an inch of physical separation. It even has its own weather. Cooler, foggier, more, you know, coastal. It has fierce devotees who regard the East side of LA with the same disdain Nina had for the West side, but as they tended to be richer, more opinionated, and deeply into things like crystals and colonic irrigation, Nina didn't worry about it.

Lydia lived on 16th Street, in a nice residential neighborhood, where presumably she could wreak havoc with her neighbor's peace and quiet. Nina's intention was to drop off the letter and walk away as swiftly as possible, but as she approached the front door, it opened and Lydia stood there.

"Are you coming to kill me?"

Nina stopped, halfway up the path. This woman was seriously off her rocker, but she couldn't help admiring her bold welcoming of possible death.

"Yes, Lydia," she said. "I am going to kill you using this deadly envelope, and then I am going to feast on your entrails."

"Paper actually has a great deal of strength, if properly folded."

"I'm aware of that. There's something called buckypaper, which has a tensile strength greater than steel."

Lydia narrowed her eyes at Nina. "How do you know that?"

"I read." Nina held up the envelope. "This, however, is a regular envelope, which I haven't treated with poison or booby-trapped in any way. I found it in the car your grandfather left me, and it's addressed to you." She shrugged. "I am merely the messenger, so, you know, don't shoot me."

A cat had appeared in the doorway, next to Lydia. It decided to irritate its owner by walking down the pathway and greeting the visitor. It was extremely friendly and looked like a leopard.

"Is this a Bengal?" asked Nina, bending to stroke its head.

"Yes," said Lydia, watching from the door.

The cat had grown tired of being petted and now sat next to Nina's feet and started washing itself.

"What's its name?"

"Euclid."

"The founder of geometry?"

"No, Euclid O'Hara, who works at the pizza joint on Montana." Lydia snorted. "Yes, the father of geometry." She turned, suddenly, and went into the house. "Come on, then, come in."

Nina started walking in.

"Bring the cat," said Lydia, from somewhere in the house, but the cat was already coming. Cats hate to miss anything.

The hallway of Lydia's house was dark but opened into a large, sunny room at the back that made Nina stop short. Books lined every wall and stood in stacks on several large tables. Books were open on a desk, books were piled on the floor, and there were even two books open on the arms of a chair that looked potentially as comfortable as hers.

"Wow," she said and stopped herself from saying, *I guess you like books,* because it was something people always said when they came to her place, and it irritated her.

Lydia turned to face her, catching her gazing openmouthed at the shelves. "I like books," said Lydia. "I don't like people."

"Me neither."

Lydia shook her head. "That's not true. You've already become closer to my family than I am, and you just met them. You might be shy, you might be introverted, even, but you like people."

Nina opened her mouth to object, but closed it. Lydia might be right.

"Now, a true misanthrope," Lydia continued, "hates and despises people, and I don't hate them. I simply don't like them much, in the same way I also don't enjoy oysters. Unfortunately, they're harder to avoid than oysters."

Nina nodded in understanding, gave a small smile, and held out the envelope. Lydia stepped forward to take it.

"Thanks."

There was a pause, then Nina asked, "Aren't you going to open it?"

Lydia gazed at her aunt for a long moment, then sat down on the chair with the two open books. Nina sat down on the sofa, and Euclid jumped up next to her.

"Do you have a cat?" Lydia asked.

"Yes," Nina said. "His name is Phil."

Lydia said nothing, just raised one eyebrow in the exact way Nina did. So Nina did it back at her, and suddenly Lydia laughed.

"I may have to admit that you're related to me after all. You like books, you like cats, you clearly enjoy a useless fact, and you raise your eyebrow exactly the same way I do." She looked at the envelope. "I don't know why I'm going to open this. There's almost nothing it can contain that will make any difference to me."

"Maybe it's a really good recipe for banana bread."

Lydia snorted. "Or maybe it's a bomb."

"Why would your grandfather leave you a letter bomb?"

Lydia looked at her witheringly. "Why would he leave me a recipe for banana bread?"

Nina shrugged. "Maybe it's an apology."

"For being a crappy grandfather? Too little, too late, don't you think? Unless this envelope contains Hermione's Time-Turner and a promise that he'll actually pay attention to me this time around, it's just paper."

"But don't you want to see?"

"No," said Lydia, but then she opened the envelope and tipped the contents into her lap. She sat silently and looked, then picked up a birthday card.

"I gave this to him when I was ten or so." She picked up a friendship bracelet of red and yellow threads. "And I gave this to him much later." Finally, she picked up a folded piece of paper and opened it up.

" 'Dear Lydia,' " she read, " 'If you're reading this, I'm dead, I'm afraid.' "

"Huh," said Nina. "He said that in my note, too."

Lydia looked at her over the piece of paper. "Well, it was true in both cases, right?" She continued to read:

You were always the smartest of my grandchildren, and the one that made me most nervous. I worried you saw right through me, saw how shallow I was and judged me for it. Now I think I was wrong, and I am more sorry than I can say that I never got to know you better. You're a very special person, Lydia, and I hope you can forgive me. I realize you'll probably say this is too little, too late, and you'll be right. But it's the only thing I can do, because

no one can turn back time. Except Hermione, of course.

Lydia looked at Nina and her mouth
twitched. "That's creepy."

Nina shrugged. "People make book references. What can you do?"

Lydia continued reading:

By the way, you and Nina would probably really get along. You should have dinner or something. I've put a gift card for
AOC in the envelope. Hopefully, it's still in
business and you two can start to be
friends.

Lydia looked up at Nina and frowned.
"Such a manipulative bastard, even dead.
It's funny how people behave badly their
whole lives and then think they can say
sorry and it's all erased. Not that AOC isn't
a great restaurant." Euclid left Nina and
wandered over to jump on Lydia's lap. "He
left my mom and her sister when they were
really young, and my mom was kind of
ruined by it. My grandma is a total witch
— did you catch that?"

Nina nodded. "It was subtle, but yeah, I
noticed."

"She made my mom's life difficult, and

414

my mom made my life difficult, and now I make other people's lives difficult, and maybe it's time the whole cycle stopped." She sighed. "I just find people so . . ."

"Scary?" asked Nina, sympathetically.

Lydia looked at Nina for a long time. "No," she said. "Deeply irritating and fun to torment."

"Oh," said Nina.

Suddenly, Lydia tore the letter from William into a dozen tiny pieces and threw them in the air. "So much for Grandpa." She grinned. "Fancy a cup of tea?"

At the back of Lydia's house was a wide, curving garden. Sitting there, sipping an excellent cup of tea, Nina smiled cautiously. "What do you do for work?" She waved inside at all the books. "Are you a teacher or something?"

Lydia shook her head. "No, I work at the RAND Corporation. Do you know it?"

Nina nodded. "Originally started by the Douglas Aircraft Company to research new weapons, it is an international think tank that has produced over thirty Nobel Prize winners." She paused. "RAND is actually short for research and development." She paused again, and hesitated. "I'm actually a little bit obsessed with RAND, because they do all this secret stuff and probably have a room with one of those big maps on the floor with lights and tiny models."

Lydia laughed again. "I can take you there, if you like."

"Really? There's a room with a map and tiny little models?"

"No, but there's a reasonable cafeteria."

Euclid walked to the middle of the lawn and sprawled, making sure everyone could admire him.

Nina asked, "What do you do at RAND?"

"Oh, it's thrilling," said Lydia. "I research global traffic patterns."

"Wow," said Nina. "That really is incredibly boring."

Lydia laughed. "Not to me, which is why I do it. I don't see cars; I see patterns. And it's not even only cars; it's how people move around in general." She sipped her tea and reached for a cookie. "I love it. Do you love your work?"

Nina thought about it. "Yes, I guess I do. I sort of fell into it, rather than chose it, but it suits me very well. I live a very quiet life, I walk to work, I read a lot, I have a trivia team, and I have a cat." She turned up her hands. "It's all pretty good."

"No boyfriend? Or girlfriend?"

Nina shook her head. "No. There was

someone but I messed it up."

"How?"

Nina took a deep breath. "I get anxiety," she said.

"Like Archie?" asked Lydia.

Nina nodded. "I broke up with him before we'd even really started. I got overwhelmed and threw him out of the boat." Suddenly, her eyes were prickling. "It's so stupid."

"It's not stupid. Anxiety is the most common mental illness in America, with over forty million sufferers."

Nina stared at her.

Lydia shrugged. "I share an office with a mental health researcher. RAND is actually full of people like us, nerdy obsessives with good memories." She took another cookie and started eating it. "But why don't you explain to him and see if you can start it up again? Do you want to?"

Nina nodded, then shook her head. "I don't know. I really like him, and being with him actually feels good, but there's too much going on. I thought I was pretty much alone, and I was OK with it. Good with it, even. Now I have all of you guys to deal with, and a boyfriend was too much."

Lydia gazed at her. "You're an idiot. We're family; you can ignore us completely. We're like succulents: Minor occasional attention

417

is entirely sufficient. You should absolutely get him back."

"He's ignoring my texts."

"Have you considered the old-fashioned, in-person conversation?" Lydia put down her teacup.

"No," said Nina. "Besides, he's competing in a trivia competition this evening; the final of the Southern California Quiz Bowl. I don't want to put him off."

"Wow," said Lydia. "That is both the lamest and the nerdiest excuse for inaction I've ever heard. I can't decide whether to smack you across the face or burst into applause."

Nina opened her mouth to respond, when her phone rang.

"Can you come right away?" It was Liz, and she sounded frazzled. In the background, Nina could hear yelling.

"What's going on?"

"Well, Meffo came by and posted a notice that the store was closing and was going to be replaced by a pot-infused makeup emporium called Puff and Pout."

"You're joking. A pot dispensary?"

"No. Artisanal makeup, custom made for each customer from a range of natural minerals and pigments, infused with CBD oil and locally sourced organic marijuana."

"Did you memorize that?"

"No, I'm reading from the notice. Their slogan is *Look fantastic, feel even better.*"

"Wow."

"Then people started reading the notice, and all of a sudden there was a crowd outside with placards, and now the police are here and it's all gotten a bit out of hand."

There was the sound of breaking glass.

"Oh dear. Gotta go."

"Was that our window?" Nina had visions of crowds of zombies swarming the store, which didn't make any sense, but that's what popped into her head.

"No, Meffo's windshield. I stashed him in the office for safety, but there wasn't much I could do about his car." Then she hung up.

Nina turned to Lydia. "How fast do you think we can get to Larchmont Boulevard?"

Lydia grinned. "In K.I.T.T.? With me driving? Twenty minutes."

Nina shook her head. "No, in a regular Trans Am, because K.I.T.T. is a fictional character, during rush hour, and with me driving."

Lydia made a face. "Forty minutes."

"Fine, you drive."

TWENTY-EIGHT

In which things get a little out of hand.

Here's a useful tip: Driving through Los Angeles in a fast car with a genius researcher is not enjoyable, unless you are one of those people who drinks five Red Bulls and snorts coke before getting in the front seat of a roller coaster and sticking both arms in the air. Nina started reciting "The Love Song of J. Alfred Prufrock" as they sped through Beverly Hills, and by the time they reached Larchmont, she was reading the line about rolling the bottoms of trousers, and that tells you how fast they were going. Furthermore, apparently the way to beat traffic in LA is to treat straight lines as abominations and Tetris your way through the side streets. It didn't help that Lydia was calling out street names as she went, like a pool shark calling a pocket.

As they turned onto Larchmont Boulevard, it was immediately clear something was wrong. Pedestrians on both sides were looking south, toward the bookstore, and Nina began to get what Han Solo might have called a Bad Feeling. She was still nauseous from the car ride, but this was something more.

There was a crowd of maybe twenty people in front of the store, plus two cops, all of whom were watching an argument between a middle-aged woman who Nina recognized from the store (historical fiction) and a younger woman who was wearing a long, fringed skirt, a top made of birds' wings and macaroni, and a large felt hat with a brim the size of Poughkeepsie. Birds could have perched comfortably on it, if they were able to forgive the bird wing corset.

"I question your assumption that makeup is less culturally valid than literature," the young woman was saying, as Nina and Lydia got close. Ah, thought Nina, it's a Larchmont Liberal Street Fight.

The older woman frowned. "I am not in any way questioning the validity of your products, culturally or otherwise, and far be it from me to cast aspersions on the career goals of a fellow woman, but this bookstore has been here for nearly eight decades and is a cornerstone of our community."

"Progress is inevitable," replied the woman.

"That is both true and irrelevant to our discussion," said the older woman, whom Nina was mentally referring to as the Reader. "We don't need another beauty products store on Larchmont, and we certainly don't need a pot shop."

"We're not a dispensary," replied the other woman, whom Nina had internally named Bird Wing Betty. "We create makeup infused with potent botanicals that make you feel as good as you look. We are one hundred percent organic, local, and legal."

There was murmuring in the crowd. Clearly, Bird Wing Betty had some supporters. As if to prove it, a group of about a dozen similarly dressed young people suddenly appeared.

"We saw your post on Instagram," said one, coming up to Betty and touching her upper arm. "I'm so sorry the boomers are harshing your vibe."

"Total drag," said another. "I brought you some royal jelly and an apple cider vinegar shot to alkalinize you." She handed over a tiny bottle that reminded Nina of *Alice in Wonderland*.

The cops sensed an opening. "Ladies,"

said one of them, an officer who looked like this was a pleasant change from moving homeless people off the streets, "I'm afraid you don't have a permit to protest, so you need to break this up and go home."

"No," said the Reader. "We're staying here to show our support for reading."

"Dude, we're all about reading," said one of the new young people, "but bookstores are so nineties. Stories live in the cloud now, free like birds. Don't tie them down in the physical realm."

The Reader snorted at her. "You're stoned."

The girl snorted back at her. "You're old, but at least I'll sober up."

Another guy in the crowd said, "Go back to Santa Monica, you wannabe hippie counterculturalists." Which, let's face it, are fighting words, albeit unnecessarily long fighting words.

And then it happened. Someone — no one was ever sure who it was — threw a ball of cardamom, fig, and Brie ice cream, which hit Bird Wing Betty right in the . . . bird wings. Finally, thought Nina, they got that ice cream trebuchet working.

One of Betty's friends turned and tossed a shot of cayenne and lemon juice in the face of a bookstore supporter, who cried,

"My eyes," and staggered backward. Another ball of ice cream arced overhead and nailed one of the cops, who didn't take it very well. Nina turned to see who was throwing the frosty artillery just as another scoop glanced off her head and hit Betty, this time in the face. Betty stomped her foot.

"I. Am. Lactose. Intolerant!" she cried.

"No, you're just completely intolerable," replied the Reader, and pushed her.

Nina reached up and felt her head, which was sticky. She heard giggling. Lydia was amused.

"You've got a little . . . something something . . ." Lydia wiped a little drip from Nina's forehead and tasted it.

"Huh," she said. "Mint chip. Surprising." She opened her mouth to continue and took a gluten-free cupcake right in the cake hole, which was also surprising. She sputtered.

Nina grinned. "Don't talk with your mouth full, Lydia." A mini cupcake — or it might have been a brownie; it was moving too fast to tell — whizzed by and knocked off the Reader's glasses.

The cops, who had been well trained (though, admittedly, not for a food fight), started pushing through the crowd, looking for the troublemakers. This made the people on the outside of the crowd, who couldn't see very well, assume something more serious was going on. They started to run or, at least, move swiftly away. This was Larchmont, after all; no need for unseemly panic.

The ice cream bandit sent a last volley over the heads of the thinning crowd, and both Nina and Lydia were in the line of fire. Professional hit, double scoop.

Lydia, who had decided to see the funny side of it, clutched her arm, which was covered in sprinkles. "I'm hit," she cried, and staggered backward.

"Cold . . . so cold . . ." said Nina, channeling the heroic death of so many matinee idols. She made it to the bookstore front door and did a creditable death slide down it. Then she remembered why she was there.

"Come on," she said, scrambling to her feet. "We'll go around the back."

"Really?" whined Lydia. "But this is so fun."

"Quit it," said Nina. "Let's go."

They darted across the melee and ran down the narrow lane behind the stores of Larchmont Boulevard. Nina pulled out her keys and once inside the store discovered Liz and Mr. Meffo hiding out in the back room. Even though the ice cream had been outside, the atmosphere in the room was decidedly frosty.

"Are they gone?" asked Liz.

"The crowd is dispersing, yes."

Liz turned to Mr. Meffo. "Well then, sir, you are free to leave."

Mr. Meffo got stiffly to his feet. "Thank you for the brief sanctuary, Elizabeth."

Liz shrugged. Wow, thought Nina, I bet it was fun in here for the last hour or so. Mr. Meffo looked at Liz and seemed as though he was about to say something, but simply turned and left the store.

Liz sighed. "I wanted to ask him to give me more time, but I couldn't find the right words. It's always so easy in books and so hard in real life."

"Ain't that the truth," said Lydia. Then she turned to Nina. "However, that is no excuse for not at least trying to go talk to your boyfriend." She held up her finger. "You may have hoped I had forgotten what we were talking about, but I haven't. You need to gird your loins, screw your courage to the sticking place, and remember a turtle only travels when it sticks its neck out."

Liz and Nina looked at her. "It's a Korean saying," explained Lydia, shrugging.

"You're right," said Nina, suddenly feeling bolder than she'd ever felt before. Lydia was a woman of action, and she was related to Nina, so Nina must have woman-of-action genes somewhere. Besides, now Nina had a family. She had friends. She had money. She had a bitching car. She'd survived a terrifying drive in that bitching car, and there was nothing she couldn't do, or at least try to do. "Let's go."

She and Lydia turned and left. Liz watched them go, then went to get paper towels and window cleaner. Fortunately, all-natural, artisanal ice cream is much easier to clean off than the factory stuff.

TWENTY-NINE

In which Nina takes things public.

You would have thought there was something monumental going on, judging by the crowd outside the bar. Mermaids wrestling in creamed corn. Kitten juggling. Instant Pot flash mob. Something. But it was really only the Southern California Quiz Bowl Final, and after ten minutes of wriggling, Lydia and Nina managed to push their way to the front.

Howard the QuizDick had really gone above and beyond for this one, and there was even a camera crew from a local affiliate station. Howard had decked himself out in a silver sequin dinner jacket and successfully bid on eBay for one of those microphones that looks like a half-finished lollipop on a long silver stick. Whatever it was, he was bringing it.

Nina could see both teams sitting on

either side of the podium, which was bigger and more impressive (and hopefully drier) than the last one.

"Ladies, Gentlemen, and the great Undecided, welcome to the Final of the Southern California Quiz Bowl. For the first time we have a challenger from San Diego, the California Quizzly Bears, facing off against local heroes, You're a Quizzard, Harry."

Nina looked along the Quizzard team bench . . . no Tom.

Lisa was there, though, and she noticed Nina. She frowned and got to her feet.

"Competitors must remain in their positions," said Howard.

"Don't be silly, Howard," replied Lisa. "I'll be back in a minute. I have to see why we're a team captain short."

"There are no substitutions once the clock has begun," warned Howard officiously.

"Don't get your panties in a bunch," said Lisa, over her shoulder.

She and Nina met by the bar.

"Where's Tom?" yelled Nina, over the hubbub. "This is my cousin, Lydia. She's an expert in traffic patterns."

"Hi," said Lisa, looking surprisingly interested. "You picked a good city for it, although the biggest traffic jam ever took place in Beijing in 2010."

"I know," said Lydia with relish. "Sixty-two miles long, and lasted for twelve days." She looked at Lisa carefully, never having met anyone else who cared about traffic. "I went on vacation last year to São Paulo. They have enormous traffic jams all the time; it was great."

Lisa smiled at her as if that hadn't been a ridiculous thing to say, then turned back to Nina. "Tom isn't here, but he's supposed to be. He's been totally off his trivia game. Why did you break up with him?"

"Because I was scared," said Nina. "I want to apologize, but he's not answering his phone."

"I know, I've been trying to reach him." Lisa looked mildly concerned. "Hey, do you want to play for our team? Without him we've got no chance, even if he is playing at half strength."

"I can't. I don't think it's allowed."

"Well, let's ask."

Nina hung back. "No, I'm sure Tom will be here."

"I am here," said Tom, coming up behind them. "Sorry, Lisa, I was working and lost track of time." He looked at Nina. "Hi, Nina." Then he took Lisa by the arm. "Let's go. They're going to start."

"Tom, Nina wants to talk to you," said Lisa.

Tom looked at Nina. "That's nice," he replied. "You have ice cream in your hair." Then he walked away and Lisa followed, shrugging apologetically. Nina smelled that sawdust smell that always went with him, feeling herself take a few steps without even realizing it.

She had made such a mistake.

"He's cute," said Lydia from behind her. "Go get him, tiger."

Nina watched Lisa scramble back to her seat on the team bench, next to Tom, who was studiously avoiding her gaze.

"I'll try," she said, "but I think I'm more of a pussycat."

"House cats share 95.6 percent of their DNA with tigers," said Lydia. She paused. "According to one study, anyway."

QuizDick stepped forward and raised his hand for silence. "Let's review the format. In the first round, I'll be asking the teams sets of questions in various categories. Anyone on the team can answer, but only one answer will be accepted. A correct answer receives two points. An incorrect answer means that question will be offered to the opposing team. If they get it right, they'll get one point. If nobody knows, it will be offered to the audience, and if they get it right, they can give one point to whichever team they're supporting."

As the audience was largely supporting the local team, this seemed popular, but the California Quizzly Bears had also brought a sizable contingent of fans, who were wearing bear claw gloves and Smokey Bear hats. It was a look.

"Are both teams complete?" QuizDick looked over the competitors carefully, presumably to check none of them was secretly Ken Jennings. "In order to reduce the chance of cheating, we're pulling categories at random. Our first category is Sports in the USA."

Both teams did pretty well with Sports, but Quizzard took the lead in the next round, which was Real Life Couples who Played Couples on TV. Then the Quizzly Bears dominated Minor Countries You've Never Heard Of (a statement that clearly didn't apply to them), but Quizzard swept the board in Sitcoms of the Eighties, bringing the scores level as they entered the final round.

Nina was watching Tom's face, and it was impossible not to notice how effectively he was ignoring her. It became almost comical, the lengths he was prepared to go not to meet her eye. Lydia started muttering commentary and answering the questions under her breath, and Nina made a mental note to see if Santa Monica had competitive trivia, because Lydia would crush it.

"In this final round, it's team members one by one, head-to-head and toe-to-toe with their opposition. Each pair will get six questions, two from each category, and twelve points are up for grabs, no fancy business."

Lisa was first, and totally creamed her Quizzly Bear opponent, having apparently memorized the lives of Early American Presidents, the Periodic Table of Elements, and Cartoon Cats and Dogs. Quizzard wasn't so lucky in the next round, and their team member was only able to garner two points for correctly identifying Fresno as the Raisin Capital of the World. In the last round of team member play Quizzard got all the questions about Egg-Based Recipes correct, but were unable to beat the Quizzly Bears on Cocktails or Dog Breeds.

The Quizzly Bears were getting cocky and had started celebrating imminent victory. The bar floor was awash with broken glass and beer, because it turned out bear claw gloves are cute, but not good for holding slippery pint glasses. Presumably, this is why bears prefer kegs.

"Here we go," said Howard, who had grown into his role as host and was handling things pretty smoothly. "With the scores tied we come at last to the team captains, who have to buzz in to answer ten rapid-fire questions drawn from any of tonight's categories." He pulled out his little bag of categories and withdrew a slip of paper. "The same rules apply: two points if they get it, one point if their opponents get it, and the option of throwing it open to the audience if all else fails."

Tom stood up and came to the podium, as did the Quizzly Bear captain, who was a woman not much bigger than Nina. She was wearing an entire grizzly bear head as a hat. It was bigger than she was, and occasionally, she had to grab the podium for support. Either the head was really heavy, or she'd removed her bear claws in order to drink better. Either way, she was ready to throw down, if she didn't fall down first.

Howard cleared his throat and assumed a serious expression, making sure the camera was getting his better side. "Who has the most wins as head coach in the NFL?"

Tom answered, "Don Shula."

Nina had never even heard of Don Shula, but it was nice to know he was doing so

434

well. Tom looked around at his teammates and grinned, but still somehow managed to avoid looking at Nina. Lisa was clearly getting annoyed with him, as she pointed two fingers to her eyes and then pointed them at Nina, but Tom wasn't having it.

"Next question: Who played Chandler's father on *Friends*?"

Tom answered again. "Kathleen Turner." Nina was pleased to see he was well versed in the classics.

Then the Quizzly Bears got five in a row. Then Tom got the next three.

QuizDick, delighted things had gotten so gripping, and glad to see the cameras were still rolling, cleared his throat. "Unbelievably we have a tie! For the championship, the honor of declaring yourselves Trivia Champions of Southern California, five hundred dollars for the charity of your choice, and free pizza from Domino's for a year . . ."

"Only for team members . . ." shouted a guy who was presumably from Domino's. "Not for everyone you know."

"Yes, free pizza for yourselves; we have to go to a challenging tie-breaker." He looked around the room and held up his hand for silence. Eventually he got it, and into the hush he said: "Who can tell me the famous

435

last words of Arthur Conan Doyle?"

"Who's that?" asked the Quizzly Bear captain.

"The man who wrote *Sherlock Holmes,*" replied QuizDick, surprised.

Quizzly Bear shrugged her shoulders. Everyone looked at Tom, who also shrugged. The teams both shrugged; it was a complete shrug-fest, and finally, QuizDick turned to the audience and asked if anyone knew the answer.

Nina raised her hand. Howard pointed at her, and she looked at Tom, who was finally looking at her.

"Nina can't answer," he said to Howard. "She was on an opposing team."

Howard looked at Nina. "Yes, but her team was disqualified weeks ago." He looked at Tom. "You were there; you saw it." He shuddered. "I sustained a paper cut that took days to heal."

Nina spoke. "The rules are clear, Howard. If no one else can answer, then it goes to the audience."

"Yes, but apparently the team captain doesn't want you to answer." He looked perplexed. "Although you could give the point to any team you wanted to, so maybe if the Grizzly Bear . . ." His voice tailed off.

"I'm not sure the rules cover this eventuality."

"We can put it to a vote." Nina looked around the bar. "Show of hands?"

"No," said Howard. "This isn't a democracy; this is a Trivia Bowl Final." He turned to the team captains. "I'm afraid that means it's a tie. We have no winner."

"Wait!" Lisa jumped up. "Let Nina answer the question, Tom. You're not the only member of the team." She was clearly trying to come up with a good reason. "I really . . . love pizza."

"You're a vegan," said Tom.

"We make vegan pizza!" yelled the guy from Domino's. He must have been drunk, because then he added, "It tastes like cardboard, but it's vegan!"

Tom hesitated. He looked at Nina.

"Please let me answer," she said.

Tom sighed. "OK."

Howard looked annoyed but nodded. "Go ahead, audience member. I'll repeat the question: What were the famous last words of Arthur Conan Doyle?"

Nina stood up tall. "His last words were, 'I have made a terrible mistake, Tom. There is room for you in my life, plenty of room. Please give me a second chance.' "

Total silence. QuizDick frowned and

flipped over the card in his hand. "Uh, that's not what I have here."

"Wait," said Tom, "he also said, 'What about the next time you freak out? I don't want to be with someone who's ready to throw me under the bus every time she loses her composure.' "

"He has a point," muttered Lydia.

"Shut up," said Nina.

The Quizzly Bear captain said, "Wait a minute, are you allowed two guesses?"

"I know," replied Nina. "I'm sorry. I can only promise to try harder." She swallowed and raised her voice. "Being with you is as good as being alone."

There was a pause, then Tom stepped away from the podium and walked over to Nina. "That's the nicest thing anyone has ever said to me," he said, and wrapped his arms around her, lifting her off her feet and kissing her deeply. He was vaguely aware of a woman jumping up and down nearby, saying, "Conan Doyle's actual last words were to his wife. He said, 'You are wonderful.' " And then, as Nina and Tom showed no signs of stopping, "The longest kiss on record was over fifty-eight hours long!"

While Tom and Nina didn't set a new record for kissing, they did cause the clip of the Trivia Bowl Final to go viral on You-

Tube. Weeks later, when QuizDick's Trivia Channel was launched on YouTube, he acknowledged that if it weren't for this peak romantic moment, his success never would have happened. He wasn't about to share the advertising revenue, of course, but still, he appreciated the boost.

Once the contest was over, and the Quizzly Bears had graciously bought everyone in the bar a beer, Tom and Nina made their good-byes. Lydia and Lisa were deep in discussion about fantastic traffic jams in history and barely noticed them leaving.

"I want to take you to my place," said Tom. "It's actually not far from here." Nina nodded, and they walked through the dark streets in perfect happiness, holding hands and saying nothing.

They reached a low building, and Tom pulled a key from his pocket. "This is where I work," he said, "rather than where I live, but I need to show you something."

He unlocked the door and led her inside, along a narrow hallway to a large room at the back of the building. Nina followed him, wishing she were still holding his hand. The room they walked into was filled with wood and pieces of furniture. It smelled wonderful, of sawdust and linseed oil. Of Tom.

"This is my workshop," said Tom, switching on the lights.

"You said you were a carpenter."

"I am," he replied, smiling at her. "But not the house-building kind. I'm a cabinet-maker. I make furniture." He pointed. "In particular, bookcases."

"You're joking." Nina looked around; he clearly wasn't joking. There were several large, beautiful bookcases in the room. They weren't simply shelves; they had doors and glass and drawers and little wooden twiddly bits that probably had a proper name.

Tom shook his head. "No, really. I talked to Peter about it that day at the Festival, and we agreed it was too corny to tell you. I was kind of waiting for the right moment and then . . . you know . . . we broke up, so it didn't matter."

Nina gazed at him. "It's . . ."

He blushed. "I know. It's ridiculous, a man who makes bookcases dating a woman who sells books."

"Yeah."

"How about I refocus on cupboards and dressers?"

She smiled. "I could quit my job."

"I could carry on making bookcases, but make them really badly so the books keep falling off."

440

"Knight's could switch to selling audio-books only."

They looked at each other. "See," said Nina. "I'm willing to change."

Tom stepped closer to her and took her hands. "I don't want you to change, Nina. I want to take care of you. If you get less anxious, great, but if you don't, then that's fine, too, because that's who you are." He shrugged. "I'm never going to be a huge reader, I'm never going to know all about the stuff you know all about, but that's who I am."

"I like who you are," Nina said, not feeling anxious at all. "And you know plenty of stuff I don't know. Like Don Shula. I don't even know who Don Shula is."

"You don't? Well, maybe this won't work after all." He grinned. "Look, I cleared you a corner." Tom pointed to an area near a large window. It was dark then, of course, but in the daytime it would get plenty of light. "I was going to surprise you and put a comfy chair there so you could sit and read while I worked, and we could, you know, hang out." He tugged her closer and kissed her. "I want to be with you the way you are, the way you're going to be, and the way you end up. Every way you are is beautiful to me."

They kissed, and then Nina said, "That was the cheesiest thing I've ever heard."

Tom laughed. "Really? I worked on it in my head for days."

Nina was going to make fun of him again, but didn't. He wasn't a poet, but whatever. She wasn't a competitive skier. It didn't matter what they weren't; it only mattered who they were.

"I could be in love with you," she said.

"I could be in love with you, too," he replied.

"We're very romantic, aren't we?"

"Very," he said, and kissed her again. "Let's go home and be alone together."

THIRTY

In which Liz loses her mind, finds a
friend, and gains a partner.

The next morning, Nina woke up to find
Tom already awake and looking at her.

"Good morning, creepy boyfriend," she
said. "Have you been staring for long?"

"About thirty seconds," he replied. "Your
cat registered a complaint by standing on
my eyeball."

Phil was sitting on the chair, washing his
paw with the air of a cherub grooming his
wing.

Nina grinned and got up to feed him. She
went to get the coffee started and found it
already set up, water in the reservoir, coffee
in the filter. She paused.

"Did you do this?"

Tom turned over in bed and nodded. "I
was inspired by my brother's wedding
vows."

Nina was opening her mouth to comment positively on this when her phone rang. She looked at the clock. Oh. Ten o'clock. Not exactly the crack of dawn.

It was her friend Vanessa.

"Hey, I think you better get over to the bookstore."

"Why are you in the bookstore? And why are you whispering?"

"I'm not." Vanessa sounded suppressed, like she was either about to laugh or cry. "I'm hiding from the manageress because we're not supposed to be on the phone at work, and I think you should hurry up because there's a crowd outside the store and occasionally Liz appears and hands out books."

"Sells them?"

"No, gives them away." Vanessa paused. "Enthusiastically."

"I'll be right there."

When Nina arrived, she and Tom found Liz sitting in the middle of the store, with Mr. Meffo, in the midst of chaos. Every book in the store's inventory was off the shelves, and Liz sat in the middle like the Caterpillar on his mushroom. Meffo, who reminded Nina more of the White Rabbit, was perched by the register. Both of them seemed to be

444

having a marvelous time.

"Ah, Nina!" said Liz. "You're just in time."

"For what?" said Nina carefully. "It looks like I missed the main event, which was apparently trashing the store."

"Not at all! We've been having a literary discussion requiring illustration," replied Liz, fluidly. "It was necessary to refer to multiple volumes."

"Are you all right?" Nina picked her way over to Liz, who pushed aside a stack of books to make room. She patted the carpet beside her.

"I am fantastic," Liz said. "Pull up some rug and pop a squat."

Mr. Meffo giggled, which was alarming.

"Did you have breakfast?" asked Liz, holding out a bakery box. Inside were a selection of brownies, cupcakes, and muffins.

Nina took a mini muffin and popped it in her mouth. "Wow, these are good." She took another. "Where are they from?"

"I can't remember. Do you know," Liz continued, leaning closer, "that books have been the cornerstone of my life?"

"Yes," said Nina, chewing.

"I distinctly remember the first time I recommended a book — it was *Snow Crash,* by Neal Stephenson, and I recommended it because the customer enjoyed both William

445

Gibson and S. J. Perelman, and I thought, hey, *Snow Crash* is futuristic and hilarious . . ." Here she seemed to lose the thread for a moment, but after a second remembered where she was going with all this. "And he came back to the store and said he'd loved it, and I was hooked."

"On science fiction?"

"No, on introducing people to books. To reading books, knowing people, and putting them together. Love *Bridget Jones* AND *Rebecca*? Try Mary Stewart, who crushes the romantic suspense genre and wrote over a dozen fantastic books." Suddenly, she reached over and grabbed Nina's arm. "Do you know the best feeling in the world?"

"Uh . . ." Nina shook her head, despite having some ideas.

Liz glowed. "It's reading a book, loving every second of it, then turning to the front and discovering that the writer wrote fourteen zillion others."

"Fourteen zillion?"

"Or a dozen!" Liz turned to Mr. Meffo. "Mr. Meffo came by to help — isn't that lovely of him?"

Liz was definitely losing her mind. Nina looked at their landlord. Ex-landlord. He looked sheepish.

"I was passing," he said, somewhat defensively, "and I heard noises and investigated. It was Liz." He cleared his throat. "Singing." He smiled at Liz. "And she invited me in and we had pastries and coffee and talked about books." He was almost happy. Nina had never seen him like this. "It turns out we have a lot in common."

"We both worry about Curious George, for example," said Liz. "Why doesn't the Man with the Yellow Hat take his responsibility seriously? Why does he keep leaving George in these obviously dangerous situations and then walking away?"

"No, no," said Mr. Meffo. "You're looking at it wrong. The Man with the Yellow Hat is the victim. George keeps promising to behave, but he never does. Not to mention," he said, warming to his theme, "that Curious George basically teaches kids it's acceptable to damage property as long as you do something cute afterward." He threw his hands in the air. "What kind of message is that?"

Nina glanced over at Tom, who had been leaning in the doorway listening quietly. He was looking at Liz and Meffo with narrowed eyes.

"Where did those muffins come from?" he asked.

"From the lovely, lovely lady who's stealing my store," Liz told him. "I think she felt badly about the fighting and the ice cream, so she came over last night and dropped off a peace offering." She reached for the last mini muffin. "I ended up eating some for dinner, and then I decided to reorganize the books." She looked around. "I started well, but then I got distracted."

There was a pause.

"You're stoned," said Nina.

"Don't be silly, Nina."

"Liz, she sells pot-infused makeup. Someone who thinks pot should be in eye shadow certainly isn't going to hold back when it comes to baked goods."

"Huh," said Liz. "Well, that might explain my pressing desire to raise goats and live in harmony with nature." She turned to Mr. Meffo. "My apologies, Mr. Meffo, I appear to have given you adulterated muffins."

"Adulterated Muffins is a great band name," he replied, giggling again. "Plus, we're adults, so adulterated is completely appropriate."

"You're funny," said Liz. "I should never have called you Mephistopheles."

"And I shouldn't have called you Slippery Liz." His eyes softened. "I will miss our monthly cat and mouse. Of all my delinquent tenants, you were my favorite."

"But wait," said Nina to the landlord. "Do we really have to close so soon? I have money now. I want to buy into the store, pay you back, and help Liz run Knight's for another twenty years." She looked at her boss. "I wasn't sure until just now, but I love readers, too, and books, and there's nothing I want more than to spend my working life making introductions."

"Are you sure?" Liz looked worried. "I mean, I get that the universe whirls in mysterious yada yada, but wouldn't you rather travel the world?"

"No, I'd rather stay home and read."

"What about investing in real estate?" asked Meffo.

"In this market, are you mad?" replied Nina.

"What about your photography?" asked Liz.

"I'll buy a nicer camera, but I'm not quitting my day job." Nina grew exasperated. "What is with everyone? I don't want to travel, I don't want to buy a house, I want to run a bookstore, and this is the bookstore I want to run." She turned to Tom. "You believe me, don't you?"

Tom nodded. "Baby, you do you."

"Well, I don't know . . ." Mr. Meffo was frowning. "Puff and Pout signed a lease."

"They just got you guys high without warning you! I think a strongly worded conversation should encourage them to back off."

Liz looked around. "It's going to take a while to reorganize all this."

Nina felt triumphant. "That's OK, Tom and I are going on a road trip, anyway."

"We are?" asked Tom.

"Yes," crowed Nina. "To Mexico. I just decided. I like being spontaneous!"

"Oh my God," said Liz, who was clearly losing her buzz. "You're like a character in a book."

"Lizzy Bennet? Katniss Everdeen?"

"No, the stubborn guy in *Green Eggs and Ham*. After all the irritating and obsessive planning, it turns out you like to wing it after all." She adopted a singsong tone. "I do! I like being flexible! And I will do it on a train, and I will do it in the rain." She turned to Tom. "I guess that makes you Sam-I-Am."

He shrugged. "I'll take that. Persistent and loyal are pretty good character traits."

Nina laughed out loud. She'd found her purpose — not reading as many good books as possible, but helping other people do so. She was going to make Knight's a huge success; she was going to add a big, shiny coffee machine, and put her photos on the wall, and get a store dog and call it Admiral Frontispiece . . . or maybe it was just the muffins kicking in.

"Come on," she said to Tom, jumping up. "Let's go!"

So, dear reader, that's precisely what they did. And once they'd finished doing that, they lived happily ever after.

today is the day

DATE _GRAND OPENING DAY!_ M T W Th F S Su

SCHEDULE

7>8	Pick up Lon @ airport
8>9	
9>10	Finish decorating
10>11	
11>12	Pick up Cakes - Polly
12>13	
13>14	
14>15	DOORS OPEN
15>16	
16>17	PARTY!
17>18	
18>19	
19>20	
20>21	

TO DO LIST

- [ ] Cupcakes
- [ ] wine
- [ ] cheese
- [ ] bread
- [ ] Pocky!!
- [ ] KNIGHTSHILL BOOKS ← Find a designer!!
- [ ]
- [ ]
- [ ]
- [ ]

GOALS

Don't run out of wine!!
Taco Truck Guy
323 197 2419

NOTES

Tom
Peter - bring dog
Lydia & Lisa?
Lili + kids + Guy?
Becky & John

+ BREAKFAST

+ LUNCH

+ DINNER

+ WORKOUT

ACKNOWLEDGMENTS

Writing books is both a solitary job and a team effort. I would never have finished *The Bookish Life of Nina Hill* without my trio of early readers and my wonderful editor. Leah Woodring, Candice Culnane, and Ali Gray read it waaay before it was ready, and made comments and changes that improved it immeasurably. Then my editor, Kate Seaver, dragged it over the finish line. All four of you are goddesses and snappy dressers, and I'm lucky to know you.

The beautiful planner templates Nina uses are from happydigitaldownload.com, and my thanks to P.S. Lau for permission to use them here.

ABOUT THE AUTHOR

Abbi Waxman, the author of *Other People's Houses* and *The Garden of Small Beginnings,* is a chocolate-loving, dog-loving woman who lives in Los Angeles and lies down as much as possible. She worked in advertising for many years, which is how she learned to write fiction. She has three daughters, three dogs, three cats, and one very patient husband.

The employees of Thorndike Press hope you have enjoyed this Large Print book. All our Thorndike, Wheeler, and Kennebec Large Print titles are designed for easy reading, and all our books are made to last. Other Thorndike Press Large Print books are available at your library, through selected bookstores, or directly from us.

For information about titles, please call:
(800) 223-1244

or visit our website at:
gale.com/thorndike

To share your comments, please write:

Publisher
Thorndike Press
10 Water St., Suite 310
Waterville, ME 04901